THE DAY THE SKY OPENED

a novel of the Great Flood

Andrew R Guyatt

THE DAY THE SKY OPENED by Andrew R Guyatt
Scripture Union, 207–209 Queensway, Bletchley, MK2 2EB, UK
e-mail: info@scriptureunion.org.uk
www.scriptureunion.org.uk

Scripture Union Australia: Locked Bag 2, Central Coast Business Centre,
NSW 2252
www.su.org.au

ISBN 184427 220 6

First published in this substantially revised edition in Great Britain by
Scripture Union 2006. The original text previously appeared in 'Noah'
published in 2001 by Cromwell Publishers/First Century.

Cover design by David Lund Design of Milton Keynes
Internal page design by Creative Pages: creativepages.co.uk
Printed and bound by Creative Print and Design (Wales) Ebbw Vale

Scripture Union is an international Christian charity working with
churches in more than 130 countries providing resources to bring the
good news about Jesus Christ to children, young people and families – and
to encourage them to develop spiritually through the Bible and prayer. As
well as coordinating a network of volunteers, staff and associates who run
holidays, church-based events and school Christian groups, Scripture Union
produces a wide range of publications and supports those who use their
resources through training programmes.

Because Noah had faith, he was warned about something that had not yet happened. He obeyed and built a boat... In this way the people of the world were judged, and Noah was given the blessings that come to everyone that pleases God.

...the water under the earth started gushing out everywhere. The sky opened like windows, and rain poured down for forty days and nights ...

Hebrews 11:7; Genesis 7:11,12 (CEV)

About the author

Born in Carshalton, Surrey, Andrew Guyatt read science at the University of London, was a research assistant at the Royal Postgraduate Medical School, and a postdoctoral fellow at the Universities of Florida and Edinburgh, before spending 15 years investigating the effects of smoking at the Midhurst Medical Research Institute in West Sussex.

Italian and choral singing are among his hobbies, as are listening to cricket on the radio and playing early and classical music very loudly to drown out his children's rock. He began writing novels when he became redundant. He is now the secretary of a local writers' group and is collaborating on a book of local history including research into an eighteenth-century workhouse. He preaches in local chapels, is a member of a church he describes as 'free evangelical charismatic', cooks a mean Sunday roast and battles with Weight Watchers. He is married to Sue, and they have five children.

Acknowledgements by the author

I am grateful to many friends for assistance – though any errors or omissions are my responsibility alone.

Mrs Julie Laing Muir first suggested I should write; David Rivett provided practical assistance; and my late sister Dorothy gave much encouragement. I owe a great debt to my cousin, the writer Mary Batchelor, the late Bob Chandler and the members of the Midhurst Writers' Group who patiently listened to the book being read out in instalments and made many helpful criticisms and suggestions.

I would also like to thank David Harris, who first showed me the relevance of Noah's world to our own time; the late Peter Rumsby, who gave invaluable insights into geological aspects; and the L'Abri Fellowship for the loan of books.

I am also most grateful for the encouragement and practical help given by David Selley and Judith Merrell of the Leprosy Mission, and for the sterling work done by Lin Ball in editing the book.

Finally, I acknowledge the support of my children Helen, Tom, Matilda, Alice and Barney; and that of my wife Sue who – unlike the portrayal of Noah's partner in my story – is a constant and consistent source of encouragement.

The story behind this story

Whenever I think about Noah and the Great Flood I keep coming back to the words of Jesus as he talked about his second coming: 'When the Son of Man appears, things will be just as they were when Noah lived. People were eating, drinking, and getting married right up to the day that the flood came and Noah went into the big boat. They didn't know anything was happening until the flood came and swept them all away. That is how it will be when the Son of Man appears' (Matthew 24:37–39).

Quite clearly Jesus saw the episode as historic; there was a real Noah who built a real ark to enable his family and animals to survive a flood. This set me a challenge! As a Christian I was committed to believing the whole Bible as the Word of God – but I was also a scientist who had spent his working life researching how people breathed and smoked cigarettes. So I undertook the strange step of investigating the Bible account by writing a novel, although I little thought at the time that anyone would ever read it.

The more I examined the biblical text, the more logical and exciting it became, and I was rapidly convinced of its historical veracity. For example, the ark was six times as long as it was broad: an optimum ratio to prevent a floating object spinning round in the current. Similarly, at 450 feet long it was near the maximum that can be achieved using wood. Sailing ships rarely exceeded 300 feet in length, but they had the added strains of masts and rudder, while the ark was simply a floating box.

There are still many things I do not understand about this fascinating story, and the hardest part of writing was filling in the gaps from my own imagination since I was anxious not to detract from the inspired Word of God. Paradoxically, I found myself writing a myth to prove that the Biblical account was not a myth!

Some scholars believe that the story of Noah's Ark was derived from the Babylonian deluge accounts. I lack the academic knowledge to refute this, but if I had based my novel on them it would have read like *The Arabian Nights*. The version included in *The Epic of Gilgamesh*, (English version, NK Sandars, Penguin Classics 1970) is filled with improbabilities and inconsistencies. To me it reads as a late, corrupt copy of the Genesis original, and instead I have imagined Noah using a primitive form of writing to record things properly.

Inevitably my book will arouse controversy. For example, Bible-believing Christians are split as to whether the Flood covered the whole planet or a limited area. At the risk of offending many of my readers I take the second view. The Old Testament concept of the whole earth is well expressed in Psalm 113:3: 'From the rising of the sun to the place where it sets, the name of the Lord is to be praised.' Clearly the psalmist believed in a flat earth centred on the Middle East. The Bible never mentions the Americas, Australia or even Britain. Why flood these outlying regions just to punish the sinful descendants of Adam?

Consider also the dimensions of the ark: 450 feet by 75 feet, with three decks. The lower two were probably used for storage since they had no natural illumination, and Noah needed to provide food and drinking water for his family and the animals for the year they spent in the ark, together with enough to carry them through until the next harvest. The ark could not accommodate every animal species on earth, and in any case there were only eight people to care for them all.

But I hope these arguments do not detract from the real message of the Great Flood. Many of us still think of it as a Sunday school story with a cheerful Mr Noah and his floating zoo, but actually it is one of the grimmest stories in the Bible: an account of God's terrible judgement, with a whole civilization condemned because it missed its opportunity to repent.

As I have already mentioned, Jesus compared the Great Flood to the time when he will come again. Apart from all the evildoers who will be punished, there are many ordinary people who have been lulled to sleep doing the normal things of life, ignoring God until it is too late. It is unfashionable to remember that almost all we know of hell and eternal punishment comes from the lips of Jesus himself in the Gospels or through his disciple John in the book of Revelation. The Flood is neither a pretty children's story nor an interesting myth – but a dire warning. I hope my book underlines this.

A crucial passage in the book is the vision that I imagine

Noah having while he agonises over the fate of those who have drowned. I used perhaps the most controversial passage in the entire New Testament, 1 Peter 3:18–20 (CEV):

> 'Christ died once for our sins.
> An innocent person died
>   for those who are guilty.
> Christ did this
>   to bring you to God,
> when his body
>   was put to death
> and his spirit
>   was made alive.

> Christ then preached to the spirits that were being kept in prison. They had disobeyed God while Noah was building the boat, but God had been patient with them. Eight people went into that boat and were brought safely through the flood.'

At the risk of offending theologians, I took this passage literally – and imagined Noah having a preview. Those of his servants who had already been warned still rejected the Holy One (Jesus) since it was too late for them, but some of those who had never heard had a chance to respond.

But perhaps the hardest thing for Noah was to see the rapid moral decline *after* the Flood. He may well have been tempted to feel that he had failed. However, there is a glowing obituary to him and his fellow saints in the letter to the Hebrews: 'Every one of those people died. But they still had faith, even though they had not received what they had been promised. They were glad just to see these things from far away and they agreed that they were only strangers and foreigners on this earth. When people talk this way, it is clear that they are looking for a place to call their own. If they had been talking about the land where they had once lived, they could have gone back at any time. But they were looking forward to a better home in heaven. That's why God wasn't ashamed for them to call him their God. He even built a city for them' (Hebrews 11:13–16).

For a full list of my source material, please see page 239.

– Andrew Guyatt

1

He was near the river by the altar stone where they burned babies to the gods. This time the ash and blood had gone, scoured by the torrential rain beating on the stones. He was alone, soaked to the skin and terrified. Choking mist and water hammered down in a never-ending torrent.

Above the din of the storm there was a new noise: a distant rumble like thunder in the hills. It grew nearer and nearer. Desperately, he forced himself to turn and face it. Through the gloom came a great wave of green-blue water higher than the tower of the temple.

There was nowhere to run. The last thing he saw was the foaming edge of the wave curling over, with huge trees floating on it like leaves. Then it was on him, smashing him against the altar.

It was dawn and the haunting childhood nightmare – that thing he could never bring himself to talk about – was slowly fading. He was in his room, sprawled on the floor beside his pallet. Cautiously, he sat up. An earthenware jar was lying smashed alongside him, the water spilt everywhere. He felt the pain of a stifled scream in his throat.

Through a gap in the shutter he saw the hills turning gold as the sun rose, looking as arid as ever they did in late summer. No mist, no driving rain or waves… just the old familiar world in which he had lived so long.

A noise distracted him. Zillah had woken, her hair in a tangle. She was straightening her red robe with both hands.

'Noah! What is it?'

'I'm sorry. It's… '

'… that dream again? The one you keep getting?'

He nodded, wiping his forehead. It was cool in the room, but he was as rank with sweat as if he had been running for his life.

Suddenly Zillah started sobbing. He took her gently in his arms.

'I'm so scared!' she exclaimed. 'It's an omen. Something terrible is going to happen!'

'It's nothing, love. Don't worry.'

She faced him. 'Now look, Noah. You can't fool me. You're as frightened as I am.'

'Well, yes... I suppose I am... in a way.'

'Don't you realise? Tiamat is trying to *warn* you about something!'

He jerked away, irritated.

'You and your gods! This Tiamat... this chaos monster of yours... it doesn't exist!'

'So who sends the big wave, then?'

'What? I've never told anyone my dream!'

'You don't need to! I've heard you screaming that the water's coming to swallow you. You don't know what this is doing to everyone. The servants are terrified. They're sure you've been cursed. I've lost two girls already and the rest could walk out any minute.'

'It's not that bad, is it?'

'You don't know the half of it. Even the men are scared stiff. Haven't you seen them make signs against the evil eye when you walk past? If they go we'll have no one to protect us from the Cainites.'

'So what do you suggest I do?'

Zillah looked nervous, her eyes pleading. 'You're not going to like this. But... for a start you... *we* might make a sacrifice... to Marduk. They say he's the one god strong enough to deal with Tiamat.'

'Zillah! You know I'll never worship a demon! I'll not give up my father's Holy One for anyone.'

'But no one's asking you to. All I'm suggesting is one *small* sacrifice. That's all. Just enough to keep everyone happy.'

'I can't! It goes against everything I believe!'

'It's just for appearances. I mean, if you go along with the priests now it'll make us... everyone feel a whole lot better.'

She took his arm. 'Noah, please! Just for me! And for the boys. No one will think any less of you.'

'I'm sorry! It's quite out of the question.'

'But things can't go on like this.'

Noah paused. 'I've been wondering whether I ought to go and see the old ones.'

His wife snorted. 'What! Run away to Daddy and Grandpa so that they can kiss it better?'

'I need to talk this over, I need their wisdom... '

'They'll stuff your head with stupid old-fashioned ideas, more likely. And what about us? I get so scared when you're away! There's so much violence nowadays... everywhere. They say the Cainites are on the march again.'

'I'll be as quick as I can. Anyway, I'll leave Reu with you. He won't stand any nonsense from the men.'

'But what if you get attacked? Or worse?'

'I'll be quite safe. I'll take some good men with me.'

She laid her hand on his shoulder. 'Love, do you have to go?'

'I'm sorry. I must. Besides, I want to sacrifice to the Holy One.'

'You and your Holy One! That's all I ever hear! If your Holy One's that special why isn't anyone else worshipping him? Tell me that! Just you and your doddering old family!'

'But he's the true... '

'What? Everyone gave him up *years* ago. You just find me *one* person in the city that worships him – just one I say – and I'll listen!'

There was a painful silence.

'Oh, I'm sorry, Noah. I shouldn't have said that. It's just that... I'm so worried. But I suppose you'll go anyway.'

She laughed suddenly.

'At least do me a favour. Take Tiras with you – and lose him!'

'Tiras? Why? What's he been up to?'

'The usual! That stupid granddaughter of Eber is having his brat! You know... the fat girl with the squint who keeps dropping things! Just get him out of my way.'

Noah spent the morning with his foreman Reu discussing the running of the estate during his absence. The harvest was almost in and the main concern was to mount a proper guard. Full barns were a temptation for those in the city.

He chose ten men to accompany him on the journey – loyal,

experienced fighters who would keep their eyes open and their weapons within reach. He issued each with a bow and arrows, a spear with a fire-hardened tip and a flint dagger. They took food for a week, presents for the old ones and a lamb for the sacrifice. Everything would be carried on their backs; pack animals would slow them too much.

He slept well that night but his rest was all too brief. It was still dark when his assistant foreman Seth woke him. The days were shortening and there was not a moment to lose. He took a drink from the water skin and grabbed a crust before they were off. They moved quietly to avoid disturbing the household. But Zillah was at the door as they were ready to leave.

'Look after yourself! Get back as soon as you can. Nothing's right without you!'

Perhaps it was her way of apologising for yesterday. Noah hesitated, but the men were already moving off.

Travelling through the estate they were fairly safe, but outside would be a different matter – particularly where the track passed through forest. It was broad daylight when they reached the old road running across the Great Valley from the city to the mountains. It was a good day for walking; the sun shining but the air crisp. Now the river was behind them, the land was open, with only occasional copses. The men walked silently, alert to any signs of danger.

Suddenly Seth touched Noah's arm. 'There, Master!' he whispered, pointing ahead. 'Some folk near the road.'

Noah paused, staring into the distance, then began walking again. 'Let's go on. They don't look like Cainites.'

The strangers approached, passing uncomfortably close but then disappearing into the scrub. Noah looked anxiously after them, conscious of sweat trickling down his neck and half expecting a spear in his back.

Occasionally they saw other people in the distance, gathering wood or picking the last berries of autumn, and once a group of men crossing a clearing.

Seth nodded towards them. 'No need to worry about them, Master. They look like hunters to me. Chasing deerskin for clothes, I suppose. Or after a nice fat bear to grease their stomachs.'

Noah grimaced.

At midday they paused by a stream. 'Don't get too comfortable,' Noah warned the men as they threw themselves down on the rough grass. 'We'll need to be off soon if we want to make camp in daylight.'

The afternoon seemed unending. Noah clutched his dagger inside his robe until his fingers were stiff.

'We're here, Master!'

He stopped with a jolt. He had been deep in thought, worrying about Zillah and the boys, and failed to notice that they had reached their usual camping place on a small hillside at the edge of the Great Valley. Years before, a tribe had lived here, burning the woodland and cultivating the soil till it lost its vigour. The trees had yet to grow back and there was a clear view all round.

While Seth took Tiras to check out the area, the others gathered wood which they lit from the bowl of smouldering charcoal Seth had carried slung from his neck. They ate their evening meal of bread and cheese, stretching out tired legs to the blaze. Two men at a time stared into the dusk, alert for any attackers. But there was only the rustling of nocturnal animals beginning their foraging.

Seth slept little, continually checking the lookouts and rousing men for their turn of duty. It seemed hardly any time before he was waking Noah.

'First light, Master.'

Noah pulled himself stiffly to his feet.

'It really feels like winter's coming. I won't be sorry to sleep indoors tonight!'

The men took turns to drink from the skin, grumbling as they helped each other shoulder their loads. Seth checked each one before giving the order to start.

Soon the road sloped steeply upwards and their pace slowed. Beech and oak gave way to pine and birch. The track narrowed and became more overgrown now they had left the main settlements behind. But at least they felt there was less danger of attack.

At midday Seth called a halt. It was much cooler now. After eating, the men stuffed their sandals with hay for warmth, and pulled their cloaks of woven grass over their heads. The long slow climb continued through the woods till suddenly in the late afternoon they came out onto bleak moorland, and stood blinking in the brightness. But there was no warmth in the sun and the wind was bitter.

Seth turned to Noah. 'Not long now, Master!'

'Yes. The steepest part of the climb. But at least we're in sight of the homestead now. I always feel better when I can see the watchtower.'

Up ahead some low buildings sheltered in a fold of the hill. At the eastern end a tower showed starkly against the sky. A lonely place built at the edge of the world. Forgetting their heavy loads, the men hurried up the hill to escape the biting wind. There was a shout from the tower.

'Do you come in peace?'

'Yes!' Seth bellowed back. 'Don't you recognise Noah and his men? Come on, open that gate. It's cold out here!'

As they neared the heavy gate there was the grating of bars being drawn and creaking as it opened. Noah entered first, then his men impatiently shouldered their way into the courtyard and started slipping off their loads. Noah looked round for the old ones.

'Welcome, Noah! This is a very pleasant surprise.'

It was his father Lamech. And behind him his grandfather Methuselah hobbled out of a doorway.

Noah gazed anxiously at them, but they seemed the same as ever – wizened old men, more like brothers than father and son. Years of living on this windswept hill had dried them out, wrinkling them like fruit left in a store room. But their eyes were alive, darting everywhere and missing nothing.

'You must pardon us. If we had known you were coming we would have had a meal prepared for you. I am afraid we do not have much to offer. But please be patient with us.'

Lamech turned away, clapping his hands.

'Adam! Quickly! Food for my son and his men! They look frozen after their journey. Make sure that all the fires are burning.'

Soon Noah was reclining in the old familiar room, listening to the crackling from wood hastily arranged on the smouldering peat fire. As it blazed up, he gratefully stretched towards it.

Adam – a bent old man looking as ancient as his namesake but hardly changed in all the years Noah had known him – brought him a cup of milk.

'It's good to see you again, Master. The women are preparing

14

your meal.'

There was gruel from barley grown in a sheltered valley nearby, cheese and butter made with sheep's milk, and rough bread. And – an autumn delicacy – a platter of berries sweetened with honey.

The old ones joined him, pecking at their food. He sensed their intense curiosity but, following the ancient custom, they ate in silence.

Afterwards, Lamech asked the usual questions about the family. Then, almost for the first time, Methuselah spoke with his strange old-fashioned intonation.

'Noah, you look worried, my son. Perhaps there is something which you wish to tell us?'

Noah rested his head in his hand. He was still frightened by his dream. But he had come all this way to ask their advice and there was no point in holding anything back.

'Sir, there is a dream I have had many times since I saw you in the summer.'

Lamech interrupted him.

'You must speak up. Your grandfather and I can hardly hear you if you mumble like that.'

Noah lifted his chin and began speaking slowly and much louder. The dream sounded thin and unreal as he described it. When he had finished, they sat silent for a long time. Nervously, Noah watched their faces in the flickering lamplight.

Finally, Methuselah spoke. 'It seems clear to me that the Holy One is speaking to you, just as he did to my father Enoch. He knew the Holy One far better than I do, for all that I have lived so many years.'

Then he began recounting a story so familiar that Noah knew it word for word.

'The first thing I remember is sitting on my father's knee. His robe always smelt of woodsmoke and I felt safe there. I would stay for hours while he told me of our family history, teaching me the names of my ancestors, of their children, of the years they had lived.'

Methuselah paused, looking intently at Noah. 'He always said that to understand a man you should know his name. And the name Enoch meant *to start a work.*'

He chuckled – a chuckle that turned into a cough and he reached for his cup.

15

'I often wondered why they called him that, because Cain gave the same name to his firstborn and to his city too. By all accounts, that particular Enoch was an evil man, so unlike my dear father. And I decided to ask why he had called me Methuselah. You must understand: even in those days it was a strange choice! Some of the more unruly boys used to laugh at me!'

He coughed again. 'My dear mother had no liking for the name; she had her own pet name for me. But father was insistent. He said the Holy One had given it to him in a dream while mother was carrying me.'

As a child Noah had always prompted him at this point, and now the old familiar question popped out.

'Sir, what did it mean?'

'Well, in the old language Methuselah means *after he dies it will be sent*. Father told me that I was going to be a sign to everyone, that after I die the Holy One will bring some terrible judgement on men for their evil deeds. But while I live, there is still time for them to turn back to him and ask his forgiveness.'

'But, sir, they have not turned.'

'No, indeed! And it grieves me. I hear that in the Great Valley the people are more evil than ever. I believe it cannot be too long before the Holy One punishes them. Men were wicked in my youth, but at least you could walk round your own fields unmolested.'

He paused, staring into the fire. 'In a few years I will go to my fathers. I tremble to think of the things that will happen then. What kind of judgement will follow? I never met anyone – not even my father – who could tell me.'

He looked directly at Noah. 'But tonight I begin to understand. I think the judgement is revealed in that dream of yours. I am sure the Holy One has marked you out for his purpose. If you prove faithful he will show you more, though it will not be easy. But remember that your father and I are always here to support you.'

He smiled. 'I trust that you will sleep quietly tonight. You need rest after your dream and your journey. Tomorrow we will make an offering to the Holy One and seek his will.'

2

The ancient stone of sacrifice stood on the hill overlooking the homestead. Noah gazed anxiously at the old ones.

'My men would be happy to carry you up there.'

Lamech was irritated. 'We are not so old that we cannot climb a small hill to offer worship to the Holy One. But ask your servants to gather fallen branches from the forest for the fire.'

The wood was ready to light long before the old ones reached the top. They killed the lamb with a flint knife, sprinkling the blood and burning the body as a sacrifice. There was a strong breeze and the fire blazed fiercely.

They waited till it burned low, then scattered the hot embers. Afterwards the old men laid their hands on Noah and blessed him.

That night he dreamed he was in the Garden of Eden.

He had gone looking for it many years before, but there was nothing left except an arid waste scarred with piles of salt, tree stumps, and a few straggling thorn bushes.

But now he saw it in its full glory – warm and moist from a heavy dew and bursting with life. The trees were loaded with flowers and fruit, the colours so vivid that he shaded his eyes. And there were animals. He walked towards a gazelle which calmly lifted its head to be stroked. A bear growled softly with pleasure when he scratched its shoulder. Everywhere the creatures of the Great Valley – cattle, lions, leopards and sheep – mixed fearlessly together.

Then he saw the man and woman, naked but seeming to be wrapped in light and to have a tangible joy that lightened his spirit. They were the most complete people he had ever experienced. The man was digging near a tree. He took a young shoot and tenderly planted it in the dark moist earth. The woman was holding some chicks while a hen clucked contentedly round her feet.

Then the man straightened up and looked at the sinking sun. There was a surge of excitement; the gate of the garden was open and the Holy One was coming.

Noah turned his head away, blinded by glory. Through his fingers he saw the couple running to the Holy One like excited children.

'Look at these chicks I've found!'

'See the shoots I planted. They're growing already!'

The Holy One left them to explore the garden, the man explaining each animal and plant to his partner. As they dug and pruned, they looked like children playing – till Noah realised how skilful they were. In a few minutes they did more than he could achieve in a day of hard labour. He willed them to go on, but all too soon he saw a shining figure approaching: the evil one, decked in gold and jewels, still glowing from the time he had walked among the stones of fire when the world was forged.

Noah felt a shock like a hammer blow. It was a tiny fragment of the Holy One's pain of betrayal. This gorgeous being had been the loved and trusted chief of the cherubim, but that was not enough to satisfy him. He had challenged the Holy One himself, and had been hurled out of heaven.

The woman knew nothing of this. She was dazzled by his beauty. It happened so quickly. First the insinuation of doubt; the lie about the Holy One and the sudden burning desire for secret knowledge. In a moment the fruit was picked, tasted and shared. The man and woman – now stripped of their glory – grabbed at leaves to cover themselves.

That evening the Holy One returned for the reckoning. The shining being was cut down to a wretched crawling thing. The woman's wonderful heritage of bearing new life was scarred by pain. And the man's joyful work became backbreaking toil. They were turned out of the garden to die; the gate closed for the last time and cherubim with flaming swords mounted guard. The Holy One was left alone, sobbing for the friends he had banished.

Adam, huddled in his skin cloak, raised his eyes to Noah with a look that would haunt him forever. He had never imagined such despair.

Somehow the couple began again. There was a brief happiness as Eve rejoiced with the Holy One over her newborn sons. Although the soil had been cursed, Adam had not lost his husbandry skills. Soon he was growing crops and taming a flock of sheep.

Then tragedy left them huddled together in grief. Their son Abel was dead – killed by his own brother Cain. Turned into exile, Cain carried the awful mark of the Holy One to save him from the man-creatures who would otherwise hunt him down. Noah recoiled from Cain's face, already frozen in stubborn lines, too proud to ask for forgiveness. Guilt, anger and rebellion would be a fearful legacy for his sons.

Generations passed. He saw Lamech the Cainite genius, inheritor of all Adam's imagination and skill, encouraging his sons. Jabal learned to tame wild cattle; Jubal was a musician, making harps and pipes for his new gods; and Tubal Cain forged bronze and iron to make weapons that would rip men apart.

'Strange!' Noah mused. 'This Lamech shares his name with my godly father. He's worse than Cain! He boasted that he had killed a boy, a mere stripling, whose only crime was to hit him!'

Then Noah found himself in their temple, with its deafening thud, thud, thud of drums and wail of trumpets. Through the darkness he could make out the masks of the prancing dancers, maddened by the herbs they had eaten. They were weaving to and fro, taking first one child then another... while on the altar the body of a baby still twitched...

Noah flinched, sickened, remembering the time he picked up a bundle in the dark only to find it held a rotting animal.

Now he saw his own ancestor Seth, Adam's third son, with his family. There was hope again; men were even beginning to call on the Holy One. But soon they fell under the Cainite spell and learned the terrible secrets of their gods. Men acted on evil impulse, grabbing everything they wanted and degrading everyone they desired.

Next he saw the Nephilim: huge men bursting with layers of fat, the sons of gods or demons who had forced themselves on mortal women. Their eyes probed him, gleaming with lust as if they would rip out his very soul and crush it.

Then he was outside the temple. His great grandfather Enoch stood on a stone platform, prophesying to the crowd. They bayed at him, frantic to leap on him.

'You defy the Holy One!' he roared. 'You've trampled on everything he's done. But he's coming to judge you!'

The mob boiled over in fury. Men leapt to spit in his face and tear him with their teeth. Some grubbed up stones to throw; one hurled a skull, another a clod of dung. It smashed into his face before falling to cling obscenely to his robe.

Through the oaths, someone shouted, 'If your god's any good, why isn't anyone worshipping him?' Noah winced. It had been Zillah's question. But nothing would silence Enoch.

'Look! The Holy One's coming to judge you... every one of you! No one will escape. And he's got an army: hundreds of thousands of men like me that love him. They'll judge you for every filthy thing you've ever done or said, down to the curses you are shouting now!'

The crowd surged forward trampling on those in front. Noah flinched, fearful of what would happen, but somehow, incredibly, Enoch faced them down. Slowly the noise died away to a grumble, then a long silence broken only by his footsteps as he strode off unharmed.

But the people wouldn't be stopped. No longer content to practise their fearful rituals in the dark, they flaunted them in the full light of the sun. At the altar Noah saw his own uncle tearing with a knife at the chest of his baby son, ripping out the tiny heart in the name of some foul god...

The dawn light brought little relief. The fears of the night crushed him. He lay in a pool of sweat, helpless as a baby.

'Zillah's right!' he moaned. 'No one believes in the Holy One now! I might as well let go and die!'

❖

The day passed quietly. Night again, and Noah dreamed he was standing in the Great Valley. It was autumn and he sensed the passage of many summers. He noticed a mass of cloud spilling over the hills where the sun set. The cloud's black edge steadily cut off the sky.

There would be a terrible storm.

'I must escape! But where? If I could somehow cross the valley and make for the hills... '

He ran till his heart was bursting, but he was too late. The rain fell, crushing and blinding him. Now he knew what would happen next. The dream was becoming that terrible nightmare. In a moment the wave would smash him.

But instead he was flying like a bird over the valley. Mass after mass of black rain clouds swept in; earthquakes released underground springs; the sea surged over the land.

He saw men panicking, wading and swimming through torrents, frantic for a boat or piece of wood to save them. Some clung to buildings till they were submerged. Others tried to scale the mountains but were beaten back by great cataracts. Soon all that was left of the Great Valley was a few bloated corpses in water that stretched as far as the eye could see.

'Holy One, it's horrible! Horrible! It can't be happening! Stop it!'

Silence. Emptiness. A question seeped into his mind: 'Perhaps it really is Tiamat's doing?'

He imagined him lurking in the deep, smirking and relishing the destruction. He shuddered. 'What's come over me? How could I possibly think such lies? Even for a moment? No, it must be the Holy One doing this. His chance to get his own back on everyone! His revenge – and he's loving every moment!'

Even as the words formed in his mind he was ashamed. Once more he felt the piercing grief of the Holy One. It was as if a precious vase had been smashed and the Holy One was sitting on the ground sifting through the pieces. He picked up each shard, looking for the beauty that had once been there, before throwing it aside.

'That's just how we're destroying our world. We've spoiled our people, our homes, even the Great Valley itself. And however the Holy One looks at it, he can't find anything worth keeping. What can I do? Just *one* man?'

He saw the flood again: driving rain, thick mist, surging waves. But now there was something else… something floating on the water. A huge dark shadow unlike anything he had ever seen before. Not a boat. More like a huge coffin or chest, what the old ones called an ark used for storing clothes. But this ark was floating on the water; it had high wooden walls and a thatched roof with rain cascading off it.

Then he found himself inside. It was huge; hundreds of paces long. There were two levels packed with stores and jars and above a third, holding every kind of animal and bird. There were oxen, sheep and goats in pens, doves and pigeons in cages.

21

To his dismay he saw there were also vultures, ravens, wolves, lions and even biting insects.

People were moving between the pens and cages, tending their occupants. There was Zillah, her hair turned white; and their sons, fully grown. Those must be their wives and that stooping figure…

'Surely I will never look that old?'

The great ark floated on, till at last it landed and the people and the animals emerged safely. It was like Eden all over again.

'But where do I find this thing? This ark?' It was simply enormous, bigger than his homestead. Far greater than anything that had ever floated on the river. Why, it would stretch from one bank to the other and still overlap the shore!

Then the vision shifted. Near the river he saw a mass of scaffolding. Behind, not some great building, but wooden walls. There he saw himself, directing a gang of men sweating over a great tree trunk, rolling it into position.

He was appalled and lay babbling excuses into the darkness, staring at nothingness.

'O Holy One! You don't mean me? I could never build it! I'm just a farmer… a simple man! You'd need a son of the gods, one of the Nephilim to do that job. I'm too old. I've had my time. I'm tired. I've worked hard all my life building up an estate to leave to my sons. And it's so huge! I mean… where on earth would I get the wood? Even if the whole city decided to help me, they'd never be able to lay their hands on that amount of timber. And that's just the beginning of all the things I'd need.'

The night pressed down on him. He tossed and turned in his bed.

'Even if… well, it would take years – far more years than I've got left! And how would I pay for it? It would take everything I own! And my neighbours… What would they say? And the men in the city I do business with? They'd think I'd gone mad… stark, staring mad!'

Suddenly he was looking at more raging waves on a dark sea. But these were ancient waters; the seed from which the world itself had sprung. And something hovered above it, like a bird over its nest.

It was the Holy One's Spirit. He saw the Spirit working with the Holy One to bring everything into existence... light and darkness, sky and sea, the land covered with plants, the sun and moon and stars singing for joy. The sea, land and sky teemed with creatures. He saw the man, at first lying senseless, and then the Spirit breathed life into his nostrils. And Noah knew that the same Spirit was breathing into him. The power of the Holy One himself was released in his body.

3

Next morning Noah climbed the hill alone to the stone of sacrifice. As a boy it had been his favourite haunt. It seemed no time at all since those summer days when he lay here gazing out across the moor to the forest and the Great Valley. Beyond a few plumes of smoke there had been nothing to show that anyone lived there. In his daydreams he was the first person to set eyes on this land and explore it.

One day Methuselah had come with him. He was more nimble then, of course. He carried a staff but used it mostly to point out things.

'That is where we lived when I was a boy,' he explained. 'The family had lived in that same house since the time of Enosh. It was a fine old building indeed, with thick walls that made it cool in summer. All round it we had wide fields. We were well respected too, for all that we did not worship the idols.'

'But Grandfather, why aren't we there now?'

'Well, everything changed after my father Enoch prophesied against the sinners. They were very angry – very angry indeed. Often we were threatened. Once I was hit on the head by a stone. And our barns were burnt down. We even had to mount a guard over our crops all year round.'

'So you moved here, Grandfather?'

'Not to begin with. We stayed where we were while Father was with us. Then the Holy One took him, and my grandfather Jared decided to find somewhere safer.'

'So why did you choose this place?'

'We looked at many sites, but this was the best. Here, on the edge of the world, we feel safe, and far from the idols and wickedness.'

'It's a lovely spot – the best anywhere!'

Methuselah laughed. 'You should have seen it then. I remember how your dear grandmother wept when she first came here! It was so cold.'

He twisted himself round so that he could point to the mountains behind them.

'When we climbed up and looked towards the setting sun, we saw a valley filled with ice and snow.'

'I'd like to see that!'

'Maybe. But most men were frightened even to come this far. They believed that over that mountain there were ice demons who feasted on human flesh. Grandfather had a hard task persuading any servants to stay with us and on winter nights when the wind howled they would huddle together chanting their spells, terrified to stir. But at least the stories served to keep our enemies away!'

'Have you ever seen an ice demon, Grandfather?'

'No! And I do not expect to do so! It was just a silly story put about by men who did not believe in the Holy One. I am sure you remember how once I took you right over into that valley. I would not have done that if there was any danger!'

'All I saw was grass and bogs and pools of water.'

'It is much warmer than it used to be and the ice has gone, though even now sometimes, if you climb the mountain near sunset and look across, you can just see a glow in the far distance.'

'Is that the ice?'

'Indeed it is. But so far away that few men could ever reach it.'

'Grandfather, will the ice come back one day?'

'I hope not! It was such a relief to be free of it. The wind was less cruel and we could plant more crops. By the time you were born, it seemed as if everything had come right for us. The Holy One had given us new life.'

'And that's why you called me Noah?'

'Yes. Your father thought it a good name. *Comfort.* The Holy One was comforting us and helping us to raise crops from the ground he had cursed.'

Methuselah put his hand on Noah's head. 'We are so blessed that the Holy One has given us a faithful son who will build up the family. He will make our home a refuge for true worshippers and a place of prayer.'

But as Noah remembered those years his fists clenched. They might have been content to live in their isolated homestead, but he was desperate to explore the big wide world. As a young man he had bombarded the servants with questions about what lay down the hill, until one day in autumn his enthusiasm boiled over.

'Father,' he asked, 'why don't we move back to the Great Valley? The ground here's so poor we'll never grow anything. We'd do much better near the river.'

Lamech was dumbfounded. Red in the face, he stuttered to find words.

'How dare you! How dare you! Let me never hear you speak of that again! The Holy One put us here in this place, not down there among those filthy idolaters! All you want is a full belly and slave girls. And to forget everything we have ever taught you!'

'But... '

'You are just like all the rest! What have I done that the Holy One should send me a faithless son!'

'But there's no harm in just looking, is there?'

'Looking! Looking! Listen to me. Once you get among those dreadful people you will be serving their gods before you can turn round and... '

He raged while Noah stood with head bowed. But the longing would not go away. All that winter whenever the weather permitted he would climb the hill to look at the forbidden land. Lamech knew where his son's heart lay, for one evening in early spring he spoke again about it.

'Do you really want to leave us and go down to the valley?'

The question caught Noah by surprise. He flushed to the roots of his hair and it took him a moment to find his voice.

'Well... yes, Father, I would like to. But only, of course, with your blessing.'

Lamech sighed. 'We had such hopes for you, my son. You were the Holy One's comfort to us, to carry on the worship once we were gone. But you want to throw it all away!'

'No, Father! I only want to see what it's like down there! I still believe in the Holy One. I won't be like all the rest.'

Lamech shuddered. 'Sometimes I almost wish you would die! I cannot bear to think that after we are gone there will be nobody left following the one true God!'

'But I'm not forgetting him. In fact, I think it's him who's telling me to go!'

His father summoned him the next day.

'Your grandfather and I were discussing your future late into the night. We have decided that you may go to the Great Valley – but you may only have until autumn to see if you can make a success of your new life. If not, you must come straight back. We will be calling on the Holy One for your safety.'

A few days later Noah set off with two servants. It had seemed so natural at the time, but, thinking back, he was amazed.

'It was incredible, simply incredible that we didn't come to harm! And I don't know how I found the courage to go. I could never do anything like that again. Then, being given that farmland by the river... I couldn't have done better if I'd hunted for years!'

It had been a distant uncle who had given him his start, a man who had left the family many years before. Although he no longer worshipped the Holy One, he was pleased to help a relative. He lent the land to Noah for three years.

And Noah prospered beyond anything even he imagined. He had planted a new crop – wheat. There was a bumper first harvest. It paid off most of his debt in that first year and he still had several bags of grain to take home.

His family were amazed to see how he had changed. In a few months the slender boy had broadened into a man with firm muscles and a confident air.

'I never thought I would say it,' confided Lamech, 'but the time in the Great Valley has done you good! So long as you avoid idolatry and keep worshipping the Holy One.'

Noah had winced; they still did not trust him. But it made him more determined than ever. In all the years since that time he had been faithful to the Holy One. He also kept his promise to visit the old ones every year. Once, he was even able to persuade them to come down to see his land. The farm was expanding and he could tell they were proud of him. A highlight was the moment he showed off his herd of cattle.

'Here they are! All bred from one bull and some cows I got from the Cainites.'

Lamech looked amazed. 'How did you manage that?'

'Oh, I don't know. Perhaps I caught them by surprise. Anyway, they take care to geld any males they sell now, and my neighbours bring their cows here when they want them served.'

The old ones gaped when they saw how much milk came

from each cow – far more than from the sheep that supplied their dairy needs. Then he showed them the oxen hauling heavy loads, and finally the donkeys.

'This is the animal to use up in the hills to carry loads,' he explained. 'They're more nimble than oxen and you can even ride them yourself if they are properly broken in.'

But Lamech was impressed most of all by Noah's men. 'They seem to be very happy in their work, my son. You are very fortunate.'

'Well, I think that's due to your example. I remember how you looked after the men at the homestead and I try to copy you. Feed them well and treat them like free men.'

'It must be a relief to have them around in these lawless times.'

'Oh, yes. They're my eyes and ears. They make sure no one steals or damages anything. And they're pretty useful in a fight. I don't get much trouble from outsiders!'

'Do they believe in the Holy One?'

'I fear there's not much sign of it yet. They reckon I'm old-fashioned not to worship their new idols. But they're polite as long as I don't force my ideas on them.'

The old ones left for home after a week, taking several donkeys with them. They were pleased with what they had seen and promised to come back. But the years had passed and now they were too frail to make the journey.

An even bigger change in his life was when he married Zillah.

She was the daughter of a local farmer who was delighted to get such a successful son-in-law. The family home was full of idols but to please him Zillah agreed to worship his Holy One.

'Are we going to live in this hut?' she asked. Noah had always been too busy to build himself a proper house.

'Once harvest is over, I'm going to give you the best place in the whole valley!'

And he was as good as his word. In the next few years he built up the settlement, with a tall watchtower, granaries and sheds for the oxen. But the centrepiece was the farmhouse with five separate rooms, a thing of wonder to his neighbours, whose whole families were crammed into a single hut.

Those had been exciting years, watching the farm expand into an estate till he became one of the richest men in the Great Valley. He never seemed to have a bad harvest and his main problem was finding space for his food and herds. Every few years he bought more land.

After years of waiting they had three sons. He called the oldest Shem or *name* to remind him of the name of the Holy One. Then there was Japheth or *expand* – a tribute to the way that the Holy One had blessed him materially. The youngest, born with a mass of black hair, was Ham, a name that meant *hot* – a name that completely suited his nature. From the moment he could crawl, he was into everything!

Looking back, Noah had much to praise the Holy One for. He recalled a conversation with Zillah the previous year.

'I'm really pleased with the boys this summer. They've been a real help to me.'

She nodded. 'Well, they're growing up. They'll have wives and families of their own before we know it.'

'Yes, I suppose they will. Maybe it's about time I started turning some of the responsibilities over to them. It would certainly give me more time to be with you.'

She smiled. 'That would be nice.'

'I enjoy my work, of course. But I won't be sorry to take things a little easier. I'm getting tired of having to push myself.'

'You've earned some time off. You're not as young as you used to be.'

He stretched out his legs. Perhaps he was a bit stouter nowadays and looked forward more keenly to his midday rest. It was good to look back and savour his successes.

But that had been the very night the nightmares had started and everything had changed. So much for retirement!

The ash of the sacrifice began to blow around as a breeze sprang up. Noah set off back down the hill towards the homestead.

'Is it possible?' he questioned. 'The homestead looks as if it'll last a thousand years. But if that dream is really from the Holy One, one day soon it'll vanish under water.'

He stared at the buildings, straining to fix every last detail in his mind. He heard his father calling his name and, with a shock, realised that he would never be intimidated by the old ones again.

'I think I've spent my life trying to win their approval, worried about what they would think,' he mused. 'Even when I went down into the Great Valley, I was still trying to prove I hadn't let them down. But now the Holy One's given me a mission of my own and I don't have to keep justifying myself.'

That evening they sat together in silence. The fire burned low and one lamp spluttered out but they made no attempt to refill it. Then at last Noah told them of his latest vision, of the immense boat.

Afterwards there was a long pause before Methuselah spoke. 'We must thank the Holy One for giving this task to you. The Holy One will keep his promises and he will help you, just as he did my own father Enoch.'

Slowly, reverently, he turned to Noah and blessed him.

Noah and his men left next morning as the first rays of the sun lit the watchtower. The old ones hobbled to the gate to see them go. They looked so very frail, bent over their staffs. But Noah sensed there was something different about them, a new excitement. Suddenly he felt an almost unbearable surge of love for them, a longing to stay and share their last days. But there was work to do. He waved once more, wondering if this was the last time he would see them.

Soon they left the sunlit moors and plunged into grey, misty forest. He found himself questioning his visions as he thought of home.

'Perhaps things aren't so bad after all,' he thought. 'I'm sure the Cainites get up to some horrible things, and those rumours about what happens in the city... But my neighbours... well, they're all right. It's just a pity they don't worship the Holy One... '

They saw no one all morning as they trudged on. They had almost reached the clearing where they would take a midday break when Seth, leading the way, motioned with his hand. The men froze while he listened intently, cupping his hand behind his ear. Then he hurried back to Noah.

'Master! Do you hear that?'

For a moment Noah was only conscious of the small sounds of the wood, the drip of water from the mist-bound trees and the odd crackle of leaves. But slowly he became aware of a strange pulsation, first as a feeling in his legs and belly and then as a noise that seemed to come at him from every direction. He felt the hairs rise on the back of his neck. Forcing himself to speak calmly, he turned to Seth.

'Sounds like a drum.'

Seth nodded grimly. 'I think it wouldn't do any harm to check out what's ahead of us before we run into trouble.'

Tiras was already moving forward expectantly, so Seth beckoned to him and two others and they disappeared down the path. The others stood impatiently, flexing their shoulders, anxious to shed their loads.

Suddenly there was the sound of running feet. The men were reaching for their weapons when Seth and his companions appeared through the mist. They made straight for Noah. Seth struggled to catch his breath.

'Master ... bad trouble ... ahead ... bodies ... killers can't be far... '

Noah glanced round nervously. The trees were thick here, only a few paces from the path – an ideal place for an ambush. The drumbeat had ceased. Perhaps they were already being stalked.

'Let's move on ahead to the clearing. At least we'll be able to see to defend ourselves.'

They went forward, the men clutching their spears, staring into the undergrowth. As they reached the open space they saw two bodies, so mutilated they were hardly recognisable as human. The heads and legs were missing and chests gaped open.

Seth was at Noah's elbow. 'Look at that. I reckon whoever did that was after ripping out the hearts.'

'You mean it was a sacrifice?'

'No, they ate them, more than likely. They say it makes you a better fighter, taking in the spirit of the man you've killed. And they've taken the legs too; there's some good meat on them!'

Noah was horrified. 'But that's only a story. The sort you tell naughty children to make them behave.'

Seth shook his head. 'All too real, I'm afraid. Look! Here's their fire.'

There was a pile of embers with blackened bones. 'See, Master, there are the leg bones. They've cracked them open to get the marrow. And here's bits of skull. I reckon they've roasted the heads whole to cook the brains.'

Noah stared at the fragments of bone in horror, retching.

Seth took his arm. 'Master, we'd better go before they come back.'

Noah shook his head. 'No, let's bury these men first. It doesn't feel right to leave them for the birds.'

The men were terrified, but he insisted. They dug one large shallow grave and lifted the bodies in using their spears, then shovelled in the bones from the fire. They scraped the earth over hastily.

Noah stood for a moment, his head bowed in prayer, but aware that the men were desperate to be gone. All thought of a midday rest was forgotten. As they left the clearing he looked back at the mound of earth and shuddered. He had no more doubts about his vision.

4

'I'm so glad you're back! You've no idea what it's been like! A gang came up from the city two nights back! The first I knew, they were breaking into our granary!'

'Zillah, are you all right? The boys?'

'Yes, we're fine! Reu got the men together and they killed two of them, but the rest got away.'

She burst into tears. 'I've been so frightened without you! I didn't know what to do. I've even got the men guarding my door!'

By the time she had calmed down and told her story in detail it was nearly sunset. Noah just had time for a quick look round. As far as he could tell there was only minor damage to the buildings, while Reu and his men were unhurt apart from a few cuts.

He almost welcomed this distraction. He had been wondering how to explain his visions to his wife. The more he thought about it, the harder it seemed. Now they would have to wait. Once they had eaten it would be time to sleep.

The next few days provided fresh opportunities for delay as he busied himself dealing with the aftermath of the raid. But then one morning he found Zillah alone and knew it was time to say something. He swallowed a couple of times and was just clearing his throat when she turned her head away.

'Noah! I know what you want! You're longing to tell me all about your wretched nightmare! But I really don't want to hear any more about it.'

He clenched his fists. 'I'm sorry, my love. But this is important.'

'Can't you leave it for now? I've got a lot to do... '

'We've got to have this out sooner or later.'

She sighed and looked at him sullenly. 'All right then. I suppose I'll have to listen. Only, be quick about it.'

She sat staring fixedly at the wall, never once looking at him, while he struggled through his account. Eventually, he tailed off in the middle of a sentence.

She rose. 'Is that it? Can I go now?'

In despair he watched her leave, wondering if she had understood anything. There was no one else to share things with and the enormity of his task pressed heavily.

These nights he was battling with fresh nightmares. He dreamed he was struggling to build the ark single-handed with the rain already beating down. Often he woke in the darkness in a cold sweat.

Zillah was scornful. 'So much for gallivanting off to see your precious family! They were no help. You're worse now than before you went!'

But how to begin the work? Of course, he knew all about boats. They were always ferrying goods and livestock on the river. He had a number of coracles covered in cowhide and two craft made of reeds with high curving prows and sterns. For really heavy loads he relied on rafts made of tree trunks lashed together with reed rope. Going downstream they were steered using long pieces of wood, but when coming up against the current they had to be towed by a team of oxen.

'But this is about something much bigger!' he worried. 'I shouldn't wonder if it'll be larger than the Great Temple itself. And I've never seen a raft with side walls, specially one that's three floors high with a roof on top!'

The problem remained unsolved throughout the long winter. When spring came Noah began taking solitary walks along the riverbank; it was the one thing that calmed him.

'It's odd,' he muttered to himself. 'I almost feel as if the Holy One is coming along with me. I think I begin to understand how they said Enoch could walk with the Holy One. But I still wish he'd show me what to do!'

Zillah found his walks irritating. 'I've put up with you and your moods all winter. It's bad enough when you get under my feet – at least I know where you are. But now you're disappearing half the day just when the men need you!'

'I'm sorry, dear, but I've got to be alone with the Holy One.'

She snorted. 'That's rich! I've got enough things to do here without running your precious estate as well. You mark my words! If you keep on wandering off like that alone, some day someone will stick a spear in you! Then where will I be?'

The spring days were lengthening when his next vision came.

He was drifting down the river in a boat, watching the sky and overhanging branches. Someone, somewhere was speaking to him. 'Noah, this is the place to build your ark.'

He recognised the field as one just inside the estate boundary, about a morning's walk from the settlement. The main road from the city ran close by.

'But,' he objected, 'it's the last place I'd choose. People use that road all the time. They'll be able to see everything... No, I know just the spot... in the middle of the estate. It would be nice and safe there, out of sight.'

The voice came again, quiet but insistent. 'I have chosen you to warn everyone of the danger that is coming. They must know what you are doing.'

'But... just there? Couldn't we move it beyond those trees?'

'The ark must be in plain view. It will be a constant reminder both that judgement is coming and that there is a way to escape it.'

'But how can I possibly protect things while we're building? When we grew crops in that field they were always being vandalised or stolen.'

'The ark will be safe – and so will you.'

The vision took him to the riverbank. The field was flat, covered with large piles of branches where young trees and scrub had been cut down. Many years earlier the river had changed its course here, leaving a blind inlet. This water was covered by rafts, while oxen dragged heavy loads up the gently shelving bank.

He walked across the field to a large pit. They had dug clay from here to make bricks when he was building the settlement. Now in his vision the kilns were busy again. He turned and saw his men building an enormous structure. Along its length were little towers of bricks breast high, supporting a great lattice of timber. Some men were rolling tree trunks and tying them together. Others were filling the gaps between the logs with reeds and pitch. At last he understood.

'It's a cradle! We're going to build the ark on top of it so that we can get at the underside, and also keep it clear of rot and termites!'

He looked again. The logs the men were handling were larger than any on his estate. Immediately, he found himself in a cypress forest. The trunks stretched straight up, far over his head. Instinctively he knew he was in one of the great forests of the north. In the distance between the trees he saw an odd-shaped mountain, looking as if it had been split down the middle into two distinct peaks. He stared at it, burning the outline into his memory.

◆◆◆

He awoke alert and eager. Zillah was relieved to find he had shaken off his strange moods.

'Now's as good a time as any to start,' he told himself. 'Things are a bit slack three months before harvest. We can look at the site today, and maybe make a start on clearing the trees.'

He sat counting off on his fingers the things he had to do.

'I'd better take Reu with me this time. It should be all right to leave Seth in charge here; he did very well on that last trip. If the worst happens at least we're not too far away.'

It was a short journey, just a walk along the riverbank while a raft loaded with supplies floated down in the current behind them. The men enjoyed this pleasant break from their usual routine, but Noah was unable to rid himself of a feeling of unease. Twice he stopped the men while he listened carefully. When they had almost reached their destination, he called another halt.

'Reu. Can you smell anything?'

The foreman paused a long time before replying. 'I reckon someone's lit a fire, maybe just up ahead of us.'

'But that's on our land and none of my men are down here.'

'That's what I'm thinking, Master. Leave this to me. I'll go to take a look.'

Motioning with his hand, Reu formed the men into a defensive ring before crouching down and slipping forward to investigate. Through a gap in the bushes he glimpsed a small clearing bordered on one side by the river. Several rough shacks were clustered round a dying fire, with a plume of smoke still rising lazily. Some women were washing clothes in the river while children played in the water.

Noah noticed a dog coming his way. It began barking and Reu tensed his muscles, expecting discovery. Instead, a man emerged from a hut and cuffed it till it ran away howling. Thankfully, Reu wriggled backwards until it was safe to stand, then hurried back to the others.

He divided the men into two – one group guarding the raft while the others crawled to the edge of the clearing. He beckoned them to stand up and walk forward, holding their spears at the ready.

Reu whispered to Noah, 'Squatters! City folk! You can smell them from here. Look at all that rubbish everywhere – and the flies!'

They achieved complete surprise. A woman screamed as they reached the shacks. Five or six men came tumbling out naked and stared at the newcomers in astonishment.

'Any more of you?' Reu shouted. 'Come on out! We want to see you!'

Several others emerged while two of Noah's men rounded up the women. The squatters stood in a sullen line while their children hid behind them.

Noah began, 'You've no right to be here! This is my land. There's plenty of other places you can go.' And he jerked his thumb towards the boundary stone.

One of the squatters belched loudly and the rest started sniggering. But the laughter died as Noah's men moved forward menacingly.

'Get out!' Noah growled, 'and take all your stuff with you.'

Several men looked ready to object, but the spears held close to their throats quelled the protest. Soon, reluctantly, they were trudging down the road towards the city clutching their bundles of possessions. Suddenly an old woman darted back, ran right up to Noah and spat in his face. Two of his men whirled round to run her through, but Noah knocked their spears up.

'Let her be,' he ordered.

The woman didn't flinch, but jabbed her finger at him. 'I curse you! I curse you by the gods of river and forest and by the sickness that comes at full moon. I curse you for turning us out!'

Her strange sobbing sounds seemed to fill Noah's head. Out of the corner of his eye he saw the men turning away, trembling at her curse. Then Reu pulled his sleeve.

'Let's kill her! Better be on the safe side!'

Noah shook his head. 'I don't want her blood on my hands.' Turning to the woman, he ordered, 'Go on! Get out!'

She cackled, 'I wouldn't get too comfortable if I was you!

We'll be back! We've got enough men to make short work of you – and your fancy soldiers!'

She hobbled off, turning once to lift her shoulder as if daring Noah's men to throw a spear at her.

5

'Pile everything into the shacks and set fire to the lot!' Reu ordered. 'Then clean yourselves up in the river.'

Clearing up was a foul job. The squatters must have been there many months. It was sunset by the time they finished – too late to build shelters, so they would have to sleep in the open, taking turns to keep watch.

Noah woke suddenly at first light and got up stiffly. Something had disturbed him, but he could only hear leaves rustling and the low murmur of the river. The spring morning was cold and he pulled his robe about him as he walked round the men. Both watchmen were asleep.

Suddenly a twig snapped. He reached Reu. Putting his hand over his mouth to stop him crying out, he shook him awake. Then they roused the others and ordered them to pick up their spears.

There were more noises from the river. Someone ran through the gloom. They just had time to form a defensive ring; then men came at them from everywhere.

It was a desperate battle. Their enemies loomed out of the pale light, their screams cut off by the sickening jolt of spear tearing into living flesh. Inside the ring Noah glimpsed a white figure ducking between two defenders, and instinctively lunged at it with his dagger. He hit harder than he knew he could. It was all he could do to drag the blade out before the body slumped writhing to the ground.

Suddenly the attack was over. There was distant shout and the enemy melted away. For a moment, the men relaxed; then Reu called urgently, 'Stay alert! They may try again!'

Then there was a weary wait as the light grew stronger and the excitement of battle ebbed away. In the distance they heard a man crying in agony.

At long last Reu ordered them to stand down. A count showed they had only lost one man. Seba had appeared a few months earlier looking for work. He kept himself to himself and no one even knew if he had a woman to mourn him.

Reu checked the wounded. He had a reputation as a healer and was always in demand at the settlement.

'Nothing to worry about,' he reported to Noah. He took some dry leaves from his pouch and began chewing them. Before long he had made several poultices and bound them to the wounds with thread spun from a climbing plant. But he could do nothing for the man they had heard crying. He offered him water but he was too weak to swallow and died soon afterwards, calling for his mother. There were six other dead bodies scattered around.

'They're the squatters, all right!' Reu called. 'I'd know this man anywhere. He's got a scar right down his cheek and one ear's missing. And I fancy I know that one over there, too.'

It was the person Noah had stabbed. The body lay sprawled face down. When Reu unceremoniously tipped it over with his foot, Noah stared in horrified fascination at the woman who had cursed him.

Reu turned away. 'The sooner she's underground the better!'

Noah had an overwhelming urge to escape. 'Reu, can you tidy up here? I'll be back soon.'

'Be real careful, Master. Those squatters may still be around.'

He wandered away by the river. All he could see was the woman's face twisted in fury and the dead eyes staring accusingly at him.

'Why didn't she just go away?' he burst out. 'I didn't mean her any harm. I never intended to kill her!'

He returned as the men finished laying the dead in a large hole. The grave was already half full of water. He watched as they piled the earth back. There was a lot to do and he would have little time to brood. He walked over to the raft.

'Let's get this unloaded,' he told Reu. 'Then we can get some shelters up.'

They erected wooden frameworks, stretching reed matting over them and pegging it down with stakes. Then they took the precious sacks of grain and beans from the raft and stored them inside. Three men were delegated to make a lookout post on a tall tree near the road. They lashed timber together for a platform high up among the boughs, cut footholds in the trunk and hung a rope so that men could pull themselves up. The post would be manned day and night.

That evening the men took a long time to settle, sitting round the dying fire late into the night. Noah lay on his straw listening to snatches of their conversation. 'Will they be willing to stay here after all this?' he worried. 'What if the squatters do come back?'

But he grappled also with the vision which had bought him here. 'If the Holy One really meant me to build in this field, why did he let those people come in? Why did we have to kill so many of them? Is this plan really from him?'

He fell into a troubled sleep. Thankfully, when he awoke the men seemed cheerful and had already started work grubbing up bushes and felling trees. Their only difficulty was the lack of tools. Between them they had just two precious bronze axes. The only people who knew how to make them were the Cainites – and they were hard bargainers, charging what they liked for their tools.

They also had five flint axes. Although the stone for these had to be brought from the mountains, at least the tools could be fashioned at home.

Their best craftsman was old Eber. He worked outside in all weathers, generally with a mob of children round him listening to his stories. He wore an eye patch and if the boys were cheeky he would push it up and grin at them with his empty socket.

'That's the price I paid the gods to make me a craftsman!' he would cackle. 'Got a bit of flint in the eye when I was a lad, and it hurt so bad they had to take it out. Reckon I'm a bit more careful now – that other eye's got to see me through!'

Noah never tired of watching him twisting a lump of flint in his hands, then putting it between his knees, tapping it with a piece of stone. Without warning he would strike it hard, splitting it cleanly in two. A few more blows blocked out the rough form of the tool, then he shaped it by removing flakes, pressing on them with a piece of bone. Finally, he ground the edge on a flat stone covered with olive oil. Once satisfied, he carved a collar of deer antler to fit the blunt end of the flint, forcing it into a socket cut in a wooden handle. Then he bound it all together with damp plant sinew which tightened as it dried.

Although he never seemed to hurry, Eber worked far faster than the other men, reckoning to make an axe a day. The one thing that angered him was a bronze tool.

'I've no faith in these wretched newfangled things!' he would say, spitting on the floor in disgust. 'I can make anything you want from flint, and far cheaper than those Cainite robbers charge for that unnatural stuff!'

He had certainly kept Noah well supplied with axes, adzes, spears, arrow heads, knives and awls. He even made saws, melting resin to hold flakes of flint onto a piece of wood. But the flint tools were not as strong as the bronze ones.

※

All seemed to be going well with the work till near midday, when Noah was summoned.

'Master! We've found a shrine! This is holy ground; the gods will be very angry if we work here any more!'

His heart sank as he looked at the small altar stone with the carved figure of a goddess. His first impulse was to throw it into the river, but his men would be outraged. In fact none of them would even go near it; he had to take an axe himself to clear away the undergrowth.

He had hardly finished when there was fresh trouble. One of the precious bronze tools had disappeared. The culprit was brought to Noah, sweating with fear.

'Where's it gone?' he snapped.

'Master, I swear to you I don't know. I had it just now. I was one of the few trusted to use it.'

'What happened?'

'I was thirsty, Master, so I put it down. I swear to you by Marduk I was only gone a moment and I kept my eye on the place. It must have been one of those thieving city scum that had it. His own mother won't know him when I catch him!'

Reu picked up a spear, twisting it in his hands. 'Shall I kill him, Master?'

The man fell, clutching Noah's feet. 'No, Master, no! I've got a wife and three little ones – they'll starve without me!'

'Let him go,' said Noah. 'Killing him won't do any good.'

Soon afterwards one of the flint axes shattered. This at least could be replaced. But Noah began to hear mutterings.

'... Cursed I tell you... this place is sacred... the goddess will kill us all if we don't stop... '

That evening Reu came over to speak to Noah, looking

distinctly nervous.

'Master, pardon me bothering you, but... but there's something that might help. My wife... well she knows all the ancient rituals. If I were to... well if I were to fetch her tomorrow she could make the proper offerings so that we could appease the goddess. Then we could move the shrine.'

It was a hard decision; a betrayal of his beliefs. But what else could he do? He nodded reluctantly.

'Well, I suppose... if you must. But don't expect me to give you any help.'

He kept away from the site the next evening. By the following morning the shrine had vanished and the men were back at work.

It was a turning point. Things began to go smoothly. Eber was making fresh axes and soon the site was cleared. The large timber was piled on one side while the brushwood was chopped up for fires and charcoal. A gang of men moved away into the adjoining land to cut more wood while Reu set others to level the site. They piled a bank of earth all round, then flooded it with water carried up from the river. As this ran away or evaporated in the sun, they shaved off each mound of earth as it appeared above the surface.

Yet other men started burning charcoal. It was a regular chore at the settlement, but now they needed more than ever. The brushwood was piled in great heaps and covered in damp clay; then a flaming brand was thrust in at the bottom. They watched it day and night, replacing any clods of earth that fell off, since otherwise the hot wood would burst into flame.

They nearly lost the first batch when they stripped off the clay too soon. The pile flared up and the men ran round the camp yelling for others to help. Several nursed burnt hands that evening.

Reu had followed Noah's instructions faithfully but now he looked more and more puzzled. 'Why do you want all that charcoal, Master?'

'We're going to fire a lot of bricks', Noah told him.

'But wouldn't it be simpler to use sun dried ones?'

'They wouldn't be strong enough for what I want. When we've finished we'll be moving a lot of heavy logs over them and they'll crumble unless they're really hard. And if you don't fire them well they'll wash away when it rains.'

43

'But won't the roof protect them?'

'Roof? We're not building a house.'

Reu stared at him uncomprehendingly.

'No, we'll be building a whole lot of brick towers. About so high.'

Noah motioned with his hand, tracing the outline that he wanted.

Reu still looked utterly confused. 'Well, if that's what you want, Master.'

For a moment Noah was about to blurt out the whole purpose of the work, describing the building of the cradle and the way the boat would rest on it. But his courage failed him. What would this tough, no-nonsense foreman make of the vision?

'These bricks of yours, Master. Where are you going to store them until they're fired.'

'Well, we'll need a shed.'

'That's no problem. We'll build one. It won't take very long, Master.'

The work progressed. Gangs of men dug out clay, mixing it with chopped straw to make it easier to handle. Soon the first bricks were moulded and stacked in clamps, piles surrounded by charcoal and shrouded in damp clay. Once the fire was lit it would be weeks before they would be cool enough to handle.

Yet now harvest was coming and most of the men would be needed back at the settlement. For a few weeks Noah could turn his thoughts to the familiar gathering in of the crops. But in his mind one topic was dominant. How would he explain what he was building?

6

When men die, their spirits wander in the land of pitch.

It's an awesome place. Flames burst from the ground and mix with steam from the black, stinking pools. The sun is blotted out by a strange choking mist. Ears are filled with the rumble of distant thunder and the cries of souls in torment. Even birds flying overhead drop dead out of the sky.

Not even the scorpion lives there. Just men – worshippers of the terrible gods of fire. They find ecstasy sitting motionless day after day in the blazing heat like great birds of prey watching the sacred flame until their eyes cloud over. Their skin is yellow, rough as leather, covered in bleeding sores and tumours from the boiling tar.

Even the men of the city dread the place, recalling the time one of their youths witnessed the rite of the dead, the terrible full moon feast. The fire worshippers had snatched him from his parents and mutilated him. Somehow he escaped before he was thrown into a lake of fire, but when he returned home his hair was white and his family had to tie him up like a dog.

Noah was a boy when he heard this story from a trader selling pitch to Lamech. He had looked at the man awestruck. Surely the trader was the bravest person in the whole world, to go again and again to that accursed land!

Every night for weeks afterwards he cowered in his bed, fearful of being kidnapped and dreaming only of terror. Once, when he awoke screaming, Lamech came to him, sitting on the straw and putting his arm round him.

'What is wrong, lad? Why not tell me about it?'

Noah stuttered a bit before repeating the trader's story.

'Next time I see that man, I will give him a piece of my mind!' Lamech said. 'Fancy filling your head with all that superstitious nonsense!'

'But it's true,' Noah had protested. 'The trader has a friend who knows the family well!'

'Hmm... Strangely enough, I heard that same yarn when I

was young. Only then it was one of the Cainites who had been snatched. A servant told it to me when I had misbehaved and after that I used to lie awake shaking with fear. And what is more, your great grandfather Enoch knew the tale too. Only then the unfortunate young man lived near the hills and lost an arm in the fire!'

'So you mean... it isn't true?'

'No, of course not. But you must remember that your trader has a good living and is anxious to keep it. If people lose their fear of the land of pitch, they will go there and get their own supplies rather than spend a fortune buying from him.'

Noah thought for a moment. 'But that's a really good idea. Why don't we go and dig our own pitch? Then we won't have to pay him!'

His father suddenly looked uneasy. 'It is not worth it for the little we use. And I think it is time for you to sleep.'

Young though he was, Noah realised that Lamech was frightened too.

Ever since then he had followed his father's example and bought what pitch he needed from the traders. The land of pitch was one of the few places in the Great Valley he had never seen. But now he was building the cradle he needed a vast quantity of pitch to bond the bricks together, to say nothing of what he would use later to seal the ark. It would cost far too much to buy.

'There's only one thing for it,' he thought. 'I'll have to go myself with some of my best men. And it won't be just the one trip; we'll have to go time and time again before we're through!'

Once harvest was over, he fasted for three days, asking the Holy One for direction. The next morning he explained his idea to twenty of his trusted servants. They were horrified.

'But, Master!' Reu objected. 'You're not really asking us to go there! You know we've always done what's right by you, but this is different... '

'What's different?'

'Well... none of us would ever come back! It doesn't bear thinking about what they'd do if they caught us and.... '

'That's nonsense!'

The voice came from Pallu, one of the older men.

'Don't worry, Master. I've dug pitch many a time. It's a messy old job right enough but it's safe. There's worse places to go.'

Noah stared at him. 'You've actually been there?'

'Yes, and you can get almost all the way there by river. I reckon it'd take about eight days towing a raft, though it's quicker coming back with the current. You stop off at a village on the left bank which is the nearest point to the pitch lakes. That village is where all the business gets done. You go and dig the pitch, then they charge you a toll on each load you bring out.'

'Do you have to pay in gold?'

'You *can* do that. But we found it was just as easy to barter. They can't grow much round there, so they're always after grain and oil. And they're partial to a bit of fruit – grapes, figs, that sort of thing. I'd better warn you, they drive a hard bargain! You have to go a long way to find any other supplies and they know it. If you do barter, make sure you keep your stuff out of sight beforehand or they'll cheat you. Keep 'em guessing if you can!'

Noah quizzed Pallu about what they'd need for the expedition.

'There's the raft, of course, with something on top to hold the pitch. A wooden box does very well if you seal all the cracks with clay, otherwise you'll lose half of it on the journey. And I'd have at least two oxen teams so you can rest one while the other's towing. Then there's the baskets.'

'Baskets?'

'Yes. That's what the men use to carry the pitch out to the raft. It goes on your back with a strap round your forehead. The trouble is you sweat so bad you need to pad it carefully or it'll have all the skin off your face. There are several women round here who are very good at making that sort of thing. And one other thing: once you start digging it'll take a good three or four days to fill the raft, so be careful you don't arrive just before full moon!'

The discussion went on late into the day, but at the end Noah had eighteen nervous volunteers lured by his offer of double wages. Enough to man two rafts.

◆❖◆

The journey went surprising well. Once again Reu stayed behind in charge of the estate, leaving Pallu to enjoy his new status as

47

guide and foreman. Early on the eighth day he shouted, 'Master, see that smoke right over there! That's from the pitch lakes. Reckon we'll arrive soon after midday. We come to a sharp bend in the river and once we get round that we'll see the quay.'

As the morning progressed the men grew quiet and Noah could almost smell their fear. He kept a wary eye on them in case they panicked and headed back down the river. It was quite a relief when they reached their destination and could tie up the rafts and unyoke the oxen. The village appeared deserted apart from a few children who stared at them from a safe distance. At last a fat man emerged from a hut, wiping his hands on his greasy robe.

He wasted no time. 'Enkidu's the name. Come for pitch?'

Without waiting for a reply he continued, 'By the look of it you want a lot. Most folk don't bring two rafts. And you've got grain to offer, I hear.'

Noah glanced quickly at the rafts. They were completely shrouded in matting.

Enkidu grinned. 'Oh, yes. We don't miss much. We've been keeping an eye on you for days. What's your olive oil like?'

Somehow Noah kept the surprise out of his eyes. 'Everything I have is of the highest quality.'

'We've had a lot in recently. All we need for this year. Still... if you've got something special perhaps... we might make an exception. But it had better be good! A man of your experience will realise that all our pitch is already promised. The dealers don't take kindly to outsiders butting in.'

Pallu caught Noah's eye. 'Don't waste your time, Master. There's plenty of other agents who can fix a deal.'

Enkidu rubbed his hands together.

'Occasionally – very occasionally, mind you – we have been known to, shall we say, stretch a point? But you must realise that's just for exceptional customers.'

Noah turned, but Enkidu, moving surprisingly fast for a man of his bulk, blocked his way. 'In fact, let me suggest... '

Noah shook his head. 'I'm sorry, but I need to discuss this.' He walked off along the bank with Pallu. Out of earshot, Pallu suggested he should negotiate with Enkidu alone.

'He knows you're new to this and is looking for some way to cheat you.'

Reluctantly Noah watched Enkidu usher Pallu into his hut. It was almost sunset when the two of them emerged smiling.

'I've got what you wanted, Master,' Pallu explained when they were alone. 'I've got him to agree to let you load both rafts and you'll still have more than enough grain left to feed us all until we get home.'

'You've done a fine job. We can all rest easier tonight.'

'Not too easy! You'll have to be extra careful about setting a proper guard here. I don't like the way the locals are eyeing the oxen.'

◆

Despite their early arrival the next morning, the quay was already busy,. Noah heard two scowling traders muttering as he passed.

'... no right to be here. Enkidu knows not to let outsiders in without consulting us first.'

Noah turned to Pallu.

'As if I hadn't enough to worry about. And I'm dreading meeting those fire worshippers!'

'Don't lose any sleep over them, Master. They're no problem. Anyway, you've met one already.'

'I have?'

'Old Enkidu.'

'But I was expecting... '

'They're just ordinary folk, doing quite nicely out of selling pitch. But I do think it'd be worth making a sacrifice to their gods for the sake of peace.'

'A sacrifice? I can't do that! It's against my beliefs!'

'I understand, Master, but the men want it. You'd best just look the other way.'

Pallu led them to a shrine. Each man made his offering with his head touching the ground in front of two hideous idols.

Noah walked away, dejected. Once again he had compromised with idolatry. He wanted time to be alone with the Holy One. But the prayers died on his lips.

He returned as Pallu was giving final instructions. 'I know it's hot, but you'll have to cover yourselves to keep the pitch off if you can. Tie those rags round your legs, feet, and arms.'

They walked in single file along a narrow path. It was hard

49

going; there were drifts of sand and black patches of spilt pitch.

Their destination was a desolation of sand and dark pools lit with occasional gouts of flame. But not a fire worshipper in sight.

'Start over there,' Pallu ordered, 'where someone's already been working. Take turns digging and holding the baskets.'

There was no trouble finding pitch, but it was solid and needed the full weight of a man on a wooden shovel to cut it up. It was a dreadful job working in filthy black scum under the full sun, and the men cursed steadily as they worked. One man even sank to his waist in a pool of oil hidden under the sand.

But at last they filled their baskets and helped each other hoist them up. Despite all their care, oil dribbled down their backs and legs. Two men were left to mind the shovels while the rest staggered off down the path, heavily weighed down and frantically trying to maintain their balance on the rough track, blinded by the sweat pouring into their eyes.

Back at the rafts they upended their baskets, then waited their turn to take deep draughts of water before stumbling back for another load. After four trips they were exhausted.

That evening they tried to clean themselves, rubbing their bodies with sand and bathing in the river. But they still stank as badly as before.

Five exhausting days later they had their full load. The rafts were almost submerged, leaving oily trails in the water.

'At least we're travelling downstream,' Noah told them. 'But I'm afraid most of you'll have to walk, there's no room on the rafts.'

Four men guided each craft and kept an eye on the oxen which spent most of their time in the water, swimming behind. The men on the bank had difficulty keeping up, but they had a new spirit now that they were going home.

7

Now Noah could begin constructing the cradle.

Following his dream he had made sketches on clay tablets which were then baked hard. He showed the overall plan to Reu as they walked across the site.

'It'll lie that way,' he said, pointing downstream with his staff, 'with the long side facing the inlet of the river.'

Noah carefully pushed a stake into the ground. 'This should do for one corner.'

While one of the men hammered it in with a large stone, the others took a rope marked off in cubits and began stretching it out.

'You haven't got it taut,' Noah warned. 'You've got to make sure it's straight.'

Once he was satisfied, they hammered in another stake twelve and a half cubits from the first, then a third and fourth, and on till they had placed twenty-nine in all.

After making a final check, Noah nodded in approval. 'Now for the tricky bit. We need to lay out the two ends. They'll be one hundred cubits long so we'll need another eight stakes for each. But first we need to know if we're going in the right direction. Find me another piece of rope.'

They watched mystified as he cut it into three pieces, six, eight and ten cubits long with a little over to knot the ends together. He stretched it out on the ground so each piece was taut with the shortest of the three sides lined up with the stakes.

'Now, if you look down that next shortest side', he explained, 'it'll show you the way to go. I learnt that trick off an old Cainite slave when I was a boy.'

There was some head scratching, but soon the men agreed it looked right. They measured out the two ends. By now they understood what to do and they laid out the other long side by themselves. Finally they filled the centre with more stakes, each twelve and a half cubits from its immediate neighbours.

It took two full days of hard work. Just before sundown Noah stood looking at the forest of stakes.

'May the Holy One help me,' he murmured. 'The job's huge. And I haven't even started on the ark yet!'

❖

It was time to build. Two skilled bricklayers arrived from the settlement to train the men. Noah took them on one side to explain what was wanted. Each pier would consist of a square of bricks with a central core of clay. The foundations were two cubits deep with brickwork three cubits high.

There was a puzzled debate among the men that evening.

'What on earth's it all for?'

'No idea – but it's going to take for ever and a day!'

'I counted well over two hundred stakes out there! We'll need a mountain of bricks!'

'And those columns are so short, you'll never get a roof on top.'

'I suppose it must be for some religious rite or other.'

'Must be. I've always wondered why the old man's never built a shrine or temple. He can't think much of his god!'

'Yeah! A nice building's the very least he could do. He can afford it – if anyone can!'

'He's certainly acting very strange lately. My wife knows one of his servants and they say he's not been the same since he started having those nightmares.'

'What's it matter? He pays good wages.'

❖

They started with the piers nearest the river. Reu had made wooden measures to check the height and plumb lines to keep them straight. They were using pitch as mortar but there was some argument about how to soften it.

'Can't we heat it up in a earthenware pot over the fire?' Reu suggested.

Noah laughed. 'Father tried that once, in a hut. The pitch was just starting to bubble nicely when the pot cracked. By the time we got the flames out, half the roof had gone! Leave it to me, I've got an idea.'

He returned from the settlement with two bronze bowls

52

which he suspended above a fire. Solid pieces of pitch were thrown into them and the melted liquid ladled into jars to be carried by sweating men to the bricklayers.

Once the men became proficient they were divided into gangs. It became a regular game to see who could build the fastest. As each pair of adjacent piers was completed, the men lifted a long timber to bridge the gap between them.

'Make sure it's level,' Reu insisted, checking each end with a bowl of water. Once he was satisfied, the sides were built up and the top sealed with pitch to keep the weather out.

All too soon they began to run out of pitch. There was some grumbling when Noah announced a trip to get more, but most of the men were prepared to go back. Pallu would again be in charge.

But first Noah decided to pay a belated visit to the settlement. It was a shock when he realised how little he had been there recently. When he arrived, Zillah looked decided sour.

'To what do we owe this honour? Would my lord and master deign to enter this humble home? Perhaps he would care to be introduced to his own children?'

There was a sullen truce till they were alone together after the evening meal.

'So, are you all right?' Noah asked.

'No! Of course I'm not,' she snapped. 'You promised a year ago to build some more rooms for the boys. Instead you're wasting all those bricks and the men's time on your madcap scheme!'

'I'm only doing what the Holy One told me.'

'Holy One! You're crazy! Everyone thinks you've gone mad!'

'If you're so sure that I'm wasting my time, why don't you come down and see for yourself?'

It took some time to persuade her. As they arrived, most of the men were finishing the third row of piers while others were busy burning charcoal and firing more bricks. Down by the water they were making a final check on the rafts before another journey upriver.

Zillah walked round, lips pursed, looking at everything carefully till at last she came to one of the small fires where they were melting pitch. She spotted a gleam of bronze. Grabbing her husband by the arm, she dragged him to one side.

'By all the gods, what are you up to!' she screamed. 'Are you quite out of your mind? You've ruined my bronze pans!'

'I was going to tell you... '

'What possessed you to take our only good pieces? I've been searching for them everywhere. I could weep to see them covered in soot and muck. You'll never get those scorch marks out! It'll cost half our estate to replace them. That is if we *can* get any more.'

'But I need them for the work... '

'The work! And what in the name of Ishtar do you mean by that! Yes, you've told me about that wonderful ark of yours that's supposed to save us from a flood that's never going to happen! Don't you realise you're making me a laughing stock?'

'But, my love, I've tried to explain... '

'Nobody's got the faintest idea what you're up to – and that includes me. I don't know where to put myself when I meet other women; I can hear them sniggering as I walk past. And as for the estate workers, they don't even bother to keep their mouths shut any more. They think you're stark staring crazy. Another year of this and they'll all have left us.'

'But everything's going so well at the settlement.'

'Oh, it's fine for you. You drift in when it suits you! I'm cooped up there all the time, doing your wretched work for you; raising your family! A fine husband you've turned out to be – my mother was right about you!'

'But I'm trying... '

'And what's more, you've got the best workers tied up in this foolish escapade. All I've got are boys and toothless old men.'

Noah glanced round anxiously to see if the men were listening. They appeared to be working hard, but some of them must have heard. It would be difficult to live this down.

'... and the harvest this year's been a shambles. Just when it's ready you take everyone away. We'll be lucky to get half the grain we got last year! Everything's rotting in the fields waiting for someone to reap it!'

'But I'm sure we've got enough.'

'If we go hungry it will serve you right. There's only so much

54

we women can do... And don't you care about your sons? You've spent all those years building up the estate and now you're going to throw the whole lot away because of a stupid dream! What would you feel like if I did that? If this goes on we'll finish up as slaves. We might as well move into a tent now and have done with it!'

She was getting hysterical. He tried to put an arm round her, but she pushed him away.

'Just leave me alone!' she shouted. 'I want to get back to the boys! You can carry on playing your silly games here if you like, but don't drag me into them!'

After she had left, he sat in his tent till nightfall. He felt utterly alone.

'I wanted her help and support. How can I keep going if she, of all people, won't stand by me?'

In his mind he saw the finished cradle with the ark towering above. But he realised how bizarre and strange the site looked to anyone else.

'Did I imagine it all?' he groaned. 'Perhaps everyone's right: I am mad. Why did the Holy One pick on me, of all people?'

After a restless night he woke with a strong conviction that he should go straight home.

Zillah must have been expecting him. She had been up in the watchtower and as he arrived she ran out and fell sobbing into his arms.

'I'm so ashamed of myself,' she gulped. 'I knew all the time you were right... the flood... the ark... I've let you down in front of all the men.'

She buried her face in his robe. When she looked up again her eyes were brimming.

'How can you ever forgive me?'

8

'Bronze! Where can I get some from?'

It was dusk and Noah was striding across the site, totally preoccupied with the latest hold-up.

The men were gambling down by the river.

'Master's got something on his mind,' Reu grunted as he picked up the throwing sticks for his next wager. He made a cast, then got up in disgust.

'I'm cleaned out! I can't win a thing tonight! I might as well go and see what's upset him!'

Noah was back in his tent, sitting head in hands, muttering. Reu waited till he looked up.

'We really need some decent tools.'

'Decent tools? But what's wrong with Eber's?'

'There's just not enough of them, not even if there were five Ebers working from dawn till dusk!'

'We've got quite a lot of axes now.'

'Oh, yes. And they're fine when it comes to cutting scrub, but they're not much good on the bigger stuff, the sort of trees we need for this job out here.'

Reu's eyes dropped to the ground and he watched his foot tracing in the dust. 'You know, I'm doing my best, Master! I keep telling the men to be careful but they're forever splintering the flint edges. We can't keep up with the repairs!'

'I'm not blaming you. But flint isn't really good enough for this job. A bronze axe – that's the thing.'

'Of course! It'll cut anything, and when it's blunt it's easy to sharpen. If only we hadn't lost the second one!'

'We really need some for the next stage of the work.'

'The next stage?'

'We'll be needing to fell and shape a huge number of big trees. We'll never do that with flint – not in a thousand years! I've asked all my neighbours to give me their bronze and offered them anything they'd like. But there are so few pieces around

56

that each one gets handed down from father to son.'

'It's the fault of those Cainites. They make the stuff and won't let anyone else have any.'

'They sell a bit, but they're wary of letting too much go. They don't want to wake up one morning and find an army on their doorstep armed with bronze spears!'

'If only we could get hold of their secret, then we could make some ourselves!'

Noah looked at him hard; then dropped his voice. 'You want to be careful saying a thing like that! If they ever thought we were prying, I wouldn't like to think what they'd do!'

'So, Master, what do you have in mind?'

'I just don't know. The obvious thing is to risk it: go straight to them and ask them to sell us more bronze tools.'

'Wasn't that what you did when you bought your cattle from them all that time ago?'

'Indeed! People had been talking about doing it for years and got nowhere. So I went straight ahead and bought them.'

'It must have taken courage to do that.'

'A little, maybe. The main thing was that I got what I wanted. But the Cainites are a lot more vicious than they used to be. They could easily kill us on sight. I don't know anyone who would risk it, not even those Nephilim thugs.'

'I suppose the Cainites might come down here again on a trading mission? Like they used to?'

'Maybe. But you can't count on it. They usually wait till they're short of food. It could be years before we see them again. I need those tools now.'

◆◆◆

When Noah woke at dawn his mind was clear. He knew that the Holy One was telling him to go to the Cainites. He battled with the idea all day, trying to find excuses. The next day he returned to the settlement. He had decided to ask Zillah. She was the very last person who would approve of this plan; she was always upset if he was away from home for any time. If she said it was a stupid idea, he wouldn't go.

To his amazement, she heard him out.

'I can't say I want you to go, but I'm sure it's right. Don't worry about us. Seth looks after us very well. Why don't you go to see your father and grandfather first and talk it over with them?'

His mouth dropped open.

* ❖ *

He was back home within a week. The old ones had listened, prayed and given him their blessing.

'I'll take a lot of grain and oil to barter,' he decided. 'The Cainites are always short of them. But I ought to take some gold as well.'

He stood looking out over his estate.

'I've still got some of the gold dust father gave me to buy land. But I'll need more than that. The only way to raise that is to sell some land, though I hate doing it. I suppose that land over the river could go. It doesn't really contribute much.'

A neighbour had wanted that plot for years and the sale went through quickly. Soon he had three gold tablets to add to his gold dust. They fitted nicely in a money belt he would wear day and night under his robe. 'I'll blame any stiffness on my age!' he laughed to himself.

Zillah was indignant; her new mood of understanding was wearing thin.

'I don't know what you think you're doing! I loved that place! I was going to get you to build a house over there for one of the boys, and now you've let it go without even telling me!'

'I'm sorry, dear. I didn't think you'd miss it. I really do need to buy a lot of bronze tools.'

She sniffed. 'Well, I warn you there's a lot of talk. The servants think you're hard up. One or two are already looking around for other employers!'

Noah's next task was to recruit a party to go with him. They would know it was a dangerous mission.

'I'm heartily sick of these unreliable flint tools,' he explained. 'And I'm sure you feel the same. So I thought we'd go and buy some good strong bronze ones from the Cainites.'

There was a long shocked silence. At last Reu spoke.

'But, Master, I thought you told me you wouldn't risk it?'

'Yes. I did say that. But I can't see any alternative.'

He looked at his men, but they were all carefully avoiding his eye.

'So I'm asking for volunteers to come with me. It's a long way and I can't pretend it'll be easy. But I'll make it worth your while.'

Noah could almost see fear rising like a fog. It was several long minutes before the silence was broken.

'Count me in, Master! I'm not scared of any Cainites. I'm worth ten of them in a fight!'

Tiras pushed to the front. In the last year he had filled out and now he was a young giant. His arms were covered in tattoos of the gods that came alive as he flexed his muscles.

'I'll be glad to have you!' Noah's relief was enormous. He could feel sweat prickling his scalp.

Tiras nodded. 'It's high time someone stood up to them! Who gave them the right to push us around? Anyway,' he sniggered, 'I hear that they've got some fancy slave girls up there!'

Javan, one of the older men, joined him with a wry smile. 'I'll come. You've been good to us, Master, and you've got the luck of the gods.'

'That's right!' another called. 'Remember the way he dealt with the fire worshippers?'

After that a number of men, including Reu, sidled forward. Tiras seemed pleased with himself. 'Come on! Let's show these Cainites what the sons of Seth are made of!'

They took one heavily laden raft as they set off up river. For eight days the route was familiar as they retraced their way to the pitch lands, but beyond the village the men became uneasy. They passed a few huts and some moored boats, but no one seemed to be around. The river, however, teemed with life. Flocks of fowl erupted into the air as they approached, and crocodiles lazing on the bank slithered into the water. Once they saw a large pile of droppings and some huge spoor leading up the bank. There was a ragged gap in the undergrowth where an animal had forced its way through.

'Hippo, I reckon,' Javan called to Noah. 'I hope we don't run into one of those.'

'Yes,' agreed Noah. 'In the old days we had quite a few down by the settlement. It doesn't do to stir them up. I lost a couple of men and a boat once when one of them attacked.'

Two days later Tiras, walking ahead of the oxen, hurried back to Noah.

'Look! Along there, Master. Do you see? Men coming our way!'

It was a party of ten, heavily armed, marching along the bank. When they were about a hundred paces away, the leader hailed Noah's party.

'You'll have to pay a toll to come through here! What are you carrying?'

Noah felt a nudge.

'Let's kill them!' Tiras whispered. 'If you let them get away with this, everyone will want their cut!'

Noah shook his head. 'There must be more of them around, otherwise they wouldn't dare face us in the open. Anyway, don't forget we've got to come back this way. We don't want to find an army blocking our route!'

In the end they bought passage with five sacks of grain.

'We can't afford for this to happen too often!' Reu growled. 'Or we won't have anything to eat, let alone barter with.'

They seemed to be leaving the last traces of habitation behind. The river became narrower and the forest hemmed them in. One morning they crossed a large stream pouring down from the hills to join the river. In the distance through a gap in the trees they saw a strange mountain split into two separate peaks.

'The very place!' Noah gasped.

Reu was just behind him. 'What, Master?'

Noah turned. 'You'd better remember this stream. It goes up to the high forests. We'll be coming this way again to cut wood!'

On the twelfth day they reached a cataract and, a short way downstream from it, a small island.

'I remember this spot!' Noah announced. 'I came here all those years ago when I bought cattle from the Cainites. We'll have to walk now; we can't take the raft any further.'

Reu glanced towards the mountains ahead. 'Which way, Master? It looks pretty rugged to me.'

'We're heading for Tubal Cain's City. I've not been there myself, but I understand there's a track leading from the river around here.'

While they began unloading the raft, Noah took some of

his servants to reconnoitre. Suddenly a youth blundered out of the woods. He tried to run but Tiras grabbed him and brought him to Noah. He was shaking with fear and it took some time to calm him. Finally, with a lot of stammering and jerking of the head, he indicated a path through the bushes and described the route. Noah offered him pouch of grain. He looked at it suspiciously, then grabbed it and scuttled off into the woods.

When most of the cargo had been unloaded, Noah called Reu aside. 'I want you to stay here in charge of the raft and oxen.'

The foreman looked disappointed.

'I'm sorry to leave you like this, but we must be sure everything's safe and you're the one man I can trust. I'll leave you a couple of men and food for two weeks. Keep watch. And if you can get the oxen and raft across to that island by the rapids so much the better. They'll be safer there. Hopefully, we'll be away seven days or less. If we still haven't returned after two weeks, give us up and go home.'

They bundled the goods into about thirty packs. Tiras picked one up and turned to Noah.

'Why don't we take the oxen to carry this stuff?'

'I doubt we could get them along the path, and they'd be in the way if we have to escape in a hurry.'

The next morning before setting out the men made their usual offerings to the gods. Noah walked in the woods and made his own prayers to the Holy One. When he returned they were shouldering their packs.

'They look pretty heavily loaded,' said Reu.

Noah nodded anxiously. 'Maybe it will help to take their minds off the dangers ahead!'

The path took them toiling up one hill only to plunge into a deep valley beyond, then climbing again towards the mountains. Often they had to help each other over the steepest parts. The second night, Noah spoke to Tiras alone.

'It's strange. We haven't seen anyone since we started, but I feel that there are eyes all round watching us.'

'Yes, Master. I've seen several fresh footprints on the track, and don't tell me the birds stole that pouch of grain that went missing yesterday!'

'How do you reckon the men are doing?'

'I wouldn't worry. They don't say much but they know

they've got to stick together if they want to get out of this alive.'

Next morning they found themselves in a gorge. The track was carved out of the side of a precipice stretching high above them, while a river cascaded over rocks far below. In some places the cliffs squeezed the path until there was scarcely room to pass, then opened out again to form small valleys ringed with mountains.

Just before midday they came to a particularly narrow pass, and blocking the track was a stockade made of timbers black with age, with just one gate at the bottom. As they approached, the gate slammed shut.

'Well,' said Noah. 'I think this must be the entrance to Tubal-Cain's City. But they don't seem too happy to receive visitors!'

As he spoke, a man's head appeared over the top of the stockade. 'What do you want?' he yelled. 'Do you come in peace?'

Noah spread his arms wide. 'Yes! We've come to trade. To buy bronze tools.'

'Wait there!'

He disappeared, leaving Noah and his men standing nervously. Tiras put down his load and began stretching.

'No point in lugging that around if I don't have to!'

Some of the men laughed. Noah nodded. 'All right; this looks as if it's going to take some time. Put your stuff down, if you like. But keep your spears handy in case there's trouble.'

He walked back along the path to relieve himself. Making sure no one was watching, he pulled one of the gold tablets out of his money belt and slipped it up into his sleeve.

The men were still fidgeting and fingering their spears, casting anxious glances at the stockade.

'I hope they're not getting a squad ready to attack us,' Noah thought. 'We wouldn't stand a chance.' He took a deep breath, forcing himself to look calm.

Suddenly he heard dogs – a deep, terrifying baying. The door creaked open and a huge man emerged, armed with a large club. He beckoned impatiently to Noah.

'Don't show fear,' Noah told himself as he stepped through the gate and it slammed behind him. But his throat had contracted so that he could not swallow and his hands were wet.

He was in a courtyard with about twenty armed men who looked at him curiously, almost eagerly. The dogs, the largest he had ever seen, snarled viciously and hurled themselves forward, choking on the ropes that held them. The big man who had opened the door spat at them and as one sprang forward he smashed its head with his club, splitting the skull. In an instant the other dogs leapt on the body, tearing it apart. Noah stared horrified till the big man beckoned him inside a doorway.

As his eyes became accustomed to the gloom, he found himself in a small room facing three men. One, much older than the others, wore a black robe with a huge pendant round his neck.

'So, you've arrived at last!' he sneered. 'We thought you'd have got here yesterday!'

Noah blinked.

'Oh, don't look so surprised! We could have set our whole army on you and you wouldn't have known a thing till we slit your throats!'

'We don't mean any harm!' Noah protested. 'We're here to trade grain and oil for tools.'

'Well, I must say you're certainly different! Not many of you snivelling sons of Seth visit us! But I'm afraid you'll have to wait till I get further instructions.'

'What about my men?'

'They'd better come in and share this guardroom with you. But they'll have to give their weapons up first. You understand: we're a very *peaceable* people. It wouldn't be very nice if our guests attacked us!'

He left. Noah heard the creaking of the stockade door and the barking of the dogs rose to a crescendo. Through the doorway he watched his men being shepherded in and made to lay their weapons and baggage in separate heaps, before being ushered into the guardroom. It was a tight squeeze. They squatted on the floor with two men guarding them. One of Noah's men was clutching his arm where a dog had bitten him. After a time Noah shifted a little to ease the cramp in his leg.

'Sit still!' a guard yelled.

He forced himself to ignore the discomfort. He watched a tiny patch of sunlight moving slowly across the wall... and waited.

9

Just when Noah felt he could stand it no longer, the man in the black robe returned.

'Come on!' he ordered Noah. 'Your men stay here. They will be released soon – that is, if everybody behaves themselves. Our slaves will carry your goods for you.'

As he spoke, Noah was overwhelmed by a disgusting, fetid smell. The guards were driving some slaves to the door. Although it was cold, they were naked, their ribs visible and their limbs like sticks. They were filthy, covered in festering sores. One guard was whipping them, bringing up fresh weals.

'Over there, quick!'

The slaves shuffled over to the heap of baggage left by Noah's servants.

'Pick it up – and be careful, or I'll have the hide off you! There are jars of oil in there!'

The loads had been heavy for healthy men. These slaves could hardly lift them. Noah turned his head away in distress but could not shut out the sound of the guard's curses, the crack of the whip and the faint groans.

The man in the black robe laughed. 'Be careful, old man. It might happen to you yet! Let's go!'

He walked on, Noah a few steps behind. The slaves followed, driven by the whips and spear butts of the guards. As they left the gate behind, the valley widened out again and he could see a cluster of houses in the distance.

Then he heard a sudden scrabbling of feet and a thud. A slave had collapsed, dropping his sack of grain. The guard was kicking him; then he took his whip, bringing it down with his full force. The man writhed, too weak even to protect his head.

The guard shrugged and called to another slave. 'Hey you! Pick up that sack!'

They started off again, leaving the first slave still lying on the ground. Noah pushed forward till he was abreast of the man in the black robe.

'Isn't someone going to look after him?'

The man shrugged. 'Ha! Hardly! It's not worth it! The dogs will clear up the mess soon enough!'

'But he's still alive!'

'Not by the time they've finished!'

In the distance there was the sound of more barking. Noah could smell fear. He stole a quick look at the slaves and knew that even in their miserable condition there was worse to come. They were already imagining the teeth tearing through their flesh when their time was up. If only he could do something for them – something to give them hope!

The man in the black robe seemed to read his thoughts.

'Don't lag behind! Our masters are waiting! And keep your eyes off our slaves. We're rather particular about our property!'

Ahead Noah could see a track which branched several times before leading to holes at the bottom of a cliff.

'That must be where they get the magic rock for making bronze,' he thought. 'So close! If only I could get my hands on a piece!'

Several guards slouching by the first branch in the path scratched themselves and grinned as he was hurried past. One even made a practice thrust with a spear in his direction. Next Noah noticed two huge columns of black smoke which seemed to rise from the earth. Then, as the track swung up over a small hill, he could see the low grey building from which the smoke was pouring. More armed men were on guard outside.

'Maybe that's where the bronze is made! If I just had a few minutes inside I might learn what to do! But I suppose I'll never get the secret even if I live as long as Methuselah!'

He had slackened his pace. Black Robe snapped at him.

'Keep up! Don't dawdle!'

Just where the valley narrowed so much it seemed there was no way through, he saw the palace, nestling under a steep cliff, half hidden by trees.

'Naamah's palace, the residence of Tubal-Cain's sister. You're privileged to go there. Mind you behave yourself.'

The slaves were already lowering their burdens before being rounded up for the return journey.

'Hey you! Look after this lot – and don't let anyone touch it!'

Two men moved quickly to stand guard over the pile, while

Noah was hustled towards an imposing doorway. In a moment he was in a room larger than any he had ever seen. There was no time to wonder; he was pushed into a crowded side room. And then another wait. More guards were squatting by the wall, picking their teeth and searching their clothes for vermin. One took a flute carved out of bone and began playing a sad melody that went on and on – the same snatch of tune repeated till Noah thought he would go mad.

At last four men entered. They had to be high officials since the guards stood up immediately and bowed their heads. The first one, elderly, shambled slowly and painfully forward, bent right over and supported by two youths. Noah's first impression was of a mass of white hair, but when he sat down, cold blue eyes pierced him.

The old man motioned Noah to come close. When he spoke, it was a shock that such a frail body should produce such a commanding voice.

'What's your name?'

'Noah, son of Lamech, of the clan of Enoch.'

'Where are you from?'

'The Great Valley. I have an estate near the city.'

'What do you want of us? How many men have you got? Why are you spying for the Sethites?'

'I'm here to trade for bronze. I brought thirty men with me and I've left them at the gate. I'm no spy, I'm just a farmer… '

'What do you really want of us, spy?'

'I tell you, I'm no spy. I've come openly to buy some of your bronze axes and tools. I can offer you the finest grain and olive oil in return.'

The white-haired man jerked his head at Black Robe, who went out and returned with two guards carrying some of Noah's sacks. The old man grunted.

'I want to see everything.'

The two youths helped him up and he hobbled over to the sacks.

'Rip 'em open!'

One of the guards slashed a sack with his spear. The old man pushed his hand into the grain, letting it run through his fingers onto the floor.

'And the oil!'

A servant pulled out the clay bung of one of the jars wrapped in cloth. The old man sniffed at it.

'Nothing to get excited about! The best I can offer is one bronze axe head for the lot.'

Noah opened his mouth to protest.

'That's a final offer. Don't even think of bargaining!'

Noah groaned to himself, 'All that precious grain and oil for one miserable axe head!'

'Have you brought anything else?'

Noah had no option. He reached into his sleeve, pulled out the gold tablet and passed it to the old man who took it and looked at it very carefully, feeling its weight in his hand. Finally he bit it.

'We could give you another axe head and perhaps even an adze for this,' he said at last.

This was robbery! Noah lost his temper.

'That's rubbish! It's worth far more than that!'

Two of the guards grabbed him and pushed him close to the old man. He was smiling, but his eyes were like ice.

'Search him!'

Rough hands pulled at him. Then he was down on the floor, legs in the air with his robe pulled right up round his shoulders while his secret belt was torn off. The guards were laughing.

'Quiet!'

Noah got up slowly, angrily pulling down his robe, feeling shamed and humiliated. To his acute embarrassment he was blushing like a youth.

His precious gold was spread out for everyone to see. He moved towards it, but the guards grabbed his arms again. The old man waited, savouring the moment.

'It would seem you've not been quite straight with us. We don't take kindly to those who try to cheat us! I rather think this gold is ours by right! But… don't worry, we'll be generous!'

He called Black Robe and whispered something. Black Robe disappeared and returned carrying a small cloth bundle bound with cord. The old man took it, his shaking hands fumbling with the knots. He emptied it on the floor next to the gold. There were three bronze axe heads, a saw and an adze blade.

He smiled. 'There you are! Aren't we kind?'

Noah was speechless. Then he heard the sniggering. He turned round and the guards were all laughing at him, making obscene gestures and calling insults. The old man was enjoying the joke as much as anyone.

Noah clenched his teeth. Cheated! Cheated comprehensively and completely! All that prayer... the sale of his precious land... the journey... the dangers... everything swapped for this... this rubbish! If this were the price he had to pay, he would never have enough tools –even if he sold everything.

'You'd better take what you've got before I change my mind! And remember: you'll never leave here alive unless we let you!'

'But... '

'We could kill you right now, and there's nothing that any man – or god for that matter – can do to stop us! Then we'll have your precious gold and trifles for nothing and your men for slaves! We use up a lot of them round here.'

Noah's eyes fell.

'We've been very lenient with you, letting you come here. But I wouldn't try it again if I were you. We might not be so friendly next time!'

They wrapped up the tools and gave them to him. The bundle felt desperately light. At that moment Noah caught sight of the old man's arm. He wore a bracelet. Grey and gleaming, it was made of the most precious metal in the world – iron!

The old man sneered when he noticed where Noah was staring.

'An eye for quality, I see! But I deeply regret we do not sell it to anyone, least of all riff-raff like you. Don't you know this is the precious gift of the gods, thrown down in flaming stones from heaven? Look as much as you like, I wager you'll never see it again!'

The interview was over. Four guards hustled him outside and back down the valley. He had never felt so defenceless; at any moment they might seize his bundle of bronze and drag him away as a slave.

They passed the place where the slave had fallen. On the road was a dark red patch, swarming with flies.

At last they reached the stockade gate and his men were let out of the guardroom. They picked up their weapons under the stern gaze of the guards and filed through the gate after Noah. It crashed shut behind them. More guards waiting for them outside hurried them down the road until they were out of sight of the stockade. The officer turned to Noah.

'Get a move on! We want you away from here by nightfall,

or I won't answer for your safety!'

Noah needed no encouragement. Groups of armed men were watching them from the cliff tops. But he almost welcomed his fears; at least they kept him from brooding over his disappointment and humiliation. Time for that later.

They walked on till sunset to a point where the gorge widened out and Noah called a halt.

'We'll stop for the night here. Let's get off the road.'

They made a small fire to warm themselves. They had nothing left to eat except a few crusts. No one felt much like talking; they were all too conscious of Noah's bitter disappointment. Noah was just finally dropping off to sleep when something jolted him wideawake. He heard men running down the path, shouting commands. Standing and peering through the trees he saw flaming torches that gave sudden grotesque glimpses of an army.

Their fire was almost out, just a few embers showed; it was unlikely they would be spotted. His men were awake, crouching down on the ground, praying to their gods.

Just as suddenly, the soldiers were gone. The last glimmer of light disappeared, the sounds faded and all they could hear was the wind in the trees. Silence fell. Then there was a fresh noise. An animal was scrabbling over the rocks behind them. They froze. Then Noah sensed rather than saw a figure. One of his men leapt up and grappled with it.

Noah took a brand and poked it into the dying embers of the fire. For a long moment it would not catch and he cursed it in his impatience. Then at last he saw someone pinioned by two of his men, with a third holding his feet. Tiras had clamped one hand over the captive's mouth and held a flint knife to his throat with the other.

In the torchlight the young man's eyes gleamed with terror and despair, his chest heaved. The smell of sweat was overpowering.

'Let go of him,' Noah ordered. 'But watch in case he makes a dash for it.'

But he was past running. They dragged him to his feet, gasping for breath, but he could hardly stand. Then his knees buckled and he fell. One leg was bleeding freely. Noah bent over him.

'Get some water! Take my drinking horn!'

69

They filled it from the stream. First they slopped some over his face and when he began to revive, Tiras lifted his head so he could drink.

His breathing quietened and he drank greedily, then looked up in panic.

'You're not with them, are you? You won't let them get me? They're going to kill me.'

It was difficult to understand him with his rapid speech and clipped Cainite accent. Noah hurried to calm him.

'Don't worry. You're among friends, whoever you are. I take it you're in trouble with the Cainites?'

The man nodded.

'Well, we've no love for them either. We won't give you back to them. But I'd like to know who you are. Only keep your voice down, we don't know if anyone's out there.'

He stared at Noah, almost pleading.

'You don't know what you're doing! If they catch me with you, they'll butcher all of you! Slowly!'

'But why? You're a Cainite, aren't you?'

'Yes. Irad, son of Mehujael, named after my great ancestor, Cain's grandson. Born and bred here.'

'We're from the Great Valley. We came here to trade.'

'I know. I saw you today while I was hiding near the gate. I thought you'd had it. You can't know anything about this place or you'd never have come within three days' journey! No outsiders escape from here! The gods must love you!'

'Was it you they were chasing just now? We were scared they'd had second thoughts about us. Luckily our fire was almost out, or they'd have spotted us.'

Irad sighed. 'No, it's me they want. I've been in hiding for days. But I managed to get out at dusk, climbing round the stockade. They're pretty steep those cliffs; I nearly slipped a couple of times. Thought I'd done for myself. I'd just got clear when one of the guards caught sight of me. Another minute and it would have been too dark for him to see. After that there was nothing for it but to make a run down the road. I was scared, I can tell you! Then I tripped over and gashed my leg and that slowed me down. After that I heard the patrol… '

'Well, you've got a chance now.'

Irad shook his head. 'No, it's all up with me. They'll be setting up blocks at all the narrow parts of the gorge. As soon as it's

70

light they'll come looking for me with the dogs. They'll spread out and search everywhere. Once they start they never, ever give up.'

'What have you done that was so terrible?'

'Well, I was in charge of the foundry… '

'The what?' Noah was puzzled.

'That's what we call the place where we make the metals. I know all their secrets, that's why they can't afford to let me go.'

'What happened?'

'It started as a row over a woman. A chief's daughter, mind you. But her father didn't fancy me as a son-in-law! Sent his heavies round to warn me off. I got mad. I stuck a knife into one of them. I know it was a stupid thing to do. After that I had to get out quick.'

'You could come along with us. We'll give you a spare cloak. They'll never notice an extra man.'

'Thanks – but you don't understand. They'll kill the lot of you if they get the slightest hint you're hiding me. They'd enjoy taking days to finish you off. My best hope is to head up into the hills and take my chance.'

Noah looked down at Irad's leg.

'You're in no fit state to go anywhere tonight. At least stay with us till dawn. You'll break your neck if you try climbing in the dark. There must be… '

Tiras was getting agitated.

'Master! Do what he says! We want to get back home in one piece! We've got loved ones and children waiting for us! We can't throw all that away for a… a Cainite!'

Others murmured agreement, but Noah was determined.

'I've never turned anyone in need away yet – and I won't start now! The Holy One's sent this man to us and he's going to keep us safe. He'll show me what to do. I want two lookouts, and the rest of you can get to sleep! There's a lot to do tomorrow!'

10

The deer saved them.

Noah saw it at first light, grazing near the path.

'Can you kill it for me?' he whispered to Tiras, standing guard.

Tiras stared at him, then slowly reached for his bow and quiver. He was proud of his bow. He had spent months searching for just the right piece of yew and had twisted the string himself. The quiver was made of two layers of fur with triple stitching. But best of all were the arrows: long straight shafts with flint points and feathers set with a twist so that they would spin true in flight.

Noah prayed silently as Tiras slipped on his wrist guard, fitted the arrow and tensioned the bow. The deer whirled round just in time to take the shaft full in the throat. It reared up kicking before falling dead.

The men woke in panic.

'Quiet!' Noah whispered. 'You'll have the Cainites on us! A few of you carry that deer down to the road. Irad, come with me.'

He went ahead, checking that no one was around.

'Now, roll the body on the verge so you spill as much blood as possible. Irad, give me your cloak.'

It was a beautiful garment made of soft leather with long fringes. Noah daubed it generously with blood.

'What do you think you're doing?' Irad protested.

'I'm sorry but it's got to go.' Noah ripped at the seams. 'I want the Cainites to think a lion attacked you and dragged you into the bushes. If they reckon you're dead, we might be able to get you out of here.'

Irad nodded slowly.

'Well, take my bracelet too. I made it myself; there's not another like it. They all know it.'

He took it off, admiring it for the last time, bending and dipping it in the blood.

'Now,' Noah ordered, 'I want four men to drag the body up

the hill. Pull it through the bushes, trying to break as many branches as you can.'

Their arms were covered with scratches by the time they got out of sight of the road. Noah walked in front and beckoned them towards a hollow.

'Drop it in here and cover it with anything you can find. Then get washed in the stream.'

He had a last look round.

'We'll be all right so long as they don't try to find the body!'

Tiras had a spare woollen cloak and he gave it to Irad, though it was far too big. They began walking down the road in single file with Irad positioned near the back of the group between two taller men. They were only just in time; a Cainite patrol of about ten men cutting through the woods were suddenly upon them.

'Stop! Who are you?' the leader challenged.

Somehow Noah managed to stay calm. 'We're traders. We've just been up to the city on business.'

'You what?'

Noah struggled to keep his voice steady. 'The guards on the gate will vouch for us. Here. Look at this.'

He took out his bundle of bronze tools and started untying it, hoping no one would notice his trembling fingers. He extracted an axe head and handed it over.

The man examined it carefully before passing it back.

'Well, that's all right. I'll just count you... '

There was a cold sweat on Noah's forehead.

But just then they heard a call from up the road and another officer appeared at a run.

'We're too late. A lion's got him! His clothes are still up there! Three of you come with me. The rest get back to your posts. Quickly!'

Noah and his party were forgotten. They waited while the soldiers disappeared, then began trudging down the road again. They heard distant shouts from other patrol groups but were unchallenged for the rest of the day. But they made uneasy progress.

'You're not still worried, Master?' asked Tiras, catching Noah looking over his shoulder. 'They'd have got us by now if they were going to. That trick of yours with the deer was brilliant.'

Noah smiled gratefully. 'I feel somehow we're getting away

too easily! And then there's the problem of them having taken all our food. We'll have to look for roots to eat, there won't be any berries yet.'

'Pity we didn't bring a bit of that deer with us. I fancy a steak!' Tiras smiled as Noah turned away in disgust.

They woke hungry next morning. There was a steady drizzle as they plodded on down the track but the day passed uneventfully enough until Noah noticed one of the men lagging behind.

'Are you all right?' he asked.

The man pulled up his sleeve. His arm was grossly swollen and there were livid bite marks.

'That's where that dog got me,' he said, gritting his teeth.

Noah looked grave. 'There's nothing we can do here. You'll have to wait till Reu can have a look at it and… '

Just then Noah felt someone brush past him. Irad reached out and took the man's elbow, lifting it. It must have been agony, but he did not resist or cry out.

'First thing is to get that poison out. It's going to hurt, I'm afraid!'

In a moment he was sucking the wound and spitting out pus. Then he reached into his bag and pulled out a small twist of cloth. Inside were some herbs which he strapped to the wound, covering it with a rag.

'That'll have to do till your own medicine man can fix it. At least it shouldn't get any worse.'

They reached the river at last. The raft was in clear view by the island but there was no sign of the men.

'Typical!' Tiras jeered. 'Here are we, starved and exhausted, and they're sleeping off their last meal!'

But after a few shouts, Reu appeared and began poling the raft across. He looked worried.

'Sorry to keep you waiting, Master, but we've had a spot of trouble.'

'What's happened? Are you all right?'

'We're fine. But two days back some of the locals decided to try their luck. They came across to the island at dawn in one of those reed boats. The lookout saw them coming and we decided to lie low and wait for them.'

'What were they after? The oxen? How many did they take?'

Reu grinned. 'None at all! They didn't have the first idea

what to do. The oxen started charging around, and while they were trying to sort that out we took our chance and killed three of them. The rest jumped in the river and swam for it.'

'Have they tried again?'

'Not yet, Master! But I've a nasty feeling they're collecting their mates for another go. That's why we kept out of sight till we were sure it was you.'

That night they camped on a knoll near the river and lit a fire. Tiras stamped round, impatient for his food and making the cook's life a misery.

Reu laughed. 'Hey! You'd better leave the cook alone or you'll wait all the longer. We're giving you double rations tonight. We can't have you looking half starved for your lady loves!'

After the meal the men fell asleep quickly but Noah and Irad sat by the embers of the fire, speaking quietly so the lookouts could not hear.

'I'm afraid those tools I bought aren't up to much,' Noah confessed.

Irad shrugged. 'Why don't you let me have a look at them?'

He threw fresh wood on the fire to make a blaze while Noah brought the bundle. Irad took out each item in turn, hefting it in his hand and examining the cutting edge by the firelight.

'They cheated you, right enough. This is the rubbish that no one else will touch. The metal on this axe head's so thin it'll buckle as soon as you try cutting anything.'

Noah held his head in his hands. 'That was my last chance to get proper axes. I might as well chuck the lot in the river!'

Irad shook his head. 'It's not that bad! I could melt these down and make you a couple of good axes. At least you'd have decent blades.'

Noah stared in surprise. 'You could?'

'Of course! Didn't I tell you? I used to be in charge of the foundry where they made all this stuff.'

For the first time in days Noah smiled. 'That's marvellous! What would you need?'

'Well… stones to build a furnace, charcoal to fire it and some clay. Oh… and some wood and a piece of cow hide. But the most important thing is finding somewhere really secret where our Cainite friends will never find me.'

'You should be safe enough on my estate.'

'I don't think you understand. The Cainites know everything

that happens in the Great Valley. And if they ever found me I'd be a dead man – and anyone else they could lay their hands on. If needs be they'd destroy whole villages to keep their precious secrets safe.'

'Then I know just the place!' Noah exclaimed. 'My old home in the hills, where father and grandfather live. It's on the edge of the world. No one goes there.'

They discussed it and eventually Irad nodded. 'It could be the answer. But how do I get there?'

'Well, that's a bit of a problem. It would be difficult for you to find the way. And I could hardly take you along with my men or tongues would wag.'

Irad went with them all the way to the settlement. But after two days he made an announcement: 'Thanks for everything. I would have been dead by now without all you did. I would like to stay here but I reckon I'd best be moving on. I guess I'll try my luck downriver as far away from the Cainites as I can get. I may even take a look at the sea.'

A couple of days later Noah set off to see the old ones. This time he took Japheth and Ham with him and to the surprise of his servants some pack animals loaded with clay and charcoal.

'I'm sorry to be off so soon,' he told Zillah, 'but they're short of pottery up there and they want me to make them some.'

She was annoyed. 'Why on earth are you taking all that stuff with you? Can't you make your pots here? I'm not happy about you taking the boys either… not happy at all. I hate to think what they'll get up to once they're out of my sight!'

'I'll take good care of them. And I'll be back soon.'

The heavily loaded animals slowed them down. It was the fourth afternoon when they finally emerged above the tree line and saw the homestead.

Irad watched from the edge of the forest. As arranged, he had trailed them all the way from the settlement but now he would have to wait till dark before he could cross the open moorland. His new cloak was thin and it was bitterly cold. It seemed as if the afternoon would never end, but at last the sun touched the hills. Gratefully, he started up the path, hurrying to try to warm himself.

He could hardly make out anything by the time he reached the homestead. He sensed rather than saw the watchtower looming above him. Then he heard his name being called very softly. Noah was waiting and showed him into a room with a fire, a meal, and a place to sleep. It seemed no time before he was being woken and sent out again into the dark, carrying a large bundle of food. Noah was shouldering another pack and was there to show him the way. They climbed the moor towards the distant mountains showing black against the first grey of dawn. At sunrise they paused to drink from a brook.

'Is it much further?' Irad asked nervously.

'No. We'll be turning off the path in a moment. Just there beyond that large rock.'

They turned left onto a sheep track which ran downhill. At first it seemed to be another stretch of moor, but then Irad realised they were dropping down into a hidden valley.

'I hope you like it,' Noah said. 'Look at those trees. They're the only ones for miles around. The manage to grow because it's sheltered here. You can see how the top branches are bent over where the wind catches them. But down below it's a bit of a sun trap. It can be quite warm, even in winter.'

They walked by a stream which fell in a series of waterfalls. Noah pointed to a ruined stone hut nestling among the trees.

'It's where our shepherds used to live. It'll need a bit of work but it's yours.'

Irad examined the hut outside and in.

'It's better than it looks. It won't take long to make it weathertight and fix up a new door. And I certainly won't lack for firewood or water!'

'Good. I'll bring my sons over in a day or so with the clay and charcoal you wanted. We're telling the men we're going to use it for pottery. Hopefully they won't start asking awkward questions.'

'I'll need more food. There doesn't seem to be much up here to eat apart from a few birds.'

'I'll arrange that. Here's our old bronze axe. It should be good enough to cut the wood for the roof. I'll be back soon.'

'All right, but don't be too long.'

The words sounded casual enough, but he spoke just a trifle too quickly. It would be all too easy to believe in the ice demons in that isolated spot.

Two days later when Noah, Ham and Japheth turned up at the hut, there was no sign of Irad. He had obviously begun work, laying branches over a hole in the roof and covering it with turf. But he himself had vanished.

'Is he asleep in the hut?' Ham suggested.

It was empty. But, walking round the outside wall, Noah spotted a small clay figure with blood and feathers scattered round it. He turned away in disgust.

'Look! He's got an idol and is sacrificing to it!'

Ham shrugged. 'I wouldn't be too hard on him, Dad. You'd need something to keep your courage up if you were staying here by yourself!'

At that moment there was a cry and Irad burst from the trees at the head of the valley, laughing and shouting as he bounded down the path.

'He's gone mad!' Japheth exclaimed. 'What happens if he attacks us?'

But when Irad arrived he could only lean against the wall, gasping. Between breaths he tried to explain something, but failed, so he grabbed Noah's arm and started dragging him up the path.

At the top of the valley they pushed through a clump of bushes, stopping in front of a rock face. It looked like any other outcrop, brown at the top and bluish green below, except there were some marks where Irad had been hammering it.

'The magic rock!' he shouted. '*Ore* we call it. Just like we've got at home. I can make you *bronze* – any amount you want – right here!'

Noah rubbed his forehead in amazement. 'I just don't believe it. I've been worried sick how to get proper tools. I wasted all that time and money going to the Cainites and the answer's under my nose. And the Holy One's even given me the one man who knows what to do!'

'I could start work straight away.'

Noah stared gratefully. 'Fine. But do you need anyone to help you?'

Irad pondered. 'I'd better do this myself. If any of your men find out I'm making bronze tools, it's bound to get back to the

Cainites. You saved my life; it's only fair that I give you something back. Why don't I teach *you* all I know?'

'That would be marvellous. The trouble is, I've got so much else to do.'

'So, why not leave your boys with me? They can be my apprentices.'

'Hmm... I don't know how I would explain it to their mother. And what do I say to the servants about their sudden disappearance?'

Irad paused. 'Didn't you say shepherds used to live in this hut? If you could find a few sheep you could always say that the boys are learning to look after them!'

11

They started by building the furnace. Irad set Ham and Japheth to scouring the valley for suitable stones, then spent days matching each one to its neighbours to get a good fit.

'The smaller the gaps, the less packing you have to put in afterwards,' he explained. 'Everything's got to be right or it won't draw properly. It took us years to work out the proper shape.'

They left a hole at the bottom and another one half way up, blocked with a loose stone. Finally, they added a tall chimney.

'You put the fuel in the bottom,' Irad explained. 'And that other hole's where you get the bronze out when it's done.'

Next he showed them how to make bellows to blow the fire. He trimmed some pieces of wood with an old flint adze, fixed some cowhide to it with resin, and added a clay nozzle to stick into the fire.

'Not the best, but it'll do. Once I get some bronze pins I can fix it properly. I can't wait to get rid of those old stone tools of yours! Back home we threw them out years ago!'

He set his helpers to work making pots. They used the clay they had carried from home, rolling it thin, shaping it, adding handles and separate lids.

'We call these crucibles. They're what we melt the metal in. But before we actually start we'll use the furnace as a kiln to fire them, together with that clay nozzle I made for the bellows.'

At last they were ready for the bronze.

Irad decided to refashion the old tools first. The broken pieces were put in the crucibles which rested on ledges inside the furnace. He started the fire, crouching down to pump the bellows. As the flames roared, the sweat poured off him.

'Care to have a go while I get a drink?'

The boys took their turn but were soon flagging.

'How long do we keep this up? Ham asked.

'Till it's done.'

'But how do you know that? It's so bright in there you can't see a thing!'

'You'll get a feel for it after a time. Since we're only melting old bronze it should be ready soon. I wish I had some metal rods to get the crucibles out. I'll just have to use some green wood sticks for now, and keep changing them as they burn.'

As he pulled away the loose stone a wave of heat hit them. They screwed up their eyes as they peered inside, but Irad was calmly pushing his sticks into the handles of a crucible and pulling it out. It glowed brightly and he turned away to shield his face from the shower of sparks and steam rising from the sticks. He rested the crucible on a rock for a moment, then began pouring into the mould of an axe head he had formed in clay. The ribbon of molten metal looked as if it had been pulled from the sun. Quickly he extracted the other crucibles. One of the handles broke as he tried to lift it and he swore.

'Got to leave that one for now. Once it's cool we'll put it in another pot and melt it next time we use the furnace.'

'So do we just let it go cold now?' asked Japheth.

'No, you've got to toughen it up before it cools completely, otherwise it's too soft to cut anything.'

He waited till the metal was solid, then lifted out the glowing axe head and started hammering it with a piece of stone tied to a wooden handle.

'Keep clear!' he warned. 'A lot of bits fly off and they'll burn you. This job's going to be a whole lot easier when I've made myself a proper bronze hammer.'

He got two good axe heads out of the old metal and dropped them into the stream to cool. Then he ground the edges on a piece of rock moistened with oil and bound the finished heads to wooden handles with sinew.

'That's what Eber does with his flint tools,' Ham commented.

'Well, it works well, so there's no point in changing.'

Next it was time to make bronze from ore. Ham and Japheth started confidently on the rock face with their stone hammers, but it was much harder than they thought. They had only dislodged a few flakes of stone before they sat down exhausted, examining their blisters.

Irad chuckled. 'Now you've had your go, let me show you what to do. The first thing I need is a fire. Get me some brushwood.'

They were mystified. Surely rock didn't burn? Still, it was a chance to use their new bronze axes and they soon had a big pile of wood. Irad arranged it carefully against the rock before setting fire to it.

'While that's burning, get me as much water as you can.'

They filled several jars and two water skins at the stream. Irad waited till the fire burned down, leaving the rock glowing, then he emptied the first jar over it. A cloud of steam and ash blocked out everything, but he kept pouring.

'Quick! Fill these up again! I need a lot more.'

At last the rock was cold. Some flakes had fallen off onto the ash and the surface was cracked.

'Pick up those loose pieces, then start hammering. It'll be easier now. Cover your hands or you'll take the skin off!'

They worked for days until they had a considerable pile of rubble. The boys found it heavy going.

'You're lucky,' Irad told them. 'There's a mass of ore here. Back home we only had a thin layer to work with underneath a mass of rock. We had to dig tunnels. The slaves spent their lives lying on their sides clawing away at the rock.'

'That must have been terrible!'

'I'll say! It was pitch black in there and you had to find your way around using a piece of rope tied along the side. The rock was full of cracks and they were for ever propping it up with bits of wood but it was always falling in. Sometimes I'd go down there with a lamp and see legs and arms sticking out where some poor devil of a slave had been crushed. Rescue was too dangerous. They might have brought the whole roof down.'

Irad started sorting through the rock fragments they had dislodged. 'The pieces you want have a glint of metal in them or are greenish blue.'

Then suddenly he noticed some grey rock. 'We're in luck! See this? If we put some of this in it'll make the metal much harder!'

Finally he showed them how to crush the chosen fragments by rolling a large boulder over them before putting it all into the crucibles. Now when the furnace was fired he made them work the bellows much longer than before

'You'll make me spill it if you keep shoving like that,' he exclaimed as they crowded round while he removed the first crucible.

'This has gone quite well. There's a lot of metal here. But we'll have to get rid of the slag first – that layer on top. We let it set solid, then chip the slag away and melt the rest down again. We may have to do it several times before it's pure. But the more trouble you take, the better it is.'

◆❖◆

Irad kept them working hard all summer till they could make good tools for themselves. He even made two bronze bowls to replace those that Noah had taken. There was one awful moment when Japheth dropped a hot crucible on his foot.

'That'll teach you to be more careful, my lad. You're not the first to do that. Just let me poultice it and make you a crutch so you can get round and you'll be fine in a week or so.'

In years to come the boys would remember this as the happiest, most carefree time of their lives. They even enjoyed burning charcoal when supplies ran low. And sometimes they would spend a morning panning for gold in the stream while keeping an occasional eye on the sheep they were supposed to be looking after.

Once a week they walked over to the homestead for more food, sometimes carrying fleeces with them. It was a source of wonder to the steward just how many sacks of grain and beans they got through.

Once Irad killed a deer and roasted it over a fire.

Ham nearly gagged when he saw the meat. He had never touched any in his whole life. And yet somehow the smell was rather pleasant and when nobody was looking he cut himself a small piece to try. It tasted quite as good as it smelt.

In the evenings they enjoyed their own entertainments. Irad showed them how to make pipes from river reeds. Then he found a piece of seasoned wood and carved the body of a lyre, stringing it with gut from the deer.

'This is the music we had at home,' he told them after he had played a sad love song. 'They say that Jubal himself composed the tune.'

One late summer evening as Irad was singing, Japheth saw a shooting star. It fell towards the moor just above the valley.

'If only we could find where that came down we might get some iron. We might even make a bracelet like the one father saw that chief wearing.'

Irad grunted. 'Well, that's the story we *tell* people. We say that all iron is a gift from heaven, thrown down in the occasional stone.'

Ham was intrigued. 'What do you mean? You can't find it anywhere else, can you?'

Irad reached inside his cloak and pulled out a skin purse hanging on a piece of sinew around his neck. He opened it and took out a small piece of black rock.

'Tubal-Cain was making some pottery once and he built his kiln with this stuff. When he opened it afterwards he found some iron beads inside like the sort you get from the falling stars.'

'You mean, there's iron in it?'

'Certainly. The trouble is, the only place you can find this rock is back home. We'll never be able to get any more, worse luck. If you want iron, you'll just have to hunt for that falling star of yours.'

Japheth took the stone and looked at it carefully. It was difficult to see in the fading light so he moved over to the fire.

'I'd like to look at that properly in daylight,' he said as he handed it back.

Next day he had no doubts. 'I've seen rock just like this and not far from here! Just over the mountains in the empty valley.'

'Guarded by all those ice demons?' Irad added quickly.

'I've never met any of those! But I've seen this rock right enough! A huge cliff of it.'

Japheth and Ham spent the rest of the evening trying to persuade Irad to come with them, but he was full of excuses. The old fears were very real.

But the brothers woke next morning to the sound of beating wings. Irad was outside the hut with a wild goose he had snared. He slit its throat and let the blood flow onto his shrine.

Japheth turned to Ham. 'It's going to be all right. I think Irad will come with us to look for that iron. He's just sacrificed to his god.'

It was a steep climb till the empty valley was spread out below them, an endless tract of moorland with occasional patches of colour from the heather. A chill autumn wind ruffled the rough grass. Japheth led the way down the hill. But Irad had already spotted the black cliff. They had brought some of

84

the new bronze hammers with them and soon had as much ore as they could carry.

'It's a much longer job than making bronze,' Irad warned as he got the furnace going and crushed the black ore, mixing it with some white rock. 'This white stuff draws off the rubbish you don't want. You heat the mass till it gets soft, then hammer it to get rid of the crust. You have to keep doing it again and again till it's clean.'

Eventually he had a piece of dark grey metal. 'It doesn't look as pretty as that chief's bracelet Noah told you about, but it's the same stuff. It's even better than bronze for making knives and axe heads. But I think it's much too dangerous to use for weapons. The Cainites are the only folk who've ever owned any iron. If they ever saw the smallest bit, you'd be a dead man! We could make a couple of bracelets. Only I think we'd have to keep them up here.'

Then he reached into his cloak and pulled out the piece of black stone. 'I might as well keep this here as well. There's no point in carrying it around any longer.'

Japheth took it and looked at it again. Each surface had been ground smooth and polished till it gleamed in the sun.

'It's beautiful. It would be a shame to throw it away. Let's bury it in the floor. One day perhaps you'll be able to wear it openly.'

The winter drove them out. The wind howled through countless crevices in the hut and though they tried to block them with earth softened over the fire the room was as cold as ever. When the first snows came they found they could hardly walk up the hill.

Irad was concerned. 'We'll have to get out of here soon otherwise the next snowfall may trap us completely. We'll starve if we can't get more supplies!'

Next morning the sky was clear and the wind had dropped so, after gathering their few things together and tying up the door, wedging it shut with a large stone, they hurried up the hill. They paused briefly at the top to take one last look at the valley. The furnace stood out stark grey and black against the snow and there were many stumps where trees had been felled for fuel.

'I hope no Cainites come this way,' Irad commented. 'They'd know immediately what we'd been doing. I hadn't realised just how visible everything is from up here.'

It took all day to fight their way back to the homestead, herding the sheep along with them through the snowdrifts. More snow was falling as they arrived.

'I'll be seeing you,' Irad said. As they approached the main building, he slipped into an unused outhouse where he would hide until the journey to the Great Valley. Food would be brought there for him that night, together with some fleeces to keep him warm.

The old ones were relieved to see Ham and Japheth. It was decided they should start for home the next morning, before the weather deteriorated further.

'And just a word of warning,' Lamech added quietly. 'Be careful what you say. There have been strange stories about you this summer. Some say you have been possessed by the ice demons. It would be most unfortunate if the real truth became known.'

They set off early. The plan was that Irad would spend the winter in the city and not at the settlement since so many of Noah's men knew him. But when the two brothers got home, Ham begged his father to let him stay in the city with Irad.

Zillah was disappointed at the change of plan. 'If you must go to the city, be sure and behave yourself. I'm only agreeing to it so long as you stay with my cousin Seba. I don't want you wandering around on your own.'

Irad looked decidedly cheerful when Ham joined him at their agreed meeting place on the road to the city.

'I've had enough of being cooped up on the edge of nowhere! The solitary life doesn't suit me.'

Ham agreed enthusiastically. 'This is going to be so good. It's the first time I've ever been to the city without Dad keeping an eye on me!'

Irad put a hand on his shoulder. 'It's not all fun and games in the city. There are some dangerous people out there. You've got to keep on your guard. And don't forget that I've got enemies. If someone attacks me – just keep out of the way!'

'But I... '

'I mean it! There are folks out there who'd stop at nothing if they knew I was still alive and if that means you get hurt too I'll never forgive myself. Absolutely no heroics! If anyone attacks me, run for your life. There will be nothing you can do. Besides, I don't want my knowledge to die with me. You owe it to me to stay alive and show others how to make bronze and iron tools.'

They joined a party of travellers going to the city. Entering the gate, Irad noticed a group of temple prostitutes. He turned back to Ham. 'Are you coming?'

Ham was undecided. Thankfully, he noticed an old friend on the other side of the street and excused himself to speak to him. But as they chatted he glanced continually towards Irad. Some of the women were strumming lyres and he saw Irad take one and begin playing. He could just make out the tune; one of his favourites about a young man in love for the first time.

A commotion suddenly broke out behind him and he turned to see Cainite soldiers pushing their way through the crowd. He stared in horror! He must warn Irad. There wasn't a moment to lose!

Too late! The Cainites were already level with them.

'I pray Irad sees them and stops playing!' Ham breathed.

One of the soldiers paused, then turned towards the prostitutes.

Irad never had a chance. As they rushed forward to grab him he slipped out of his cloak, leaving it in their hands, gaining precious moments by overturning a bench in their path. He ran down one street with the soldiers in hot pursuit, dodging in and out of the traders. But more Cainites were coming the other way. He was cornered. They killed him there, hacking his body into pieces.

Ham, following at a distance, watched in horror, then turned away to crouch vomiting in a doorway, reproaching himself for what had happened.

'I let him down. I couldn't do a thing to help him.'

Ham and Japheth would grieve many months for their friend, but he had given them the priceless knowledge of how to forge bronze and iron. And the Cainites were very unlikely to find out.

12

'But this work, Master… what's it all for?'

Reu was asking the one question Noah dreaded. The longer he put it off, the harder it was to explain. He knew he owed Reu a proper answer.

'Well, it all started with a vision from the Holy One.'

'You mean… those nightmares, Master?'

Noah nodded. 'What we are doing here is just the beginning. The real job is to build an ark, a sort of boat, on top of this brickwork.'

'A boat, Master? I know the men were talking about a boat. They'd heard your wife say something. But I thought it was a joke.'

'It's true enough. And the boat's going to be huge, taking up all the area we've staked out.'

'But you'd never launch a thing like that!' Reu burst out laughing, then stopped and looked embarrassed. 'Beg pardon, Master. But it would never fit on the river. You'd need a huge flood to float it. Like the one they're always joking about.'

Noah stared at him. 'What flood?'

'The men reckon the gods are angry with us because we're so noisy and keep them awake at night. So one day they're going to drown us all.'

'There *is* going to be a flood. Only it's the Holy One who's going to send it. And it's not because of all our noise. He's punishing us for the terrible things we do.'

Reu looked puzzled. 'I don't understand. What terrible things?'

'Well to start with, how about that so-called worship down in the temple? What sort of god enjoys seeing a little baby dragged from its mother's breast and thrown into a fire?'

'But we've always done it!'

'And the poor mother has to watch it burn and try to look as if she's honoured! I saw it once and I'll never forget the look in that girl's eyes! And then there's the way you all get blind drunk and use those temple prostitutes. You all think you're having a great time but there's little enjoyment for them – just little boys and girls, most of them, and they look terrified.'

Reu was becoming angry. 'I knew you didn't approve of me selling a couple of my daughters to the temple a year or so back.'

'Weren't you worried what would happen to them?'

'They get enough to eat. And we've got a lot of other mouths to feed and it's hard making ends meet. Begging your pardon, of course, Master. I'm not saying you don't pay well!'

Noah searched for the right words. 'There's so much more to it, Reu. What about all the violence? I can't travel anywhere without taking at least ten men to protect me!'

'That's just being sensible.'

'But doesn't it upset you that people get killed for no reason at all and their bodies are dumped in the street to rot? It doesn't matter who they are: old folk, children, pregnant women – they all get treated the same.'

'I always say, stay out of other people's business and keep your nose clean and... '

'Murder's so common we don't think twice about it!' But even as he spoke Noah remembered the squatter woman he had killed.

'You worry too much, Master.'

'But the Holy One is concerned about it, too. That's why he's going to send a flood to wipe out this wickedness.'

'And is that why you want the boat? So you can escape?'

'We'll take a lot of food and water and also animals so we can restock the world afterwards.'

'But what's going to happen to everyone else? The ones left outside?'

Noah paused. 'I'm afraid they'll drown.'

Reu's eyes blazed.

'So that's all you care about us! We build your precious boat so you can save your own skin, and you leave us to die! A funny sort of god you've got! He worries about a few babies being sacrificed, but he's willing to kill the rest of us. You expect me to slave my guts out for you year after year, then you're going to turn round and watch me swim for it!'

He turned to stride off but Noah caught him by the arm.

'Listen, Reu! This boat is going to be huge. There'll be enough room for you and for anyone else who wants to join us. I won't turn anyone away!'

It was a long time before he calmed down. 'Well... even if there is a flood – and I'm not saying there *is* going to be one, I hardly think you'll want my family under your feet.'

'We'd be delighted to have you. Delighted! But if you don't fancy *our* company, you can always make your own boat. There's time! Who knows... maybe the boat won't *need* to be used, after all. When people see me doing all this they may realise that the Holy One's serious about judging them. They may ask him for mercy and he might relent – and there won't be a flood at all!'

Reu looked confused. 'But what about your precious boat then?'

'Well, it wouldn't be any use. I'd have spent all my money and I'd look a fool. But I'd much rather have that than see everyone die!'

When Reu left, shaking his head, Noah sat alone for a long time.

'Why can't he understand? He's intelligent enough. He's always coming up with fresh ideas. But I suppose I was just the same before the Holy One spoke to me.'

That evening Noah summoned his men and told them about his visions. He explained what the cradle would be for and described the plans for the ark. Finally, he offered them space inside when the flood came.

The discussion by the fire went on late into the night after he'd gone.

'I still think it would be a great trellis. The old man could grow vines!'

'Tiras reckons it's a bedstead for the gods – for them to make love!'

'Typical! That's all he ever thinks of!'

'A boat? Even he's not that stupid!'

'This flood talk is all nonsense.'

'And would *you* live in his precious boat?'

'I'd feel a complete fool!'

'Perhaps we're already fools for working here!'

Reu put an end to the talk. 'Let's play along with him even if he is queer in the head. At least it's a job and he feeds us well!'

The last piece of timber had been lifted, the last pitch smoothed down. The cradle was complete. At one end two ramps had been built and flooring laid so that the oxen could drag timber right up on top. They had even used pitch to draw the outline of the ark on the timbers.

One rather unexpected addition to the scene was the new village which had sprung up just beyond Noah's boundary. The prospect of work had attracted many people from the city.

But what was the next stage of the operation? Noah fasted three days and prayed to the Holy One for instruction. Then he summoned Reu.

'We need to start collecting all the materials to build the ark. For one thing, we'll need a lot of rope.'

'We won't have to go far for that, Master. The river's thick with reeds.'

'Fine. But when we start building we'll use it so fast that we'll always be hanging around for more unless we start making it now.'

He sketched a plan for a rope store: a long airy shed with a thatched roof, raised on brick piers to discourage termites. At one end there would be a walkway where the ropes could be twisted.

A gang of men set out to cut reeds while the morning mist was still on the water, binding their long hair on top of their heads, then wading in naked. They struggled to keep their footing in the thick slime, swatting at the clouds of midges. Each man had a wooden scythe with a flint cutting edge. They bent in the muddy water to saw off the reeds close to the roots, then gathered the floating stems into bundles. They tied them with more reeds, dragged them into the shallows, then threw them ashore.

As they stripped out each bank of reeds, wildfowl burst from cover and flew honking over the river while voles and other water creatures swam desperately from their ruined nests. Every hour or so the men came grumbling out of the water to warm themselves by a fire and take a brand to burn off the leeches.

Women did the next stage of the work, plaiting the reeds into long strings, checking the length against their arms and tallying the total with scratches on the ground. Then they plaited the strings into a cord, twisting them the other way to prevent them unravelling. Practice made them so dextrous that they hardly looked at their hands as they talked about babies or the latest gossip. It was a welcome escape from the drudgery of grinding corn and carrying water.

The children wandered around naked, making their own ropes from scraps or playing in the mud. From time to time a woman would put an infant to the breast or leap up to rescue a toddler who was too close to the water. At midday they sat and chatted in the shade or dozed till it was time to start again.

Soon the rope store was filling fast. The reeds in the inlet had been cleared and the men moved up the main river. Stems were piled on the bank waiting to be brought to the site.

Noah summoned Reu and showed him the plans for a second shed. This was also thatched with reed, but inside it had a large vat of burnt brick surrounded by waist high walls and a passageway all round for access.

'We need somewhere to store pitch,' he explained.

'But, Master, I thought we'd got all the pitch we needed.'

Noah shook his head. 'We'll need a huge amount to seal the gaps between the timbers if the ark's going to be watertight. And I want to get as much as I can together now so we are not held up later.'

'Master… it's such a dangerous journey. Don't you think perhaps we've used up our luck now?'

Noah smiled. 'Not with the Holy One with us! Anyway, Pallu knows the routine pretty well; he'll lead the group. Don't forget I'm still offering all the usual pay incentives.'

Next a new, even greater challenge waited him. The time had come to start felling timber.

◆❖◆

'This is the spot!' Noah called.

It had been a weary journey towing two heavily laden rafts high up the river almost into Cainite territory. They carried a full load of grain for provisions and barter, bundles of reed rope and, hidden carefully underneath, several of the precious bronze axes. The most difficult section was the last: the short journey up the side stream. It was shallow, with rocks sticking out of the water, while the current was much stronger than in the main river. To make matters worse there was no path alongside and the men had great difficulty finding footing for the oxen between the rocks and tree roots.

The forest was magnificent. Great stands of cypresses towered either side of the stream with their straight mature trunks rising high above them.

The double team of oxen came gratefully to a halt. The men unyoked them and tied the rafts to the trunks of the nearest trees. There was a murmuring from the rapids ahead of them. Through a gap in the trees they could see the strange mountain with its twin peaks. Noah looked around for somewhere to camp, deciding on a spit of sand with an open space before the trees which would give warning of any visitors.

Reu was doubtful. 'What happens if the stream starts rising?'

'We'll have to keep an eye on it and be ready to shift everything back onto the rafts. Once we've cleared some trees we'll be able to move clear of the water. But I don't want us to start felling until we know who lives around here. We'll set up the tents and I'll send a party out to reconnoitre tomorrow.'

'Beg pardon for asking, Master, but are you sure this is the right place?'

'Don't you remember me pointing out this stream to you while we were going up to see the Cainites?'

'Now you mention it, I do. You must have been here before.'

'No, but the Holy One gave me a dream to show me where to go. That mountain over there is the sign we're in the right place.'

Reu stared at him. 'You don't mean you brought us all the way up here to cut timber in a place you'd never been to, just because you'd had a dream about it?'

As they set up camp Noah was aware of some gossiping and odd glances from the men. The night passed uneventfully enough. But early the next morning Reu came running to say he'd seen the local shaman making his way towards them through the trees.

Noah was waiting as he emerged into the clearing, an old man shambling forward in a robe of skins and a necklace of skulls. Lifting a long wooden staff, he shouted, 'Do you come in peace?'

Noah stepped forward. 'We do.'

'Put all your weapons down.'

It was a difficult moment. Were they at the mercy of enemies hidden in the trees?

'Put your weapons down!' he shouted again.

Noah turned to his men. 'Do as he says. Pile them up over there.'

They stepped forward and dropped their spears, glancing nervously at the stranger. Then Noah walked forward his arms spread wide with Reu close behind him. The shaman ambled to meet him. His hair was matted with mud and his cloak was filthy. He stank like a stag in rut.

'There!' whispered Reu, pointing to the shadows. Noah made out the forms of thirty or forty men.

It was no time to show fear. Noah turned round slowly, deliberately exposing his back as an easy target. He beckoned to one of the youths, Reu's son.

'Cush, bring me a bowl of corn from the raft and give it to our friend here. And hurry!'

He seemed paralysed. Noah could see his lip quivering.

'Come on, lad, what's keeping you?'

Cush stumbled nervously to the raft, nearly dropping the bowl as he returned, but somehow recovering himself. He went forward holding the gift carefully in front of him. Noah could sense his revulsion. The stench was overpowering.

The shaman accepted the bowl, took a pinch of the grain and chewed it with blackened teeth. Then he beckoned to Noah.

'Come. We have matters to discuss.'

Noah wavered but already the shaman had turned and was walking back to the trees. Reu pushed something into his hand.

'Your dagger, Master,' he whispered.

Noah slipped it into his belt as he turned to his men. 'Reu, you come with me. Pallu, you're in charge here. If we're not back by late afternoon, send out a party to look for us.'

The shaman turned impatiently. Noah and Reu followed him. As they reached the trees, armed men slipped out quietly and closed ranks behind them.

13

The path turned sharply uphill, twisting between the great trees. Soon Noah was gasping as he struggled to keep pace with the others. But just as he thought his chest would burst the slope eased. Wiping the sweat from his eyes, he saw they had arrived in a clearing with a large round hut in one corner. One of the armed men hurried past him and lifted a flap revealing a very low doorway into the hut. The shaman beckoned to Noah with his hand before ducking down and crawling through the entrance. Reluctantly Noah followed.

It was dark inside – the only light coming from two lamps – and the atmosphere was suffocating. But even more palpable than the stench was the deep evil Noah sensed emanating from the shaman.

'Let me introduce myself,' he began. 'I am Ki, the high priest of the Calneh.'

'I am Noah, son of Lamech.'

'Noah. That sounds a powerful name.'

Then Noah remembered something his father had told him: 'Sorcerers never tell you their true name because if you know that you have power over them.' Perhaps he had been unwise to disclose his own.

Ki clapped his hands and a woman came in wafting another fetid odour towards Noah. The faint light accentuated the creases in her face making her look ancient but her hand was steady enough as she handed Ki a large beaker. He drank deeply then turned to Noah.

'It is our custom that our guests share our cup.'

Somehow Noah forced himself to swallow a small mouthful without gagging. It tasted of sour milk and some sweet substance that sickened him. He passed it to Reu who grimaced.

'I hope it's not poison!' he thought. 'Perhaps it's been offered to some forest demon!'

Ki eased himself onto a bench and turned to business.

'May I enquire why we are honoured with the presence of

such an important man as yourself?'

There seemed no point in delay.

'I need timber, and I see you have large forests. I believe your trees could meet my rather special requirements and I would like to fell a certain number.'

'Ah. That is indeed a pity. I wish I could have saved you a journey. The trees, as you see, are the finest in the world. But I much regret that I am unable to let you have any.'

'I will, of course, pay a fair price.'

'I do not doubt it. But every trunk is sacred since it holds the spirit of one of our ancestors. To cut it down would be to throw that soul into the abyss!'

The answer came clearly into Noah's mind and without pausing he went on, 'I quite understand. But, if you pardon me for asking, what do your ancestors do when their tree dies? Or when perhaps some great storm comes from the mountains and uproots them?'

Ki laughed, a cackle that made Noah's scalp tingle. Then the bargaining began – a discussion that left his mind reeling. The argument went this way and that, till at last Ki conceded that a few trees might be felled.

'But,' he insisted, 'before you cut any tree down, you must make an offering to appease its spirit. Then the wood is yours as a sacred gift from the gods. Yet, as guardian of the holy mysteries, I am not allowed to ask you for any reward.'

He leaned back contentedly, arms wrapped round his ample stomach. Noah stared at the floor. There was nothing for it; he must compromise again.

'I understand. Would you explain to my foreman here what kind of offering is required?'

Ki nodded to a younger man sitting nearby. 'My son will do that.'

Reu and the man left the hut.

'And are you quite sure that there is nothing that we can give you in return?' asked Noah.

The shaman's manner was offhand, almost deferential, but Noah sensed his eagerness.

'Well it's a matter of little consequence, but I did happen to notice in passing that you brought two rafts with you and some rather fine oxen. The gods might favour a gift. Shall we suggest some sacks of grain and a few cattle?'

This was the prelude to further interminable haggling. Noah tried to appear relaxed, but he was worrying about what had happened to the men during his absence. Hopefully Reu would have now returned to camp.

At last a deal was struck. Then something caught Ki's eye. He stared at Noah's waistband.

'I see you have a dagger. That's a strange thing to carry when you visit friends! May I be permitted to examine it?'

Noah cursed himself for bringing it. But he could hardly refuse. As he pulled it out, the blade gleamed in the lamplight.

'Bronze!' Ki exclaimed. 'A metal sacred to the gods! You are a lucky man indeed. And do you have any bronze axes?'

Noah nodded reluctantly. 'A few.'

'Ah, you should know that trees cut with bronze release their spirits into joy! I would indeed allow you to take more of my timber, should you use such tools. And if you could see your way to offering one or two of these axes to the gods... '

Noah groaned silently. 'We've few enough as it is,' he thought. 'And what will happen if they fall into the hands of the Cainites? They live too close to here for comfort.'

It was as if Ki read his mind. 'Of course, making bronze is the one good thing the Cainites do. Such strange people. They keep saying they're not afraid of anyone, but since I put a curse on them, they're too frightened to come anywhere near *my* forests!'

Reluctantly, Noah agreed a price of two bronze axes once the work was complete. Crawling out of the hut he was startled to see the sun was setting. He must hurry back to the camp. Ki sent men to guide him as far as the forest edge. As he crossed the sand he spat out the cloying taste of the drink. It was wonderful to breathe clean air again.

The next morning Noah and Reu looked over the trees together.

'I suggest we start with those nearest the sandbar. With six axes we should be able to tackle three at once. If we cleared the tents for now we could let them drop onto the sand. They'd be a lot easier to handle there than in the water. Once they're gone, we'll have more space to fell the next ones.'

While Reu explained to the men the ritual to appease the

spirits, Noah walked away.

'I must ask the Holy One's forgiveness for making those sacrifices. But I don't see I have any choice. I promised Ki.'

He returned to find Reu finalising the orders.

'Two men will cut each tree on the downhill side. Take turns to swing and see you don't hit your mate! And don't cut too low. We need to get a rope round the stump afterwards so we can haul it out.'

'Can't we just leave the stumps to rot?' Tiras asked.

'No. It'll make it too hard to get the next row of timber out.'

Noah was standing by the rafts checking stores when the first tree fell. He heard a shout and looked up to see it falling directly towards him. He hurled himself backwards and only the topmost twigs brushed his robe. The earth shook. Reu arrived at a run to pick him up.

'I thought we'd killed you!'

Noah smiled. 'My fault. I didn't realised how big that tree was. It's much taller than anything we've cut before.'

Reu shook with fright for some minutes. When he recovered, he yelled out to the men. 'Get those branches off. Save those bigger limbs to take back with us. Burn the rest.' While some hacked at the branches, others were digging out the stump with their deer antler shovels. The ground was waterlogged and the men were soon working up to their knees in a swamp, feeling for the roots beneath them. But before long they had freed everything and a team of oxen was hitched to the stump.

Reu had given the signal to stop work at the end of the day and was checking the tools when Noah approached him.

'The men earned their keep today, Master! Not a lot to show yet, but they're doing well!'

'I only hope they can keep it up. I've never seen them look so exhausted. I doubt we'll be kept awake tonight by singing round the fire!'

The work quickly fell into a rhythm. Soon the first row of trees had been felled and after trimming had been left floating just downstream of the spit, secured by ropes to the bank. But one morning Noah discovered that three were missing.

Reu was apologetic. 'I'm sorry, Master. We were working late last night. It was well after dark before we finished and I reckon someone forgot to tie them up properly. They must have floated off downstream.'

Noah held his head in his hands. 'They'll be in the main river by now – we've lost them for good! That's the last thing we need! We just can't afford any losses. Don't leave any more in the river. Haul them onto the bank and stack them properly.'

By high summer they had produced quite a clearing. Then one day clouds blotted out the double peak in the distance. Soon heavy rain was falling and Noah was filled with unease.

'Reu!' he called. 'I don't like the look of the weather. The river's bound to rise with all this rain. I think we'd better drop everything and shift the camp up the hill. And take the rafts as well.'

'But, Master, the rafts are far too heavy to move!'

'You'll have to break them up and shift them in sections. If you leave them where they are they'll just be swept away. And – most important of all – do something about the trees we've already cut.'

'They're already clear of the river.'

'You'll have to shift them further up. Lash them to trees that are still standing.'

It was a brutally tough job in the pouring rain. The oxen churned up the ground into a quagmire, and men and beasts floundered into the old stump holes.

By evening the river had risen sharply and the sandbar was under water. The rain continued all night and by next morning much of the clearing was covered, leaving a narrow strip between river and trees.

One team of men worked while the others sat listlessly in their shacks, watching the rain or gambling half-heartedly. Some tried to patch the worst of the leaks in the matting or stamped outside, cursing, to dig another trench to divert water cascading down the hill.

In the late afternoon Noah and Reu made a tour of inspection, squelching round in the mud, water running off their sodden cloaks.

'Well, Master, it looks like you've got your flood already!'

Noah smiled. 'It'll be a lot worse than this. You've done a good job. If we hadn't shifted all that timber, we'd have lost the lot.'

'But maybe this weather's a punishment for felling all those trees. The men are scared. They've never seen rain like this and they think ghosts are working against us. They want to go home.'

'Nonsense! The Holy One told me to come here for timber and he'll look after us. We'll be going home soon enough. Another two weeks' work should be enough, if the weather improves.'

He forced himself to sound confident but he watched anxiously as Reu returned to his shack.

All evening the rain continued and the light faded early. It was almost dark when Noah heard someone calling his name. It was a voice unlike any he had heard, almost a howl, cutting through the steady drumming on the roof.

Outside, he saw a figure emerging from the wood. After all the talk of ghosts, he flinched momentarily, then recognised Ki, looking dirtier and more bedraggled than ever.

'You're committing sacrilege, cutting down the holy trees!' he shouted. 'The gods are furious with you. Stop or they'll drown us all!'

A sudden anger shook Noah. 'No! I'll not stop! I won't let you go back on your word! We've kept our side of the bargain!'

'You're a blasphemer and violator of the mysteries! Run, or the river will swallow you!'

They stood, soaked to the skin, shouting hoarsely at each other. Then Ki began a falsetto chant.

The sound throbbed in Noah's head till he thought it would burst. He stood paralysed until at last silence fell.

'I've cursed you, old man! You'll die tonight!'

Noah shook himself and splashed back to his shack, conscious of the eyes of his men watching him. Of course, the threat was childish. But despite himself he felt unwell. Perhaps he was catching a chill? He couldn't eat. It was impossible to light a fire and his meal of uncooked grain looked unappetising.

As the cold wet night progressed, Noah began to feel burning hot. He lay down but could only toss and turn. Soon he was calling out in delirium. When his mind cleared briefly he saw the terrified face of Reu swaying in the light of a flame as he held a drinking horn to his lips.

'Take this, Master. You'll be better in the morning.'

He forced down a mouthful, but vomited it straight back.

The flame blew out and the darkness and beating of the rain overwhelmed him. He seemed to be drowning in the flood. 'I'm too late! I'm lost!' he screamed.

He saw himself at home, walking towards the cradle, up to his waist in water as rain thundered down on him. Ki was there too, laughing and jeering, his face contorted horribly, just like the evil one, still flaunting the jewels he had worn in Eden.

'You'll never see your wife and sons again! You'll be with me in death tonight! Your god's given you up! Don't struggle any more!'

The words continued, first threatening, then strangely soothing. Noah felt he was being sucked deeper and deeper into an abyss. His strength was trickling away. But then something, someone, was compelling him to speak.

'I know who you are, you liar! You don't tell me what to do! The Holy One sent me here and he'll save me! I curse you – in his name!'

The tent suddenly glowed with a strange light as a deep peace came on him and he slept.

Sunlight was streaming through chinks in the matting of his hut when he woke. Reu sat beside him, hunched and asleep, but he stirred as Noah stood.

'Are you all right, Master?'

'I feel fine.'

'I was really worried about you. Mind you, that draught of mine always does the trick. It was my grandfather's recipe and it's never failed me!'

The woods were steaming in the sun's heat. The river had already fallen and, to Noah's relief, none of the timber had been washed away. Some of the men were even singing.

'Shall we pack up, Master? Ki doesn't want us felling any more trees.'

'Forget him, Reu! We didn't come all this way to find wood for one small raft! Get the men back to work. We've lost enough time already! If his gods want to hurt me, let them come here right now and do it! I defy the whole horrible lot of them!'

Ki himself turned up around midday, looking cautiously round the camp.

'I'm here!' Noah shouted, 'and I'm not dead yet!'

A look of astonishment and horror came over the shaman's face. He turned and ran. Reu burst out laughing.

'I reckon he thought he'd seen a ghost, Master! He can't have moved that fast in years!'

◆❖◆

The next week was the most productive of all. The men knew what to do and there was fresh enthusiasm with the anticipation of going home. They had cleared all the trees close to the river and were working up a steep hill when tragedy struck. As one tree began to fall, its branches snagged in the boughs of a neighbour. One of the younger men, Meshech, jumped forward.

'I can see where it's caught! I'll get it!'

'No! Get back!' Reu shouted. 'It's falling!'

It was too late. The branches gave with a sudden cracking. Meshech tried to jump clear but slipped on the mud.

They buried him by the river, covering the grave with a piece of the tree which had crushed him. For Noah it was a double blow: not just the horror of Meshech's death, but the fear that the men would take it as a bad omen.

He summoned Reu. 'After what's happened today, I think we should go home.'

Reu nodded. 'Yes, the men think we've been cursed and they're waiting to see who's going to die next.'

'First, we remake the rafts. Then, make a couple of new ones with the wood we've cut. Float the rest of the logs down as they are. But load as many branches on the rafts as you can.'

'And the oxen?'

'They can swim or be driven along the bank as usual. We'll need them to haul any timber that gets stranded on the bank back into the water.'

It was time to settle up with Ki. The shaman looked embarrassed when Noah arrived, but much happier after he had received the promised grain, oxen and bronze axe heads.

'And will we have the pleasure of seeing you again?'

Noah hid his smile. 'Oh yes, I think so. We will return next year if that is agreeable to you.'

102

14

'Noah, are you out of your mind? Playing in the river like a two-year-old with a toy boat! And there's mud all over your robe!' Zillah stormed off, shaking her head.

Just how was he going to build the ark? Noah knew its size and that it had three floors, but when he tried to remember the details from his dream, all he could recall was a complex web of timber. But if he made a mistake with the design there would be disaster.

Then one day he had noticed some small boys playing with toy boats in a puddle.

'That's it!' he shouted. 'I'll make a model!'

He started by constructing a toy raft out of small branches tied together with straw. He found it quite difficult; his fingers were less nimble than they used to be. But he persevered. When no one was looking he scrambled down the bank to test it in the river, but it was far too flimsy! The current caught it and snagged it against a branch, where it fell apart. He tried again.

'What are you up to, Dad?'

First Zillah, now Ham. His son scrambled down the bank. Resignedly, Noah showed him his half-finished raft. Ham frowned for a moment, then his face lit up.

'It's your ark, isn't it? You're trying to work out how to make it! Once you get this toy right, you'll start on the real thing!'

He grabbed the raft and started pulling at the straw. 'It'll never work like this. You want sinew so you can tie it much tighter. And to make it firm you'll need to put another layer of sticks on top, laid the other way round.'

The next raft was more robust. It hardly flexed when Ham dropped it into the water and his knots held even when he shook it.

'Still not strong enough, not if the final thing's going to be as big as your cradle. We need another layer of sticks on top end to end again. But weren't you going to build a boat, not a raft?'

'Yes. That's what I saw. Almost a box really. Sides, three floors high, a roof on top. Somehow we've got to fit walls all round this raft. I think there were planks, laid on their sides, one above the other all up the wall. There must have been something behind to hold them but I don't know how they were fixed onto the base.'

Ham tried to tie pieces of wood round the raft, but even with his tight knots they kept falling off.

'It's no good, Dad. We'll need something to brace them; some struts slanting up from the base to the wall.'

It was a difficult task even for Ham's skilled fingers, and Noah could only offer encouragement. Finally, the boat was ready for testing. But when Ham lowered it into the river, water gushed through the cracks.

'We'll need to plug these holes. Have we got any wax? I know you intend to put pitch on the real thing, but it'll be too messy for this job.'

The new version of the boat was watertight, but Ham was still not satisfied. 'The walls aren't strong enough. Look how the top flexes when I touch it.'

Noah poked the walls and nodded. 'There's something else we've forgotten: those two extra floors to divide it up into three stories. I suppose we make each one like a raft and put them on pillars resting on the floor below.'

Then they both saw it together. Ham got the words out first.

'That's it! Those floors will strengthen the walls! The beams will stretch from one side to the other. They won't just hold the floor up, they'll make the whole structure rigid.'

'Yes, and when we put the roof on it'll be even stronger!'

Ham looked regretfully at the model in his hands. 'Pity! I've got to rip this one apart otherwise I won't get the extra floors in.'

It took him three days of hard work, but the new version was strong enough to stand on. And it floated beautifully. Even then he was not satisfied.

'This model is too small to show the details. I ought to make something much larger and that means getting help from someone who really knows about timber.'

'What about that youngster Enosh? He's a natural when it comes to working in wood.'

Enosh spent several days helping Ham. Together they built

a much larger model which was a section of part of the ark. It showed the wall with the external door, the base, floors and roof, cross bracing, partitions and internal doors.

Noah examined it carefully, twisting it this way and that to check every detail.

'Is it all right, Dad?'

Noah smiled broadly. 'All right? It's wonderful! I can make sense of my vision now. This is just what I saw, right down to the last detail!'

'So we can start work?'

'It would help if you could draw some plans on clay tablets first. And perhaps Enosh might make some examples of those carpentry joints big enough so the men have something to copy.'

It was time to reorganise the work force. Noah realised he would have to set one team to building the ark and two others to getting fresh supplies of wood and pitch. Reu would be in charge of one group, but he needed at least two more foremen.

'There's Seth, of course,' he muttered to himself. 'But Zillah would never let him go. Ham's still a bit young. Of course, there's Pallu; he's probably best put in charge of collecting the pitch. That leaves Tiras. Hmm... loyal enough, but he can be rather wild.'

Reu did not like the idea. 'Tiras? You're running quite a risk with him.'

'Maybe. But if I start him on something small I can see how he does. Most of that wood we felled is still down in the inlet. Perhaps I can get him to organise the oxen teams to drag it out of the water and up on the cradle. If he manages that all right, I could give him more responsibility.'

'I've got enough to do without keeping an eye on him as well.'

'I'll do that. Anyway, I have other plans for you. I want you to lead some expeditions to collect more timber. As my right-hand man, you're the ideal person to lead more trips to the forest. I was really impressed by the way you handled Ki.'

'But Master... it's such a big responsibility. What happens if things go wrong?'

'I'm sure you'll manage. I must spend most of my time here now we're starting to build. But, if you like, I'll come with you the next time.'

Tiras took up his responsibilities three days later. He was in his element, running around and yelling orders. The noise could be heard far upriver, with the drivers shouting and cracking their whips and the oxen milling around, kicking up clouds of dust as they waited their turn to go into the water. Others bellowed in protest as they were driven up the bank dragging the heavy logs behind them.

Noah watched carefully to see how the men responded to Tiras but they seemed to accept him. If anything, they were working faster than usual.

Then he noticed a huge trunk being dragged out of the water by a double team of oxen. The driver was really flogging them, unaware that they were being hindered by two broken branches which snagged on the ground, digging deep furrows. Noah stepped forward to warn him.

'I shouldn't get too close, Master.' Tiras sounded irritated.

'I just want to tell that driver about those… '

Just then the trace broke close to the yoke. The rope snapped back, grazing Noah's cheek and whipping through his hair. Tiras leapt forward, grabbed the driver and forced him to kneel down in front of Noah.

'Forgive me, Master!' the man gasped.

Noah was rubbing his cheek; there was blood on his fingers. 'I'm all right! But another hand's breadth and I'd have been done for!'

He stepped forward and picked up the broken rope. 'Frayed. It must have been like this for days. Didn't you check it this morning?'

'Normally I do, Master. Only Tiras said not to bother. He said there wasn't time.'

Soon they were back at work, dragging out the rest of the loose logs. Only the new rafts remained.

'Tiras, I want those broken up and the logs pulled out. But don't cut any ropes if you can help it. We'll need them again.'

It was hard work, struggling with cordage which had been under water for months. Soon Tiras was shouting impatiently at the men.

When they protested, Tiras laughed. 'Wait till the old man's

106

out of the way, then I'll find you a sharp flint!'

That evening, as Noah checked the site, he found all the logs were out of the water but only one log had been manoeuvred into position as he'd asked. Even though it had been cut from a tall tree it looked tiny, dwarfed by the cradle on which it now lay.

The next morning he briefed Tiras carefully.

'I want a row of logs right across the cradle between those pitch marks. Every second one has to stick out so we can tie it to the next row. And square off all the ends so that they'll butt together properly. Make sure the men take care; they could break a leg if they fell off the cradle.'

'Leave it to me,' was the confident reply.

When Noah returned later, he watched as the men tried to fit two logs together. He pointed at the gap between them.

'Look! That won't do! You've got to get them a lot closer. Get an adze and trim off those odd bits of branches down there that are getting in the way. And while you're at it, you've forgotten to cut the grooves round the trunks for the rope. When we tie the logs together, the ropes need to be protected. It's particularly vital on this bottom layer. When the ark floats it may well drag along the cradle or the ground and any exposed rope will be ripped off. And don't forget to cut extra grooves so you can tie these logs to the next layer.'

After a tie had been put round each pair of logs they twisted a piece of wood through the loop to tighten it, sealing it with pitch. Finally they erected a matting cover over the logs to keep the weather off during the many years before the ark was completed.

Noah inspected the work regularly. He was meticulous and often pointed accusingly at a suspect tie. 'I don't like that one! Get the pitch off and do it again.'

The next spring Noah left Tiras working on the ark while he went with Reu and his team to cut timber. To his considerable relief things went smoothly; many trees were felled and Ki carefully avoided mentioning the unpleasantness of the previous year.

Noah's one worry was Reu. 'I suppose he still resents me for taking him away from the estate,' he muttered to himself as they started the journey home. 'I hardly get a word out of him from one day to the next. I won't be sorry to see Tiras again! He may not be so reliable – but at least he's cheerful!'

Back at the site, Noah was pleased to note that the pile of timber had gone from the bank. Tiras must have made them work hard. But, although it was still mid afternoon, he could only see one man strolling beside the cradle.

'Where's Tiras?' he called.

The man sniggered. 'Off with that new woman of his, I shouldn't wonder! You won't see him tonight!'

Noah noticed that many of the new logs had been left uncovered. Up on the cradle he could soon tell that something was very wrong. In a moment he was on his knees looking at the rope ties; then he climbed down off the cradle to examine underneath.

Next morning he was up early and waiting for the men as they arrived for work. They were late, sauntering in one at a time. Last of all Tiras arrived, his pace suddenly quickening when he saw his master.

Noah gathered them together, all of them shifting uneasily from one foot to the other. Eventually he spoke calmly, almost quietly. 'I think you know what I'm going to say. I thought I could trust you.'

Some men started shrugging their shoulders, but they stopped as his voice boomed out. 'I spent months teaching you what to do! I fed you, looked after your families, even helped when you were ill. And I trusted you to do a good job!'

They looked frightened now.

'Am I blind? Stupid? Did you think I'd just overlook the shambles you've made of everything?'

Tiras started walking away. 'Tiras!' Noah thundered. 'Come back here! You've pushed those new logs in anyhow. There are huge gaps between them; you haven't even squared off the ends. And you've even used the scrap logs I'd kept for scaffolding!'

He waved a piece of rope in front of them. 'This is one of your ties; it came off in my hand! They're just a waste of precious rope. And not a trace of pitch to be seen! You couldn't build a raft fit even to carry cow dung if you tried!'

Now he spoke quietly again. 'I'm not letting this go. Either you take everything out and start again, or I promise you you'll never work for me again. I'll get this right – if it's the very last thing I do!'

He took full charge of the work. It was a grim day, finding out just how much needed to be done again. The men were sullen and embarrassed by turns. None could look him in the eye. One notable absentee was Tiras. No one had seen anything of him since the morning and once Noah's anger had cooled he began to worry. A check late in the afternoon showed that his hut was empty and that at least a dozen other young men and several women were also missing.

Reu looked grim. 'Well, Master... don't say I didn't tell you. I reckon he was just making a fool of you. All he's good for is swilling wine and chasing women. He'll never grow up.'

There was no news for weeks till Pallu returned from a visit to the city.

'That Tiras! He got what was coming to him!'

Noah was suddenly alarmed.

'It was like Reu guessed. He and his precious friends went to the city, bold as you please, like they owned it. He always said it was the one place big enough for him. And Tiras got himself a new woman. Only not any woman! He had to choose a concubine belonging to one of the Nephilim! He must have been out of his mind! The next day there was a posse sent out looking for him. They say he killed eight men before they got him. I think a lot of husbands and fathers will sleep easier tonight!'

Noah hardly spoke. He turned away and went into the woods for a long walk.

15

Noah chose Ehud as his new foreman, a veteran of several of his expeditions though still young. He was level-headed, the sort of man others turned to when things got difficult.

'It's a tough time to start,' Noah warned him. 'We lost a lot of men over the Tiras affair and it'll take a long time to tidy up this mess, let alone start new work.'

Ehud looked straight at him. 'I'll do my best, Master.'

'And the older men will make a fool of you if they get half a chance; they resent having someone younger put in charge. With things having got so slack, it'll be hard to motivate them to work properly again.'

'Would it be all right to ask Kenan to help me?'

Noah reflected. Kenan was another young man and rather diffident at that. Still...

'We'll give him a trial. He's a good friend of yours, isn't he? Just as long as he's firm with the men.'

Ehud and Kenan were really tested during the next few weeks, forging a new team from the men who were left and driving them on in the summer heat. Every log that had been laid by Tiras was hauled out and checked. Some of them were dumped while the rest were trimmed, shaped and fitted back into position before being tied and sealed with pitch.

It was nearly harvest before they finished the re-working. Noah found Ehud and Kenan one evening, leaning exhausted against the cradle.

'You've done a magnificent job in difficult circumstances. I must admit I had my doubts about you to start with – but the men really respect you both now.'

A yearly rhythm developed, with seasons for cutting reeds and twisting rope, felling timber in the high forests and collecting pitch. Row after row of logs were added until they reached the boundaries marked on the cradle and the last logs were cut to fit the curves of prow and stern.

Then one morning, after a full moon, they found the dead goat.

There was panic! The din brought Noah hurrying from his tent. The men were milling around, terrified. Noah had to shout at Ehud three times before he took any notice; he too was shaking with fear.

'It's... it's... by the cradle!'

Ehud was quite incoherent so Noah hurried across to see for himself.

The thing was so bizarre that he took some time to recognise it. A goat's head had been impaled on a stake and propped against one of the piers. Blood was daubed over the brickwork and the body lay on the ground below with the belly slit open and the entrails spread out carefully to form a fan.

By the time he'd made his assessment, Noah realised all the men had disappeared – heading back to the settlement. He hitched up his robe and started running after them.

'What's all this about?' he gasped. 'What's got into you?'

They turned, making signs against the evil eye. At last old Javan spoke. 'We're cursed! Don't you recognise the sign?'

'You know I don't believe in that rubbish!'

'Master, the whole site's been cursed by Marduk. It's full of demons! If anyone even walks there, they'll shrivel up and die!'

Noah deliberately shrugged his shoulders. Still out of breath, he forced his voice to sound calm. 'I'm sending those demons back where they belong! To say nothing of clearing up that horrible mess before it starts stinking!'

Javan looked shocked. He groped for an amulet hanging round his neck. 'If anyone so much as touches it, they'll be disembowelled on the spot!'

Noah felt sweat prickling his brow and panic rising from his stomach. Then he remembered the night that Ki had cursed him.

'Come back with me – and I'll show you how much that curse is worth!' he growled.

Though still shaking, most of the men followed him back.

It was getting hot; the goat's blood already smelt sour and the body was thick with flies. He was used to handling live animals but, as someone who never ate meat, the sight revolted him. He paused, breathing deeply, then forced himself to grab the stake holding the head. He carried it to the river and hurled it into the main current. Returning to the cradle, he pulled the animal's body together, pausing at intervals to retch. He made it into a rough bundle and dragged it towards the river.

The men watched in dreadful fascination as Noah staggered towards the water. He sensed them waiting for something to pounce and rip him open. He almost felt the fiend breathing down his neck. He backed in chest deep, pulling the horrible remains behind him. He let them go, then ducked his head under the surface, rubbing himself and his clothes to get rid of the filth.

Dripping, he walked to his tent, collected some old rags and filled a leather bucket. He began to scrub the blood from the brick piers. It was a long job and he refilled the bucket several times before he was satisfied.

As he emptied the last of the dirty water he was aware of the men still staring out at him. He pulled back his sleeves and lifted his hands. His voice reverberated round the site.

'Holy One of my fathers, Adam and Enoch, I call on you to protect me, my family, my work and everyone here. And Marduk – foul god of the goat – I defy you! I defy you! If you really are a god, strike me down dead here in front of all these men!'

He paused, his arms wide open, then laughed. 'You've got no power! This place belongs to the true Holy One!'

He left his men still staring as he went to his tent to find a dry robe. He spent the rest of the day in the woods, praying and thanking the Holy One. He wondered what he would find on his return. To his relief, he saw the familiar flickering of the campfire through the trees.

When the men started work the next morning he made a point of standing where the goat had been found. The men look sheepish – but they set to work.

❖

On the night of the next full moon Noah woke suddenly from a deep sleep. Confused, he smelt woodsmoke and knew instinctively that the ark was in danger. He could hear chanting in a high-pitched voice, reminiscent of the sound Ki had used when he had cursed him.

His first urge was to lie still and surrender, but angrily he forced himself up. Stumbling out of his tent, he saw a group of dancing figures silhouetted in flames by the cradle,

The lookout was lying on the ground, rigid with fear, so Noah hurried from shack to shack rousing the men. They crept towards the cradle, clutching spears.

The dancers seemed oblivious to everything. As he got close he saw they were women, six or seven of them, stark naked and lifting blazing torches as they interwove in a complex dance. Their bodies gleamed in the firelight as if they had bathed in oil.

At last they saw the men approaching. Shrieking, they ran to meet them, launching themselves at them and fighting like wild cats.

'I want them taken alive,' Noah screamed.

The men slowly drove them back with the spear butts into a corner by one of the storage sheds. Panting with exertion, their heaving bodies were covered in tattoos of snakes and strange animals and their heads were shaved. They had been doused in blood, which had run down their faces and between their breasts. The air was heavy with a deep musky smell.

Despite himself, he was roused and found himself gazing greedily at them. The men, their fears forgotten, were laughing and cheering. Kenan jumped forward and grabbed one of the women by her breasts.

Only then Noah remembered the fire burning on the cradle. He tore his eyes away and grabbed a spear. 'Stop!' he shouted, striding forward and driving the butt viciously into Kenan's ribs. He swung round, holding the spear out.

'I'll kill the next man who touches them!' he roared. 'Ehud, get some rope to tie them up and put them in that empty hut! Shem, get three others and stand guard. The rest of you – get that fire out!'

Many of the cradle timbers had caught light from the blazing brushwood bundles. If the resinous wood of the ark itself had begun to burn, there would be no holding it. The men frantically hammered at the brick piers to release the burning timbers.

By dawn a pile of smouldering wood lay on the riverbank.

Noah inspected the site with Ehud.

'It could be worse. One end of the cradle will have to be rebuilt, but we've saved the base of the ark.'

'We were lucky, Master, but it'll take months to repair.'

'Well, from now on, set a proper guard!'

It was time to check the prisoners. Noah could hardly suppress a surge of excitement as he walked to the hut, his mind filled with memories of their bodies writhing in the torchlight. They sat on the ground, their hands tied behind their backs to some large posts hammered into the dirt. Shem had found some sour-faced women as guards. They had brought some old clothes to cover them and had tried to scrub the blood off their heads and faces. Noah was shocked to realise they were scarcely more than children. One girl seemed to be the leader. She gave Noah a hard stare, then wriggled her shoulders till her robe fell round her waist.

'Take a good look, old man! Better have me while you can! If you're still man enough!'

Noah turned away quickly. 'Cover her up!' he ordered and one of the women guards rearranged the robe, holding an arm up in a vain attempt to shield herself from the girl's spittle.

Noah looked at her again. She was staring straight at him, but her eyes seemed empty, as if there was no soul behind them.

'Why did you do it?' he asked.

She twisted her face into a mocking grin. 'Little old man building your boat! What could you understand about the sons of the gods? How could you know what it's like to be bedded by one? We'd have shown your boys a thing or two, but you stopped things last night just as the fun was starting! Soon there'll be hundreds of us dancing, dancing, dancing... with the drumbeats going faster and faster... '

She was going into a trance.

'We're the called ones! We'll dance for him till he chases and catches us with his black cloak!'

'You mean the evil one?'

'Oh, yes! He sent us from the city to destroy you. He hates you and he's not going to let you build your boat. You were lucky last night! But it won't be like that next time. I swear to you, old man, there's going to be hundreds of us coming... to finish off what we began last night!'

114

He forced himself to look her in the eye. 'You've got no power to do that. The Holy One is protecting us!'

She spat. 'Holy One! Do you remember that goat? We planted that! You thought you'd got rid of it, didn't you? But I tell you, by Marduk, it was a curse. The curse is running, old man, and one day it'll reach you! No one will be able to hide in your boat when the flood comes – because there won't be any boat!'

Noah turn away towards the other girls sitting sullenly in their rags. He had a compelling sensation that they were dead. They might breathe, eat, speak and move – but inside they were as empty as ghosts. The evil one had sucked all the life from them, robbing them of their childhood. Now when he looked at them he felt grief instead of his guilty desire. He turned his head away to hide the tears in his eyes.

'You'd better go and get some sleep,' he said to Shem and the guards. 'You've done an excellent job.'

He chose two of his older men to replace them; they were unlikely to stand any nonsense. Late in the afternoon he returned to the hut. To his surprise, the door was wide open. It was empty. Scattered over the floor were the rags the women had been wearing, together with the ropes that had bound them. There was no sign of a struggle. They found the body of one of the guards lying by the road, badly mutilated. They never found his companion.

Despite his brave words, Noah was frightened. He forced himself to carry on with the work, repairing the cradle and planning fresh journeys for wood and pitch. But all the time he was waiting for the women's return.

'It's no good!' he told himself. 'Even if I have twenty guards out there every night – or fifty or a hundred – if they bring the whole city with them we stand no chance!'

On the next three full moons he kept watch himself. But nothing happened.

By the fourth full moon, fear had left him exhausted. Despite everything he fell into a deep sleep. Some time after midnight he was called.

'Master! Wake up! They're coming! The lookouts report a huge crowd coming from the city. They've got soldiers with them! We've got to get out of here! Quick!'

Noah pulled his cloak round his shoulders.

'No, Ehud! We stay. At least, till we get the men up.'

In a few moments the men had all been roused and grabbed their spears, but Noah reckoned they were more likely to run than to put up any sort of fight. Already they could see torches approaching. There was a growing noise. Hundreds seemed to be screaming and shouting. Noah's men crouched in the moonlight, rigid with fright.

Then slowly, incredibly, the lights from the torches began to vanish and the noise died away.

'What's happened, Master?' Ehud whispered.

'I just don't know. Let's wait for a bit.'

There was silence apart from the wind and the distant sound of someone crying. Then they heard the lookout, walking across the site, singing out his name in case anyone speared him by mistake.

'Master!' he shouted. 'They've gone! The whole lot of them.'

'But why? What happened?'

'I don't know. There were hundreds of soldiers and them women – the dancing ones – with torches. Suddenly they all started shouting their heads off. The next I know, they're making a run for it. Not that they were running *from* anything. I could see as plain as anything in the moonlight. They just started chucking everything away and running like hell.'

'I'd better take a look. It may be a trick.'

Slowly Noah climbed the ladder to the lookout post, gritting his teeth as he got higher, trying to forget the drop below. But once he reached the platform, the sight was extraordinary. The road was littered with spears, cloaks, bags and spent torches.

He turned to the lookout, who had followed him up. 'Stay here and shout if you see anyone coming.'

He reached nervously with his foot for the top rung and forced himself to climb down again.

'Get some men,' he called to Ehud. Once they had gathered a group he began leading them along the road. About two hundred paces out they found a young girl crouching in a bush, gibbering with fear. She looked like the others – naked, tattooed and daubed with blood – but she had a broken spear sticking out of her thigh.

They broke off some branches and made a litter. But as they

116

carried her towards the huts, she began screaming and throwing herself around so violently that she nearly fell out. Then she fainted.

'If only Reu was here. You'd better leave that spear alone till daylight and we can see what we're doing. Cover her up for now, and give her some poppy juice if she wakes up.'

In the morning she looked deathly pale. She had lost a lot of blood, and seemed filled with some horror. It took a long time to coax out her story.

'We came to burn your precious ark. Yes, and the god had told us to sacrifice all of you too.'

She began sobbing so Noah urged her on.

'We were almost here when there was this horrible thing! A great awful shining man! Higher than the trees he was... with a huge flaming sword in his hand!'

She lay shaking, 'You won't let him get me, will you?'

'You're safe with us.'

'Everyone ran like blazes and damn anyone who got in the way. This stupid clumsy fool of a soldier trips me up and sticks me with his spear. Just left me there, he did!'

She died that evening. Her wound was no worse, but her eyes were blank with terror and her body tensed, trying to escape the thing that had come to take her.

Noah remembered his vision of Eden and the cherubim guarding the gate. Now they were protecting his ark.

16

'Ready, Master?'

Noah nodded to Ehud above him on the scaffolding. Above Ehud's head was a wooden bar over which ran heavy ropes connected on one side to a team of oxen and on the other to a great beam.

A whip cracked and the oxen lurched forward. The ropes tightened and with a violent creaking the scaffolding took the weight. Slowly the team pulled away and the heavy timber rose a little at a time till it was level with Ehud's head.

'Hold it there! Now, just a bit more.'

The oxen strained forward.

The beam raised a hand's breath.

'Now sideways!'

Five men pulled on ropes to swing the beam across.

'Let it fall! Gently now!'

The oxen shuffled backwards and the beam sank on top of a pair of wooden pillars. Ehud clambered along the scaffolding, checking that the wooden tongues projecting from the uprights fitted the holes cut to receive them.

'That looks fine! Now get those joints lashed!'

Men clambered up the scaffolding with bundles of rope. The first support to hold the next floor was in place.

Enosh, supervising the carpentry, was cheerful. 'Wow! It fitted first time!'

Ehud laughed. 'You've got the luck of the gods! I'm surprised you could see to fit anything after that night in the city!'

'I could do this work with my eyes shut!'

'It looks like it too! But let's get on.'

A forest of pillars was rising at one end of the ark. They rested on the lowest tier of logs and round their bases two more layers of timber were being laid. Ham seemed to be everywhere, rushing round with his model and clay tablets and giving urgent instructions to Ehud and Kenan.

'Make sure you get all the struts and cross-braces in! If you forget anything it'll be very difficult to fit later.'

'Enosh!' he called. 'Those pillars to support the deck – make sure they're nine cubits long, and see you square them off properly. And cut all the sockets for the cross members.'

And to the women, Ham called out, 'Before they bring the next load of timber, I want you to pack all the gaps between the logs with reeds. Make sure there's no space left. Put in as much as you can, then pound them with the wooden mallets. Then, it'll be the pitch.'

At the mention of pitch the women looked resigned. Their hair and clothes would reek for days.

Ham was down on his knees examining the logs. 'Where's Enosh? There's a bit here that needs trimming.'

One day Noah found Ham fast asleep with a half-eaten chunk of bread in his hand. He woke with a start. 'Sorry, Dad!'

Noah shook his head. 'Don't think I'm not grateful for all you do. But don't wear yourself out!'

'I'm fine. I want to get this job right. Yesterday I caught some of them fitting another layer of logs before any reeds had been packed in.'

'But isn't Ehud checking that?'

'Well, he's supposed to. But he tends to put things off. He always reckons he can fix mistakes later. But me, I like to get it right first time.'

Noah looked at him carefully. 'Don't forget: I've put Ehud in charge. I understand he's rather annoyed about the way you keep interfering.'

Ham looked surprised. 'I didn't realise there was a problem.'

'He says you won't let him alone. Last night he was even talking of quitting. I've managed to calm him down for now.'

'Sorry. I'll try not to bother him again.'

'I was just thinking… Our tools are getting a bit worn. How about you and Japheth making some more?'

'Are you trying to get rid of me, Dad?'

'I thought you could do with a break. And we really do need more tools.'

Some weeks later Ehud proudly took Noah to one end of the ark.

'Look, Master, this is what it'll all look like when it's finished: three layers of logs and everything's tied in and sealed. We've even levelled it off. All it needs is sand to cover the pitch.'

Noah tapped carefully with his foot. 'Excellent! This feels really solid. But make sure it's all as firm as this. Don't forget the oxen will be dragging logs over it. But by the way, what about drainage?'

Ehud sounded puzzled. 'Ham didn't say anything about that.'

'There'll be a lot of water down here from leaks and spray. If you leave some gaps in the top row of logs, the water will collect there rather than slopping around the floor: it's what they call bilges. Make sure they're big enough so you can get a bucket inside to bail them out.'

◆

Noah made his usual visit to the old ones in early summer. Going to the secret valley, he was alarmed to find Japheth had lost most of his hair.

'It's nothing, Father. I'm fine. A bit of a problem, but it's all sorted out now.'

'What *bit of a problem*?'

'We sort of set fire to the roof of the cottage. But we got most of the stuff out before it fell in! We were thinking the whole forest would go up too, but fortunately it started raining and we managed to beat it out. We were running short of charcoal, you see. Thanks for bringing some more. Anyway we tried using wood instead and a whole lot of sparks came out of the top of the furnace.'

'You'd better not try that again!'

'No chance! We've built a new furnace well away from the cottage. But have a look at these axe heads! I know they're not up to Irad's standard... '

He paused. 'You know, Dad, it's funny... I keep expecting him to walk in the door. But how are things going on the ark?'

'Quite well,' replied Noah. 'But there is *one* thing that's worrying me. Fairly soon we're going to have to start thinking about the walls. The first thing to do is to put up scaffolding on the outside. Then we'll need some very long timbers, say about thirty cubits long, for the uprights and cross bracing – they can be propped against the scaffolding until we've got the ties in. For the walls themselves we'll need a lot of planks running horizontally, overlapping each other all the way up – at least three layers, tied and pegged in, and packed with reeds and pitch to make them watertight.' He paused, deep in thought. 'I'm worried about cutting all those planks.'

'Dad, it wouldn't be so bad if we could use *bronze* saws. They'd be much better than the flint ones Eber makes.'

'Hmm… But we don't want anyone outside to know how much bronze we've got. Perhaps if you made just a couple for now?'

Noah was silent as he sat with the old ones that evening.

'You are worried, my son,' said Lamech.

'I just don't know whether I will be able to finish building the ark.'

His father peered at him. 'Am I not correct in believing that the Holy One called you to this work? What, then, is your difficulty?'

'Well, I just don't think I have enough resources. I still need a huge amount of wood. It costs so much. I've already promised most of our next harvest to Ki, the shaman, in return for the timber we felled this year. Each time we go, he charges us more.'

Lamech pondered. 'Could you use other wood?'

'I was told it must be cypress. It lasts well and is very easy to work. And that's the best place for it. Anyway, no one else will sell to me. They've all got this superstition about the spirits of their ancestors living in the trees.'

'And Ki does not believe that?'

'Yes, he does. But when it comes to a deal, he's more interested in enjoying the good things of life. These days I don't hear much about sacrilege. He's doing very well out of me. Each year he seems to have more gold and I've heard he's got the biggest harem in the Great Valley.'

Noah had a troubled night but when he woke at first light he was resigned to making a difficult decision.

'I'll have to sell some more land,' he told his father. 'I hate doing it, I'm so proud of my estate… and I dread to think what Zillah will say! She's still talking about those fields across the river I sold. A whole tract upstream of the settlement will have to go. Several of my neighbours have wanted it for some time. We get some very good crops there.'

'Will that be sufficient to meet your needs?'

'For the present. But I fear that one day I may have to sell the settlement as well. It will be particularly hard for Zillah; it's her whole world. She loves every clod of earth. I just don't know how I'll be able to tell her. Probably, in the end, I'll have to sell *everything*. The trouble is, the more land I get rid of, the smaller harvest I get and the fewer the men I can employ. Sometimes I wake in a panic thinking I'll never have enough to complete it!'

'You will finish it, my son. The Holy One has not led you so far to fail you now. We will continue to pray for you – and for Zillah.'

The sale was finalised soon after harvest.

To his surprise, Zillah took the news calmly. She sat for a long time staring at the floor; then began speaking quietly.

'I can't say I'm surprised. I've expected it ever since you let that other land go. I knew you'd ruin us eventually. You're a stubborn, hard-hearted old fool! I suppose I should be thankful we still have the settlement! At least I've got my own bed, even if we are surrounded by strangers. Did your father put you up to it?'

'It was entirely my idea. If I'm ever going to build the ark...'

'The ark!' She spat the words out. 'That's all you care about!'

'And you know why. I thought you shared my vision.'

She nodded wearily. 'I suppose so. But it's all so many years ago. All I can think of now is that we're losing everything we've got. Soon we'll be back in a tent slaving our guts out, working for our neighbours!'

'But can't you understand? We're selling the estate so that we can get a whole *new* world in exchange!'

She pushed him out of the way and hurried outside. He could hear her sobbing, but he hesitated to follow. Every time he tried to say something it made things worse.

Often during that next year he heard her muttering about how small the estate had become. But the next harvest was so magnificent it was hard to find room to store everything. Even she relented.

'Well, Noah... you've been lucky this time,' she told him. 'But next year,' she added, 'we'll probably starve.'

Ehud had set up four teams of sawyers. Two men worked together, one standing in a pit pulling on the big double saw while the other pushed down from above. The men took it in turn to use the bronze and flint tools. There was fierce competition, since Ehud had promised extra rations to the pair who did the most work.

It was a favourite spot with Noah; he loved the smell of the freshly sawn wood.

'What are we doing with all the sawdust and wood shavings?' he asked Ehud one day.

'Nothing, Master. When it gets too deep we dig it out and burn it or dump it.'

'Could you collect it for me? Put it in a bin somewhere where it'll be dry? I'm only sorry I never thought of it before.'

The base was complete and work was under way on the second deck. Ramps had been built at either end, up which teams of oxen laboured with fresh building supplies. The uprights for the wall stood like the ribs of some sea monster rising high above the scaffolding. The men were planking the outside walls. Halfway along the side facing the river a gap of eighteen paces had been left for a door. Ham spent a long time discussing its design with Ehud, Kenan and Enosh.

'This is the weak spot of the hull. The door's going as high as the wall and it's made the same way with upright members and planks across. I reckon the best way is to hinge it at the bottom, pivoting round a large wooden pole. When we need to close it we'll pull it up with ropes, winding the loose ends around bollards on the top deck. We'll need two on each side. But most of the time the door will be open, and we'll walk across it when we bring things in.'

Ehud looked puzzled. 'But if this flood you keep talking about ever happens, how will you stop it leaking?'

'We'll put plenty of bracing in to make sure it's rigid as well as a proper framework on the hull for it to butt onto. There'll be some bars inside to hold it shut. And just before we finally

123

close it, we'll put a thick layer of pitch all round for a seal.'

'It's a big opening,' Ehud commented. 'Will it hold?'

Ham had another puzzle for Ehud. He took him through the gap into the bottom floor of the ark. It was dark inside now the walls and deck above were nearly complete. His voice echoed in the void.

'This is going to be a storage area.'

'All of it?' asked Ehud. 'It's huge.'

'In fact, we'll be using the floor above, too. There'll be a lot of us, and we may be in here for a long time. We'll need it for food and water. Almost all the space needs fitting out with bins. We'll fill them from the top, but there'll be doors in front so we can get at the stuff easily.'

'And water, you said. Won't you be floating in the stuff?'

'It may not be clean. What I had in mind were racks with large jars in them, glazed so they don't leak.'

'There's still a lot of clay left and we can always fire them pots like we did the bricks. How many do you need?'

'I don't know yet. I think we'll make them a few at a time and store them in here. We'll fill them at the last moment to keep the water as fresh as possible.'

'What about the food?'

'I don't know yet. I think we'll wait till we've finished building. But as soon as you can get one or two bins finished we'll have somewhere to store the sawdust and wood shavings!'

'And where are you going to live?'

'On the top floor – the part we haven't built yet. The only part that will have windows.'

17

Year merged into year. Noah could hardly remember how it had all happened, but the ark seemed to grow in front his eyes. Before he knew it, the two lower decks were finished, complete with their storage bins and jars, and the men were working on the top level.

One event that stood out during the procession of years was Shem's marriage to Ishtar. Little work was done on the ark for a month before the wedding and the festivities lasted a full week.

'She's a lively girl,' Noah remarked to Zillah. 'And very pretty too.'

She sniffed. 'That's all you men ever think of! She's lively right enough – too lively, to my way of thinking.'

'She's young. She'll settle down once they start a family.'

'I shouldn't rely on it. That girl's nothing but trouble. Haven't you seen the way she eyes the men? Shem must have been mad to fall for her!'

'It's good having fresh life around the place. Though I do wish her parents hadn't named her after a goddess.'

Zillah hurried off to the kitchen. Noah sat for a long time staring after her. Nowadays they seemed to be living separate lives; it had been their first proper conversation in weeks and he could not remember the last time she had let him put his arms round her. But he urgently needed to talk to her. Once more he had exhausted his gold; there was no alternative but to sell the settlement.

He let her enjoy the wedding first. Several days afterwards he found her alone, but as soon as he started to explain she interrupted him.

'Now, stop right there! I know exactly what you're going to say. You're going to sell the settlement.'

'But how did you… ?'

'You can't fool me! I know you after all these years! I could see you trying to pluck up courage to speak. You've run out of gold again, haven't you! So you're going to sell the roof from over my head! Don't mind me... just so long as you can keep building your wretched boat!'

'We've still got plenty of other land and I've found just the place for our new home. It's well shaded... '

'And nice and convenient for the ark, I suppose!'

'Actually, it *is* fairly close.'

'I'm not leaving here till I'm carried out in a shroud!'

Suddenly a cold anger swept over him. Everything he planned was in jeopardy because his wife refused to face facts. He clenched his fists in frustration.

'You *will* be leaving! And before the end of the year! I'm selling most of the estate and that's all there is to it!'

She stared at him defiantly, then her eyes fell. 'You'll destroy everything we've got – just to get your own way!'

Her shoulders drooped and she began sobbing convulsively. Noah reached out to her but she shook his hand away angrily.

'Don't touch me! Go on! Build your new house – but don't expect me to live in it!'

Later Shem searched out Noah.

'So we're going to move then, are we, Father?'

Noah lifted his head wearily and nodded.

'Actually, we guessed a long time ago. You're going to have to sell everything sooner or later.'

Noah sighed. 'Your mother will never forgive me for this.'

Shem rested his hand on his shoulder. 'In her heart she knows you're right. She'll come round in time.'

'I hope so. 'If only she realised just how much this hurts me too. I've spent the best years of my life here. And you boys were born here.'

Noah struck an agreement with a neighbour to sell the buildings and most of the land. But Zillah spent a lot of her time lying on her bed and refusing food until the moment came when they had to walk out of the door for the last time. Noah looked back longingly. Zillah stared straight ahead as if her face was carved out of rock.

The latest sale aroused considerable interest in the Great Valley. Most people saw it as another sign of Noah's descent into madness. One morning he found some complete strangers wandering around the lowest level of the ark laughing and making obscene jokes.

'What do you think you're doing here?' Noah shouted.

'Oh, don't mind us! We're not doing any harm! We thought it was time we took a look around. We've heard some good stories about this ark of yours!'

They sniggered and began examining one of the bins. It took Ehud and five of the men to throw them out.

Another day three more came in while he was having a discussion with Kenan. They walked up to the very pillar where he was standing and began tapping it.

'Good bit of timber this! He certainly knows where to get it!'

'There's some beautiful stuff here. And all nicely finished.'

'They say he's got some good bronze tools too. Worth getting hold of.'

Noah, staring at them in amazement, at last found his voice.

'I may look old, but I'm not dead! And I'm not stupid and I'm certainly not blind and deaf. If... '

'Touchy, isn't he! I can take a hint. I know where I'm not wanted!'

But the worst moment was when two of the Nephilim arrived one morning. Noah was by the river when Ehud came and clutched at his arm, his face was white with shock.

'What's happened?'

They were strutting about inside – huge men, arrogant and as relaxed as if they owned the place. They even had their bodyguard with them, loaded down with weapons.

Ehud fell to his knees moaning and making signs against the evil eye, but Noah just gaped. It seemed as if his bowels had been turned to ice and he felt his scalp rise. He stood as helpless as a mouse waiting for an owl to snatch it up.

Then one spoke, his voice deep and menacing. 'An interesting little place you've got here, old man. How much do you want for it? Come on. No need to be shy with us. We've taken quite a fancy to your boat. It's not doing much good here, but we'd be quite happy to take it off your hands. We might even give you some gold – a bit of comfort for your old age!'

Noah swallowed twice and found his voice. 'I'm not selling. The Holy One has told me to build this ark so we can escape the flood that's coming.'

The response was a loud guffaw of laughter. 'Not a very sensible answer!' The huge man's eyes bulged and Noah saw the great muscles of his neck tighten. 'People don't often say no to us. They usually regret it – that is, if we give them time!'

Suddenly a divine rage boiled up in Noah. To his amazement he heard himself shouting, 'I'm not giving you anything. And I'll thank you to leave my land immediately!'

He thought they would kill him on the spot. One moved forward, his hands outreached, veins standing out on his forehead. For a long, long moment they confronted each other. The smell of sweat and garlic on the man's breath sickened him. Then, unbelievably, the intruder's hands dropped and he turned to his companion. 'Perhaps we should leave, since our host is not disposed to make us welcome. We would hate to be an embarrassment.'

Then without warning he faced Noah and roared so loudly that the deck shook. 'You won't get away with this, old man! We'll be back and by the time we've finished I swear to you by the gods, there won't be any trace of you or your precious boat!'

They swaggered down the ramp, their bodyguards scurrying behind them. He followed them as far as the boundary. For all Noah's deep unease over the visit, he felt certain that they would never return.

Reu left a week later. His departure was not unexpected. Noah knew he had never forgiven him for making Ehud foreman at the site. Noah went to say a final goodbye. He and his family were gathering things together for the journey.

'Reu, are you sure you won't change your mind? You know I think of you as part of the family.'

'It's best I go. You need younger men to look after things. Besides, I fancy going somewhere up river where I can be my own boss.'

'Don't forget I'm keeping room for you and your family in the ark for when the flood comes.'

Reu shook his head slowly. 'Master, I don't reckon I'll be back. Use that space for someone else. Someone who believes in all that stuff.'

'I've failed Reu,' Noah confessed later to Shem. 'I've never been able to make him realise that the flood is really coming.'

'You did what you could. It's his decision.'

Noah sat down heavily. 'It's getting me down. I can't get anyone to understand how serious this really is. Apart from Reu, I've lost a lot of good men lately.'

Shem shook his head. 'Don't worry. Most men are only too thankful for a job and enough to eat. They'd be hard put to find a better master.'

Noah stared into space. 'Sometimes when I think what this has done, especially to your mother, I get to wondering if... well, if I've imagined it all. Maybe there won't be a flood!'

Shem stared at him in disbelief. 'I know we've all had our doubts... but you! You're the one that's kept us going!'

Noah looked embarrassed. 'I'm sorry, Shem. I had no right to say what I did. I must be tired or something. The thing I can't fathom out is why the Holy One chose me – of all people. Why couldn't I have been left as I was?'

'Because you're the only man who could do it! No one else would have kept going. I know people laugh about the ark, but secretly they're amazed at what you've done.'

'If these folk believed my warnings about the flood, I'd feel it was worth it. I'll never forgive myself if we can't persuade anyone to come with us and escape.'

At last the walls were complete, extending almost to the top of the uprights, leaving a gap a cubit wide for light and air. Now it was time to fit the roof. After a long discussion with his father, Ham went off to make yet another model.

'We can't use a flat roof like we do on houses; the rain's going to be too hard. We've got to make it pitched, like this, with a slope each side to carry off the water. And it also needs to slope at each end.'

'Thatched with reeds?' suggested Ehud.

'Yes. But it'll have to be very thick, with extra ropes to hold the bundles down. Then we're going to cover it with pitch. I know it's extra work, but we're expecting stronger winds than any we've ever had. Dad reckons the rain will be a lot harder too. If the roof does come apart or leaks there's nothing we can do about it. It's not like a building where you can get outside and stick up a ladder when you want to make repairs!'

Enosh was poking at the model.

'You're going to use trusses to hold up the framework, I see. I've only ever made one roof like this and that was very small. You'll need some huge trees. Anyway, there shouldn't be any problem finding enough reeds. The beds have grown back very well since we made all that rope. How about the pitch? We've almost used up our supply.'

The roof timbers were the longest they had used. They were hoisted directly from the ground using a double team of oxen. Ehud had quite a job finding men prepared to work on them with the constant risk of falling. But one morning, to his great surprise, Ham saw Noah climbing the ladder up to the roof.

'You'd better be careful, dad. There's not much to hang onto!' he shouted.

'I must see for myself. I've got to be sure they're doing the job properly. If they leave the slightest hole it'll be awful inside once the rain starts.'

He stepped off the ladder onto a plank. He had never been so high off the ground before. A stiff wind was blowing and everything rocked gently. For a moment he glanced down and saw the men looking like children below. In a panic he grabbed one of the trusses and felt it move in his hand. When he felt calmer, he backed to the ladder, looking at the sky and feeling with one foot for the top rung.

'I'm fine!' he reassured Ham. 'And you'd better get used to seeing me climbing ladders because I'm going to check the roof every week till it's done!'

They finished the roof in late autumn. It was a moment to savour. The main construction work was over. But, with all the satisfaction, Noah also felt sadness. He could not forget Reu and the other men he had failed to persuade.

'So how are we going to celebrate, Dad?' Ham enquired.

'Why don't we give a feast for the men? And as soon as the winter is over I must go to see the old ones and offer a sacrifice in thanksgiving to the Holy One.'

But Noah was destined to make the journey much sooner. That evening four visitors arrived at the site looking for him.

'We come from the homestead,' their leader explained. 'Your

grandfather Methuselah sent us.'

'Just the four of you?' Noah asked in surprise.' It's very brave of you to come with such a small party.'

'Your grandfather Methuselah wishes us to inform you that your father is ill and thinks it advisable that you should come as soon as possible.'

Noah pressed the man for more information.

'We think he's dying. He sleeps most of the day and has taken nothing apart from a little milk. And he keeps asking for you.'

'Perhaps you want to rest tomorrow and we will go the day after?'

'Thank you, but there's no time to lose. I think we should start at first light.'

It was an unpleasant trip. Noah felt almost resentful towards his father.

'You mustn't die now!' he muttered. 'I need to talk to you about so many things! You can always make sense of my problems!'

As they climbed out of the forest on the last part of the journey they could see clouds massing in the west. It was snowing before they reached the gatehouse. Methuselah met him at the door, speaking so quietly he could hardly catch the words.

'Thank you for coming so quickly! I do not think he will live till morning. He has kept calling for you. I will leave you now; I have made my own farewell.'

They had put Lamech in his favourite room. It faced the setting sun and he had seen so many days end there during his long life. Now the only light came from a lamp.

He had always seemed small, but now he looked like a child. Noah noticed a small movement of the chest and took his father's hand. It was shrivelled and icy despite the peat fire in the centre of the room and the shawls wrapped round him.

There were so many things left to say, but it had been a long day and the warmth of the fire made Noah drowsy. He dozed several times before hearing his father call him in a faint voice, hardly more than a whisper.

'Son, you are here at last. I can go in peace. You must be strong; it will not be long now. Do not let anyone cheat you of your hope. I only wish I could have seen your new world.'

After a few minutes, Noah realised he was alone. He rose slowly and closed his father's eyes.

18

They buried him in the courtyard close to the spot where he used to sit in summer enjoying the afternoon sun.

It took them a long time to dig the grave; the ground was already half frozen. As they worked, Methuselah beckoned to Noah through a gap in the shutters. 'Be sure and dig his grave deep. And when you have finished, pile some boulders on top. He said that he did not want his body to be washed away when the flood comes.'

Noah had fresh tears in his eyes as he realised how firmly his father had believed in the vision. It was almost as if he had reached out from the dead to give him one last reassurance.

Afterwards he sat with his grandfather silently through the long afternoon.

'He must have known too many funerals in his life,' Noah mused. 'It's lonely being a survivor.'

The servants had come to light the lamps before Methuselah spoke. 'Your father and I have lived here too long. We have much to remember. But the most important thing in all that time has been the work that the Holy One has given you to do. Since you told us of your vision, we have prayed for it constantly.'

'Thank you, Grandfather. I only wish I could show you the ark.'

'I will never leave this place again. And yet you have told me so much about it that it is as familiar to me as those mountains over there.'

He dozed before speaking again. 'I was glad that you came in time. When it is my turn to die, promise me that you will close my eyes as you did for him. I do not think that I have much time left. But now you must finish your work for the Holy One.'

Noah stayed two more days. They sat in silence or sometimes spoke of trivial things; the realities of life were too painful. For Methuselah there would be a final empty loneliness without his son and faithful companion of so many years. Noah struggled to find some way to comfort him and in the end his men had to coax him away. The track across the moorland was thick with snow and more clouds were massing behind them.

There was still much to do and Noah had very little gold left. Then he thought of Heth. He was a young newcomer who in twenty years had turned some wasteland next to Noah's estate into an excellent farm. He was friendly and even Zillah liked him.

Noah met him one day while they were inspecting their common boundary. 'I don't know if you would be interested in doing a deal?' he asked after they had exchanged the usual greetings and small talk.

Heth was suddenly attentive. 'And what precisely might you have in mind?'

'Perhaps you might find your way to making me an offer for some of my land?'

For a moment Heth let his surprise show. 'You're not thinking of selling any more are you?'

'Perhaps. If I get a suitable offer.'

'Well, I did wonder about bidding when you were selling some of your land a few years back.'

'Here's another chance. It's up to you. Perhaps you might like to come over sometime so we could discuss it?'

Heth spent two days with Noah walking together through the remains of the estate and examining everything very carefully. On the second evening they came to the ark.

'I want to keep this area,' Noah explained, 'and a field or two nearby. Otherwise, if you made the right offer, I'd let the rest go.'

'But won't that leave you very short? You'll hardly have enough land to support your family.'

'It'll be hard, I admit. But there are things which take priority.'

'Like finishing your boat?'

Noah nodded.

'But, if you don't mind me asking... this flood of yours, when do you think it'll happen?'

'About five years from now... maybe a little less.'

'And then, I suppose, you'll float off and wait for the water to go down so you can start again.'

As Heth walked home, he puzzled over their bizarre conversation. 'Noah's such a solid, sensible chap,' he thought. 'If it wasn't for his obsession, he'd be the ideal neighbour. It seems unfair taking advantage of someone who's obviously mad, but opportunities like this don't come my way very often.'

He returned next day with a firm offer. 'Noah, let's just suppose I bought *everything* you've got – including the ark. I'd give you a fair price for it all, *but* I wouldn't take possession for five years.'

Noah looked at him, startled. 'But what will I do in the meantime?'

'Just carry on as usual.'

'What do you mean? I'd keep growing crops and harvesting them?'

'Exactly! I wouldn't make an offer like this normally, but you're one person I can trust. Everybody says the same, even folk in the city. After five years, sometime in the late autumn, everything becomes mine – except your last harvest.' He smiled. 'And if there's a flood *before* that, I'd expect you to save me a place inside your ark!'

'I'd want you to come with us anyway – whether you bought my land or not.'

For three days Noah fasted and called on the Holy One. Then he visited Heth.

'I'm very interested in your offer. But it would be embarrassing if anyone found out about it before you took the land. Would it be possible to make a binding agreement without involving the elders in the city?'

Heth looked at him carefully. 'Are you trying to hide this from your wife? I hear she wasn't too happy about your last sale.'

Noah dropped his head. 'That's the problem.'

Heth frowned. 'I'd prefer it right out in the open so nobody gets upset afterwards. But leave it with me; I'll see what I can arrange.'

He found a priest of Marduk to witness the contract. Noah cringed as the man sacrificed to his god, but at least he was efficient, writing two copies of the agreement on tablets in the approved manner. Finally he invoked Marduk's wrath on anyone who broke the terms or disclosed them before the agreed date.

Now Noah had the gold he needed to complete the work and stock the ark. He felt guilty about keeping the deal from Zillah, but in five years' time the flood would have begun and it would be irrelevant. Nevertheless, as he looked at the ark that evening he had a moment of doubt. He was now totally committed. If he had made a mistake about the flood or its timing he would forfeit everything he owned.

'Better wait for Ehud,' Noah said, turning to Ham, Kenan and Enosh as they stood together on the top floor of the ark.

'Late – as usual!' Ham muttered.

Noah looked around. It was an enormous space, empty apart from the pillars that held up the roof stretching high above them. The only light came from where the sun shone through the doorway and the gap above the walls.

Ehud called out his apologies as he hurried up the ramp. 'I've been getting the men started on the spring sowing.'

'Ham's bursting to tell you about his plans for this top floor!' Noah explained. 'He's got more tablets to show you.'

Ham pointed at the top of the wall. 'We need to arrange something so that we can keep watch through the window. I suggest a walkway all the whole way round, with ladders so we can get up there. At one end we'll need a larger platform with a ramp for the oxen.'

'Oxen? What do you need them for?' Ehud was still out of breath.

'For helping us shift loads of rubbish. With all the animals there'll be masses of dung and bedding to get rid of. The easiest answer is to jettison it out of the window and let the flood wash it away.'

'There'll also be a lot of waste water. Bilge water they call it,' Noah added.

Ehud looked puzzled. 'Is the ark going to leak?'

Noah nodded. 'I'm sure it will, and there'll be spray and perhaps even waves coming over the top.'

'But we're so high up.'

'Once it's loaded, the ark will float deep and it'll be easy for water to get in.'

Ham interrupted. 'Look at this sketch I've done on a tablet. We'll have shutters fitted all round. When the weather's better they'll be tied up out of the way.'

'Why have you got these bricks and clay in the middle?' Kenan asked.

'For a fireplace. It'll be far enough away from the windows not to get swamped, but we will have to keep an eye open for sparks. The main trouble is that the smoke will go right up into the roof. But we do need something to cook by and dry our clothes.'

'What will you burn?'

'Wood, mostly. We can store it in the roof space once we've got some flooring up there, and the men can make some more charcoal for us. We might even try dung if we can dry it.'

Ham looked at his tablets again then pointed to one end of the ark.

'That's where we're all going to live. There'll be separate rooms for each family divided with partitions and a bigger area where we meet together. There'll be a room for each of your families and anyone else who cares to join us.'

Noah noticed that Enosh and Kenan were looking embarrassed but Ham was too lost in his plans to see.

'The rest of this space is for the animals we are taking. Dad reckons the flood's going to drown everything except the fish and we've got to take some of every kind with us. Once the water goes down, they'll breed and restock the land.'

Ehud interrupted him. 'What sort of animals are you talking about? Oxen, sheep, that sort of thing?'

'Yes – and everything else that breathes… birds and snakes… '

'Wolves and vultures,' Noah interrupted, 'and scorpions…'

'Excuse me asking, Master,' Ehud said, shocked, 'but how are you going to manage in here with all those unclean animals running around?'

'That's where Ham's plan comes in. We'll divide the area, with cages for all of them. The birds will be kept together too and we'll make a lattice to fit over the window spaces to stop them flying away.'

'Hmm…but just how are you going to get hold of them all in the first place?'

'Well, we've got some here already – oxen, sheep and so on.

We'll take seven pairs of each. We should be able to catch the smaller wild animals and take a breeding pair of each.'

'But… the bigger ones… like wolves… ?'

'I don't know yet,' Noah replied cheerfully. 'But I'm sure the Holy One wants us to take them.'

'And what about feeding them all?'

'That's where the storage bins come in. We'll fill them with dry stuff mainly – grain, beans and figs. And a lot of hay. That'll do for bedding, as well as all the wood shavings and sawdust we've saved.'

Ehud still wasn't happy. 'So you can feed the oxen and sheep and yourselves all right. But what about the wolves and vultures? Will they take to beans?'

The question left Noah worrying all evening, but he woke next morning thinking about dried fish. It might be just the thing for the meat-eaters. He would discuss it with Ham.

'I've never tasted it myself, Dad, but I know a lot of people in the city eat it and there are always fishermen by the river. Maybe we could go down there and ask.'

Three men were in the shallows throwing nets. They were stripped to their loincloths, the muscles rippling over their backs.

'I wouldn't like to get in an argument with them!' Ham whispered.

Just then the tallest turned to see a dozen men behind him. 'Trouble!' he shouted.

They threw down their nets and within seconds were standing defiantly pointing barbed fish spears at Noah's men.

'Put your weapons down!' Noah shouted to his own people and walked forward with his arms spread out. 'I'm sorry to startle you. We're not here to cause problems. I just want to see what you're doing.'

The tall one stepped forward a pace, lowering the tip of his spear. 'Haven't you seen men fishing before?'

'Yes. But I want to learn how to do it.'

'Don't make fools of us, we've got work to do! Just let us get on with it, won't you? And while you're at it, send your men away. They make me feel nervous!'

It took time to pacify him, but a bag of grain helped. The three started fishing again and Noah watched, sending his men to sit in the shade. By midday the fishermen had filled their baskets and were checking their nets and bundling them up. The tall one looked amused.

'Satisfied? Anything else we can do for you?'

'Yes! I'd like to see what you do with the fish.'

The man shook his head. 'You're an odd one. Come along, if you must. But I don't want any trouble with your men, or it won't be just fish we'll be gutting!'

The three fishermen lifted their huge baskets as if they were empty, flicking the carrying straps round their foreheads and setting off down the path so quickly that Noah could hardly keep up. He looked back and saw Ham rousing the others. They would need to run to catch up.

They stopped at last by an untidy huddle of shacks. The smell of rotting fish was overpowering. A group of women and children disappeared as soon as they saw the strangers.

'Come out!' the tall man shouted, putting his basket down. 'Got a man here who fancies himself gutting fish. You could show him a thing or two!'

The women came out reluctantly and knelt by the baskets. Noah edged over to watch them, marvelling how quickly they seized each fish, cut its head off, slit it open to gut it and tossed it into another basket.

One of the older women tossed a fish at Noah. He jerked back but it struck his robe and fell at his feet.

'Care for a chew, dearie?' she cackled. 'Do you a power of good!'

They were all laughing, but Noah thought he was going to be sick. He forced himself to speak calmly. 'What do you do with it? Eat it like that?'

The woman looked at him in amazement. 'Where you been all your life? Ain't you heard of cooking?'

The fishermen were chatting with Noah's men. He caught snatches of the conversation.

' ... that crazy bloke, Noah... building a huge boat in the middle of nowhere... '

' ... funny kind of fish he'll catch on dry land... '

' .... pays pretty good wages though... '

The tall fisherman came across to Noah. 'I should have

139

introduced myself. Shamash is the name. Come along with me and I'll show you what we do with the fish.'

They approached some wooden racks covered in what looked like grey rags but Noah realised they were pieces of fish. Shamash picked one out, looked at it carefully and rubbed it vigorously on his bare arm before handing it to Noah. It felt hard and leathery.

'Anything we can't sell immediately we put here to dry. We wait till it goes hard like this. It lasts a good time, particularly if you put a load of salt on it.'

'Why were you rubbing it?'

'Oh that! Just shifting the maggots! You've got to watch out or they'll eat the lot. It's better doing this in winter – not many flies about then.'

'Do people actually eat this?'

'No problem! We'll get rid of this lot pretty quick. It may not look much, but once you've soaked it and got rid of the salt, it cooks beautifully. Some folk even feed their animals on it!'

Noah was excited. 'That's just what I was going to ask! Do they like it?'

'They'll eat it if they're hungry, especially in winter when there's not much else.'

'Well, I'm going to have a lot of animals to look after. I could put some work your way – if you're interested.'

19

Two weeks later Shamash and his friends began fishing near the ark, with their women preparing the catch. Soon the whole area was reeking but Noah's men did not complain; they were spending every available moment down on the riverbank.

'What's everyone doing?' Noah asked Ham as he strolled down to watch.

'Shamash is teaching us to fish.'

'What? With nets?'

'No. They're a bit tricky to handle. We're using fish spears, though next he's going to show us another way of doing it using a fine piece of cord and a hook on the end.'

Despite the distractions, the first load of dried fish was soon ready and stored in one of the bins. But when Noah talked with Shamash about more loads, the fisherman explained they were running out of salt and, though they could buy it from merchants, the price was exorbitant. There seemed no alternative to collecting it themselves. But he was unwilling to lead an expedition until Noah offered him three times the usual rate of pay. Even then he insisted on spending several days making offerings to his god and entreating him for a safe journey.

Ham had wanted to lead the expedition but Noah insisted on going instead. 'I promised Shamash I'd go with him. He's very nervous. And I've already invited Shem. He needs the experience.'

On the outward journey they began by travelling with the current and passed through the city on the first morning. But after a few days the pace slackened, the river ran more slowly as it widened out and began to divide into separate channels.

Shamash checked carefully for landmarks. Eventually he signalled for them to stop.

'This is about as far as you can go with the raft. Further on it's all mud and the oxen will sink in. We'll tie up here. This is about the only spot around here with a clear view. You should be able to see anybody approaching before they get too close! From here we can get to the sea and back in a day in a reed boat. We'll get the locals to take us; they're so poor they'll do anything for a bit of grain. But you've got to keep an eye on them. They'll slit your throat as soon as look at you!'

'How do we get in touch with them?'

'Leave it to me. There's a village close by. I've done business with them many times.'

The arrangements didn't take long. Shem was left with half the men to guard the raft and oxen while the others joined Noah and Shamash and the pile of empty sacks for the salt in several small reed boats rowed by local men.

Leaving the main river, they found themselves travelling through a bewildering sequence of small channels with tall reeds on either side. It was hot and clouds of insects followed them. Occasionally they disturbed wildfowl and once they saw a huge animal submerged apart from its dark head with small eyes staring at them.

'Hippopotamus,' Shamash remarked quietly. 'Doesn't do to get too close!'

Later Noah noticed that a cool breeze was replacing the stagnant air of the marshes, carrying a new, sharp smell. The boats began rocking as they emerged into a large expanse of water stretching as far as the eye could see. In the distance he noticed another reed boat battling with the waves, sometimes lifted high then disappearing before coming into view again.

Suddenly he had a vision of his ark tossing up and down on a rough sea without shores, fighting for survival as the wind and rain tore at it. He shuddered.

There was a slight jolt as the boat was pulled ashore. Small hillocks blocked the view.

'Sand dunes,' Shamash explained. 'The salt working is just on the other side. You'll get a good view from on top. While you take a look I'll get on with the bargaining. I know these men pretty well and what they can get up to!'

Noah struggled up the slope, feet slipping in the deep sand. As he reached the top he was dazzled by a bright light as if from a snowfield. It was the salt, spread like a shining river in front of him. Here and there men burnt almost black by the sun were shovelling it into bags.

It took several days to load the raft, hiring five boats each day to fetch the salt. Shamash grew increasingly nervous and he was delighted when they began the homeward journey. He told frightening stories of ambushes, of rafts being lost – especially at full moon – of men mysteriously disappearing, of bodies found floating in the river. When Noah told Shamash of the pitch expeditions, the fisherman was amazed at how few difficulties they had encountered.

'No rafts lost! It just doesn't make sense. I don't know what sort of god is looking after you – but he must be powerful!'

Before long Shamash and his team had filled several storage bins back at the ark with salted fish, and Noah felt happy they had enough. Shamash seemed disappointed at the thought of moving on.

'If I was you, I'd keep a good eye on the bins. I don't like to think what'll happen if there's another famine! We'll go back to where we were fishing before, I suppose. Though I doubt we'll find another place as good as this part of the river.'

'You know there's room for you in the ark when the flood comes.'

'Thank you, Master. But I'm not scared of a bit of water. When that flood comes, I'll swim or use my boat!'

There were three weddings that autumn. First, Ehud announced he was marrying Milcah from the village.

Zillah relished the gossip. 'Noah, I never would have thought it! He's not the marrying sort! And her, of all people!'

'She seems a very nice girl.'

'That's what all the men say! She's much too young. She'll never be content to be his wife! Too keen on the high life, if you ask me!'

But in a few days Zillah had more news which pushed Ehud out of her mind. Both Japheth and Ham had found brides.

'That's a relief,' she remarked to Noah. 'With all the fuss

over your ark, the family was getting a bad name. You wouldn't believe the number of women who snub me nowadays! They say we're finished socially since you let all that land go. I thought we'd said goodbye to any chance the boys had of finding decent wives!'

'Japheth's Naamah is a nice girl. But I fancy there's a bit of Cainite in her name.'

'And what's wrong with a Cainite name then? Where do you think my parents got Zillah from? I don't remember that holding you back when we met!'

'Well, it's a better name than Siduri. Another one named after a goddess. Still… so long as Ham's happy… '

Zillah interrupted impatiently, 'You should be glad to see our boys settled. They're thoroughly nice girls, both of them! And with those wide hips neither should have much trouble giving you a few grandsons! Which is more than we can say for Ishtar, after all this time!'

But as the months went by there was no sign of grandchildren from any of the three couples and Zillah began to wonder if they had been cursed. She even blamed Noah for allowing the girls to work in the fields at harvest.

'They'll never get pregnant if they're exhausted. Out every day, shaking olives from the trees or cutting wheat! If you hadn't sold all that land we'd still have enough men to do it!'

'But at least the Holy One's giving us good harvests!'

'And what do you mean by wasting a whole field growing those sunflowers?'

'There'll be a lot of birds in the ark, and not all of them will take kindly to fish.'

'Birds in the ark! I'll believe it when I see it!'

Nearly four years had gone since Noah had made his contract with Heth. Harvest was over, most of the storage bins in the ark were full and there were racks of olive oil jars and honey packed between them. Noah was making a full inspection with Ehud.

'We'd better get all these jars lashed in firmly. Once the flood begins, the ark may be thrown about all over the place. And we need to secure those water jars.'

'Shall we fill them first?'

'I'm leaving that till the last moment. If you store water too long it goes foul.'

Despite the gloom, the mass of stores was impressive.

'Nearly there,' announced Noah, pleased. 'Next year we'll grow some crops for seed so we have something to plant once the floodwaters go down.'

All that winter Noah expected news of Methuselah, but heard nothing. He sensed a strange feeling in the air, as if nature itself was holding its breath. The weather was exceptionally dry; he could see hardly any snow on the distant hills; the river was running very low.

That spring, Noah hardly had enough men to plough the fields. His mind kept turning to the animals he had been told to take. Where would they come from?

Ehud called out to him one morning. 'Master, there are a couple of boys here with something for you.'

They were about ten years old, wearing muddy loincloths and clutching some small sacks.

'What are your names?' Noah asked.

'Enkidu,' the skinnier boy replied. 'And this is Ea.'

'Well, Enkidu, what have you got to show me?'

The boy opened a straw-stuffed sack. Noah jumped back in alarm when he saw the scorpion.

'Don't you know that could hurt you very badly?'

'Oh, yes, Master. But Dad said you were going to collect every type of animal to put in your ark and I thought we could help you.'

Noah looked at them in surprise. 'Well, I didn't expect a scorpion to start with. Anyway, we're not ready yet. Who would look after it?'

'We'll do it! We'll come in every day!'

'I'm not sure about that. There's a lot of valuable stuff in the ark. It's not a place for playing games.'

They jumped up and down in excitement. 'We'd be good!'

'Hmm... Perhaps I'll talk to Ehud. But if there's any bad behaviour you'll be out! Would you by any chance know where to get hold of a mate for this scorpion?'

Noah took the boys up to the top deck.

'We could get you lots more… mice and rats and insects. We've got lots at home, only Mum doesn't like them and she wants us to throw them away.'

'Do you have any snakes?'

'Hundreds! We keep them in jars. Dad says if they bite us we'll swell up and burst. But we're their friends!'

There was no stopping them. They came every day, caring for their animals and bringing more. Enosh found them some pieces of wood and helped them make proper cages. One day Noah found them in a great state of excitement.

'Master, look! We've found a dove with a broken wing. Would you like it?'

'Just the one? I can use seven pairs if you can find them!'

Enosh spent several days extending the aviary. But the birds seemed so tame that they hardly needed to be shut in.

It was time for Noah's journey to the hills. But Zillah was very frightened.

'Must you go? Your grandfather's so old, surely he won't miss you? Why not leave it till spring?'

'I must see how he is. I have a feeling that it might be the last time.'

She caught hold of his arm. 'Please don't go! We've got so few men now and we're wide open to attack here so close to the road. A lot of people know what you've got stored in that ark. I'm amazed we haven't been robbed already.'

'Well… I suppose I could wait till after harvest. Perhaps I could hire some extra men to cover for me when I'm away. I'll get there and back as quickly as I can. I'll manage with taking Ham and just six men.'

She looked at him, her eyes brimming with tears.

'It's no good, dear. I promised.'

The harvest was as good as ever. They filled the last jars with seeds and with the extra produce Noah hired twenty men to guard the family.

It was a strange journey: utterly familiar and yet fresh. Noah looked hungrily at every clump of trees, sensing he would never see them again.

They arrived in mid-afternoon and found only one man on duty. 'We're so glad you're here at last, Master. We were expecting you weeks ago. Your grandfather will be happy to see you. He had a fall last winter, and he can't get around like he used to.'

Methuselah half rose when he saw Noah, but he was wincing with pain and his voice was faint. He peered at Noah, clutching him with bony hands.

There was little to eat at supper and Noah noticed that most of the servants had gone. Judging by the empty rooms, they had taken many family possessions with them.

But Methuselah still insisted on a sacrifice next day. They carried him up the hill on a litter and it was hard going, even though he was so light. By the time they reached the top he was grey with fatigue; the jolting had hurt him badly.

Noah called Ham away out of earshot. 'We've just got time to collect the last of our tools from the secret valley. Let's take two servants from here to help us carry everything, I'd rather our own men don't see what we're up to.'

It was years since anyone had been there. The hut roof had collapsed and it took quite a time to clear the debris away. Ham levered up the large flat stone in the floor that marked the hiding place. The tools were in full view; the sacks that held them had rotted away.

Ham counted them up. 'There's about sixty different items here, dad. Tools mostly, but a few bracelets – all bronze except for the three at the bottom.'

He reverently lifted out two iron axe heads and the bracelet.

'You'd better put that iron stuff back. It's too dangerous to take.'

20

Arriving back in the dark, Noah knew from the activity that something had happened to Methuselah.

They had put him into the room where Lamech had died. Everything looked as it had five years before, the oil lamp throwing a pool of light on the face of the tiny figure in the bed.

Methuselah stretched out his hand weakly.

'I am going at last. Remember what was promised to follow my death. You must be ready! It is almost on you! May the Holy One spare you. Do not forget the writings!'

They buried him alongside Lamech. While the servants were shovelling the earth back, Noah beckoned to Ham to follow him to a storehouse well away from the main building. Clearing a pile of firewood with his son's help, Noah located a loose stone on the back wall. Fumbling behind it he pulled out a large cloth-covered bundle. As he began unwrapping it, the fabric crumbled away to reveal some fire-baked tablets, each in its own clay envelope. Noah held them reverently.

'Ham, these are the most precious things you'll ever see.'

Ham peered at the strange old-fashioned signs interspersed with tiny sketches of men and animals.

'This is the record of how the Holy One made the world and the history of our ancestors. When I was young, Father taught me to decipher them and made me promise to teach my own children to read them too. We need to take them with us.'

That evening Noah called the remaining servants together and divided the last few things among them.

'You're welcome to come with us,' he said. 'There's plenty of room in the ark.'

They avoided his eyes; then old Adam spoke for all of them. 'We're too old to travel. We reckon we're safe up here. No flood's going to get up this far!'

It was Noah's last night in his childhood home yet he was anxious to leave. He woke at dawn to find his men were already preparing for the journey. But he needed to be alone a little longer. He climbed the hill to the ancient stone of sacrifice. He had nothing to offer but he bowed his head for a moment. There was a cold autumn wind blowing.

Suddenly he saw two young wolves bounding over the rocks towards him. He recoiled in fear; he had no weapon and his men were too far away to help. The two animals came within arm's reach, then stopped, watching him.

The men were waiting for him as he came down the hill. They shouted warnings and grabbed their spears when they saw the wolves following him, but Noah held up his hand.

'Stop! Don't touch them. I'm safe enough. Let's go.'

It was an unreal journey, like one of the legends of the gods that bards recite round the fire. The men sweated and cursed under their extra loads. Behind them the wolves trotted – like tame sheep. As if that was not enough, two young bears pushed their way out of the woods. They were bulging with fat, ready for their winter sleep. They, too, followed the men at a distance. And then two mountain lion cubs appeared. Noah pinched himself in case he was dreaming. He remembered his vision of Eden. Those animals were behaving just the same: fearless in the presence of man.

Despite their heavy loads, the men stopped only when necessary. They sat down reluctantly at midday, forming a tight group and making signs against the evil eye. The animals sat and watched them.

'The men are scared out of their wits,' Ham said. 'They think you've got a demon!'

'I'm as surprised as they are – but I should have expected it. We've been making all these preparations for the animals we're taking in the ark and now the Holy One's started sending them to us!'

When Noah called a halt for the night, the animals disappeared. But the men got little sleep, huddled together gazing fearfully into the darkness. Despite an early start, their new companions appeared and followed them all day.

When they finally reached the ark, those on the site shouted greetings and then suddenly hushed as the animals appeared.

They trotted up to the doorway of the ark and waited for Noah to lead them up to the top floor and into their new pens.

'In Marduk's name, Master, how did you tame them?'

'Aren't you scared they'll kill you?'

'You don't really mean to keep them in there, do you?'

Noah waved for silence. 'I've been telling you long enough. I'm taking pairs of every animal with me in the ark. I didn't do *anything* to attract these animals; my men can vouch for that. The Holy One has sent them. Now, rather than start using up our stores, it would be helpful if one of you could start catching me some fish – you know, like Shamash showed you?'

Shem had been busy in Noah's absence. They climbed to the top platform and onto the walkway under the window. Outside, hanging beneath the eaves, was a long trough.

'What's this for, Ham? Feeding the birds?'

'No, Dad. It's for when it rains. It'll catch water from the roof. I'm going to fit a spout on one end and use it to fill the water jars.'

'But we won't need it. We'll fill them up from the well before we start.'

Ham shrugged. 'Water always tastes better when it's fresh.'

That night Noah dreamed he was watching a mass of black cloud spreading over the western hills. And he heard a voice say clearly, 'The seventeenth day of the second month.'

He woke in a panic. 'Why, that's only a week away! In seven days the flood will start – there's still so much to do. I must move the family into the ark immediately!'

But would Zillah come? In all these years he could not remember her setting foot inside the ark. Many times he had watched her walking past it, turning her head so she would not see the thing which had impoverished them. He wondered if he'd have to drag her in by her hair and tie her up!

But, to his amazement, she smiled when he mentioned his plan the next morning.

'Noah, what are you worrying about? Do you really think I'll stay outside by myself? I don't intend to drown!'

He let out a deep sigh.

'I'm sorry I've made life rough for you,' she went on, ruefully.

'I'd got our home just the way I wanted it and it was very hard to give it up just for... an idea. But anyway, we have to move again now because of Heth.'

Noah stared at her in deep embarrassment. 'You know all about him... and our agreement? I was meaning to tell you.'

'Of course I do! You didn't think you could hide a thing like that from your own wife, did you? I don't know why you didn't have the courage to tell me years ago.'

'I though you'd be furious. But if you knew about the deal, why didn't you say anything?'

'I suppose to begin with I was just too angry. Then... well, I had that dream again – the one about the flood. I knew you were right but... I didn't know what to say. Maybe I was hoping it wouldn't happen.'

'I'm so sorry, my dear... '

She shook her head. 'We've got work to do if we're going to shift our stuff into the ark today. There's no point in hanging around any longer. We might as well get used to it.'

Noah went to talk about the plans with his sons. Ham was enthusiastic.

'After all the work we've done, I'm looking forward to it. Siduri doesn't seem to mind. I think she's glad to get away from her family. They think we've gone mad!'

Japheth sounded determined. 'I suppose I've always believed what you were saying about the flood. But what clinched it for me was seeing those animals coming to you. There's no way you could get them to behave like that.'

Only Shem was uncertain. 'If you are all moving in, I suppose we'd better do the same. I hope Ishtar won't mind too much. Her family's dead set against it and they're doing all they can to talk her out of it.'

Then Noah tracked down Ehud. 'We'll need to start moving some of the domestic animals into the ark.'

'A pair of each kind, Master?'

'When it comes to the ritually clean ones like sheep, goats and cattle, I want *seven* pairs. That'll give a good breeding stock and allow us to offer sacrifices. Just pick out the best of the younger animals. Give the rest away.'

'Perhaps I might take some of them off your hands, Master.'

Noah frowned. 'I thought you were going to come with us in the ark.'

'I suppose... I need to talk to Milcah. Not today, though. We're very busy at the moment. There's a family wedding next week and I'd like to get that out of the way first.'

'We haven't got that long. The flood's almost on us.'

'I'll think about it, Master. Perhaps I could chose a room and drop some of things off to show it's ours?'

Next Noah hurried to find Enosh, who was fishing by the river. 'There's still some work to be done finishing off those pens on the top floor. Could you get on with it today?'

'Won't it wait, Master?'

'I'm sorry, but I need it done now.'

Enosh looked embarrassed. 'To be honest... I'm not too keen on going in there. Not with those wild animals.'

'The Holy One's shown me there's only a week left till the flood starts. I want to start bringing the domestic animals in today.'

'But, Master, you'll never get cattle and sheep up there! Once they smell those wolves and lions of yours, they'll be stampeding the opposite way!'

'Let's see. Now, what about you and the family? Have you thought any more about my offer of space in the ark?'

Enosh turned his face away. 'I'm much obliged, Master. But I don't fancy being cooped up in there with all them animals. If it does start to rain, you can always leave the door open for me.'

Noah met Kenan next. 'How about you? Are you joining us?'

'It's good of you to think of me. But I don't know.... What's everyone going to say if they see me moving in there?'

'Well, we're shifting our stuff in today.'

'I'm sure it's the right thing for you, but as for me... Look! If it does look as if it's going to rain, I'll drop by and see you then.'

Heth came round to see how things were going. 'Someone was saying you're moving into the ark today. That means you won't be needing your house any more. I don't want to hurry you, but my wife's very keen on living there. I know our agreement still has a bit of time to run, but would you mind very much if she came across this afternoon for a look?'

'That's fine, we'll be gone within hours. But have you thought any more about that invitation to join us in the ark?'

'What? Well... it's like this. Everyone round here admires you very much. No one else would have been able to do what you've done. That ark! What an achievement! But... this business of a flood... '

'Don't you believe it?'

'I don't want to hurt your feelings... But if I were to move in, there would be a lot of talk... you know – from people I'm making deals with. And I'm a very busy man. I doubt if I can spare the time to even look over this ark, let alone move in. And suppose the flood doesn't happen? What are you going to do then?'

'I haven't thought about that.'

'Just don't forget that under our contract, everything belongs to me.'

That evening Noah found Zillah weeping in their new quarters in the ark.

'I'm so frightened! This thing that's coming... what's it going to be like? Will we be able to cope? I hate sitting here and waiting and waiting!'

'We're going to be fine. Look how the Holy One's helped us so far. There were times I thought I'd never get this ark built, and here we are, with everything we need. Of course, things are going to be a bit difficult. But we'll hang on somehow.'

'It's all right for you. You're so strong!'

'I don't feel it. I always had the old ones to lean on and now they've gone. I feel rather helpless without them.'

He squeezed her hand. 'But we've got to remember that the Holy One hasn't let us down so far.'

The next few days were hectic. Ehud checked through Noah's stock for the best young specimens to take in the ark. To his utter amazement, none of the domestic animals showed any reluctance to being penned in close proximity to their natural enemies.

Many birds and bats appeared spontaneously. In one morning alone Noah found pairs of vultures, ravens, two kinds of eagle, owls, quail, sparrows and partridges waiting patiently to be admitted, all sitting in the trees together. There was a strange truce between hunters and hunted.

There was also a steady stream of wild animals arriving every day: foxes, jackals, hyenas, gazelles, badgers, otters, hippopotami and even crocodiles. The men made wagers on what would appear next, although they got out of the way hastily when a pair of young leopards arrived!

Crowds of people came too. When the building work had ceased, most people had lost interest in the ark. But now there was a renewed excitement with the strange arrival of so many wild creatures. Most treated it all light-heartedly, laughing and joking as they milled around the huge cradle, their children playing make-believe games about taming monsters.

'What's new in today? A dragon?'

'Any space for me? I'd like a cuddle with a bear!'

One neighbour arrived with a pair of horses. 'Here – take them as a gift from me. I don't want anything for them. It's worth it just for the laugh!'

Noah kept on warning them. 'The flood is almost on us,' he told them time and time again. 'The truth is, you'll be dead this time next week if you don't listen. Even the animals have more sense than you. They know where to go for safety.'

He got very discouraged. Ehud was the only man who was willing to join them.

'What's wrong with everyone?' he challenged Zillah. 'They've seen me building the ark. Surely they realise that it was only possible because the Holy One helped me? But they won't believe! I'd have thought that seeing all the animals living happily together should tell them *something*. There's been nothing like this since Eden.'

'Everyone's talking about it, all right. But they're not *doing* anything.'

'I mean, something with as little sense as a wolf or lion has the understanding to come for shelter – while the men who actually built the ark haven't got a clue what it's for!'

She nodded. 'I'm sure you've told them enough times.'

He dropped his head wearily. 'I don't think they hear me any more. They come in each day to feed and muck out the animals but it's just a job. All they're worried about is finding something else once they've finished here.'

She shrugged. 'How many more animals are you expecting?'

'I think that's about it unless Enkidu and Ea turn up with some more of their crawling things. I really like those boys, I hope we can take them with us.'

But late that afternoon he heard shouting. Two women were standing by the ark arguing with Ham. As he approached they turned round in a fury. 'Where's our sons? What have you done with them?'

'Dad,' Ham explained, 'these are the mothers of Enkidu and Ea come to look for them.'

'That's right! We've come to take them home – right now!'

'I saw them going onto the top deck just after noon. You know they come in every day to look after the insects and animals they've given me.'

'We don't know any such thing! We had no idea where they kept slinking off to. But it's going to stop! Now!'

'But they're not doing any harm. In fact, they've been a great help.'

'We want to know what you've been filling their heads with, you old fool! All your blithering nonsense about a flood and building a boat! Madmen like you should be hunted down. You're not fit to be let loose! Corrupting poor innocent children!'

'How dare you speak... ' he began.

They pushed past him, shouting for their sons, and in a few minutes emerged pulling the unwilling boys behind them.

'If either of you as much as sets foot in this place again, your dads will beat your backsides so hard you won't sit down for a week!'

They were marched away, the setting sun lighting golden halos round their tousled heads. It was Noah's last sight of them as they were dragged to their deaths.

Five days after Noah's last dream, everything was done except for filling the water jars. Usually they took drinking water straight from the river, but Noah needed a purer source so that the water would keep a long time. The best supply was an old well near his boundary.

'Be sure to drop a bit of pitch in each jar,' he told Ehud as the men started work. 'It keeps better that way.'

But despite a hard day's work by men and oxen, by evening only half the jars had been filled.

'We can finish this off tomorrow,' Noah shouted to Ehud.

'Sorry, Master. I thought you knew. Young Marduk is getting married in the village. None of us will be here.'

Noah stared at him in dismay.

'The water will have to wait, Master. But we'll try to look in first thing tomorrow to give a hand with the animals before we leave for the celebrations.'

Noah called his sons together. 'I hope none of you are planning to go to that wedding, because we've got to get the rest of the water collected.'

He slapped his knee in frustration. 'How I wish we'd filled those jars before I went up to see Grandfather that last time.'

But there was worse to come.

'Before we dispose of the oxen we don't want, let's check that the door closes all right.'

'Don't worry, Dad. It worked fine last time.'

'But when was that? It's been lying open for months, with everyone walking in and out over it. If we put a rope over that beam up there, we can use the oxen to pull it up from inside.'

Ham looked thoughtful. 'If we're leaving the oxen behind, how will we pull the door up that final time?'

'We'll have to yoke some of the cows instead.' Noah stood on the edge of the cradle watching the door being raised.

A muffled voice came from inside. 'Is it up as far as it will go?'

'Yes! The top's right against the lintel.'

'Well, there's a huge gap on both sides down here. I can almost get my head between the door and the framework. It's been warped somehow.'

'Can you get the locking bars to fit? Perhaps they'll pull it all in?'

'Not a chance. You'd need to force the door in at least a cubit before they'll fit.'

They lowered the door gently onto the ground.

'About the only thing we can do is take the whole door apart and straighten it,' offered Ham.

'Quite impossible! It would take weeks – and the flood's starting tomorrow!'

'Perhaps the Holy One will delay it till we're ready!'

156

21

That final night Noah slept badly and woke with a headache. For a time he lay on his pallet afraid to face the day, but at last he got up and climbed slowly down to the open door.

An autumn morning just like any other. Or was it? There seemed to be a feeling of anticipation. The animals were subdued. Odd restless gusts of wind stirred up clouds of dust.

The men were late coming in, most bleary-eyed and pale after the late-night pre-wedding festivities.

Noah stared at them with dreadful fascination. This was the last time he would ever see them; already they were like ghosts. He had failed to save them and his final desperate words sounded weak and useless.

'Sorry! I can't stop long,' Ehud muttering, bustling about feeding the animals. 'I must get back or Milcah will kill me!'

Noah turned away to hide his tears. It seemed hardly any time before all the men had gone again.

'We've got to do something about this door!'

They tried everything: putting on more pitch; shaving wood away with an adze. Nothing worked.

Then, about mid-morning Noah saw the cloud. He knew it instantly, that terrible familiar blackness with its sharp edge. His worst nightmare was coming true at last.

Far away to the north, Reu saw it too. He was walking with the shaman Ki across the hills where Noah had felled his trees. The forest was growing back but there was still a wide expanse of sky. Ki stopped abruptly.

'Look over there! We're in for a hell of a storm. I've never seen anything like that before!'

Reu stood frozen. A horrible certainty gripped him.

'Reu! Are you all right? What is it?'

Reu's voice was cold and expressionless. 'I've been a fool! I had my chances. Hundreds of them. And I've thrown them all away!'

He ignored Ki, muttering to himself. 'Noah, old man, you were right all the time! I knew it deep down and I was too proud to admit it. I've only got myself to blame!'

'Reu! What are you going on about?'

Reu turn to face Ki. 'Remember when we were felling trees up here? Noah said he was building a huge boat to save our lives when the flood came. Well, Ki, it's just about to start! And I'm up here on this godforsaken hillside when I could have been safe and snug in the cabin he promised me. I'm going to die! We're all going to die!'

Ki grabbed his arm. 'We've got to sacrifice to Enlil. We've still got a chance!'

But Reu shook him off. 'This is not the doing of any storm god.'

He started walking down the hill to his hut. He kept his healing potions in a small leather chest. One was a tightly closed jar of poppy juice. A single mouthful masked the worst pain and gave the sufferer sleep. He opened it carefully and drank it all down.

◆◈◆

Noah started counting. Zillah was there, so were Ham and Siduri. Japheth was just outside.

'Quickly!' he shouted. 'Get inside immediately! And find Naamah. Where's Shem and Ishtar?'

Shem appeared just behind him. 'Do you know where Ishtar is?' Noah yelled.

'She's gone over to the village to see her mother. She's giving her a hand with the food for Marduk's wedding. She was pretty mad with me when I wouldn't let her go yesterday.'

'But I told you not to let her out of the ark! We've got to get her back now! Quick! I'll go with you!'

'She won't come back with us – not till after the wedding. She's been talking about it for months!'

Noah seized his arm, jerking him into the doorway.

'Look up there! That cloud! We've got to get her back now or she'll drown!'

Shem stared for a moment. Then his mouth dropped open.

'Come on!' Noah yelled. 'And the rest of you – do your best to get that door fixed while we're gone! Only make sure we can get back in!'

In those few moments the cloud seemed to have grown. They ran to the boundary marker and the road. There was a sudden chill wind blowing hard against them, but terror drove them on.

Ishtar's parents lived on the far side of the village. As they arrived, several women were coming out carrying trays of food. Desperate and out of breath, Noah ran into one, spilling her load everywhere.

'Noah, you great peasant!' she screamed at him. 'I'll smash your stupid head when I get hold of you!'

She bent to rescue the food. 'Knocks everything out of my hand and doesn't even apologise! He still thinks he owns the place!'

Shem paused by the inner door but Noah barged straight in. Ishtar was standing there half dressed. She grabbed a scarf, wrapping it round her shoulders.

'Get out!' she screamed. 'How dare you... ! I might have been stark naked!'

'You've got to come back with us now! This instant! The flood's starting!'

'Don't be so stupid! I never heard such rubbish in my life! I'm off to the... '

But Noah had thrown her over his shoulder like a sack of grain. She screamed again, trying to wrestle herself free, but it was useless. She could only drum her fists against his back as he pushed through the door.

Noah caught a glimpse of Shem's face, staring dumbfounded, then he saw Ishtar's mother bearing down on him.

'Rape! He's raping our daughter!'

Noah felt the strength of insanity. He brushed her aside and lurched across the courtyard.

'Shem!' he shouted. 'Come on! Quick! And the rest of you – follow or you'll drown! Look up at the sky. The flood's coming!'

The black clouds were covering a quarter of the sky. Noah, followed by Shem, staggered on – carrying Ishtar – till they reached the boundary stone. He turned. Ishtar's mother was still waving her fist at him, but everyone else had gone back in to the house. He was spent. He put Ishtar down, almost dropping her. She turned to run but somehow he grabbed her again. They grappled for a moment.

'Take her, Shem,' he panted.

He was never quite sure how they got back to the ark with Shem half dragging, half carrying his wife. The door was still open and Ham was standing in the opening. Noah fought to get his breath.

'Is everyone else inside?'

'Everyone. Quick! Give me your hand!'

Noah collapsed into the ark, gasping for air.

'Now get that door closed!'

'We can't!' Ham shouted back. 'We just can't. We've been trying ever since you left!'

'Then we'll drown like rats!' Noah groaned.

They stood in despair, looking out. There was an eerie glow in the sky, with flashes of lightning. And the wind was getting stronger.

Then they saw the whirlwind. A great black funnel of cloud was visible beyond the village, twisting and turning violently, rumbling and crackling like some huge animal eating its way towards them. Noah watched in horror as it reached a row of trees by the village. Unbelievably, they were swept up into the sky. For a moment he saw the trunks spinning round the funnel like straws. Then they were gone.

Someone brushed past him. Ishtar was running towards the open door. She stumbled and he managed to grab her.

'Let me go!' she yelled. 'Enlil's coming. He'll kill us all!'

'You little fool! You'll be killed anyway if you go out there!'

She scratched frantically at his face like a wildcat but he hung on, gritting his teeth, while Shem helped him manhandle her back inside. Then she went limp and collapsed on the deck.

Noah turned just as the funnel of cloud reached the line of huts. Half of them burst into fragments like children's toys. The reed roof of the rope store lifted off in one piece and flew up into the cloud.

The noise was terrible, unimaginable. He stood transfixed, staring through the doorway. The great whirling mass came ever closer till the winds were tearing at him. He grabbed onto a pillar to save himself, while pieces of wood and straw were sucked past him.

Then the door leapt up, smashing against the frame. Even

over the sound of the storm the crash was deafening. His ears rang. He felt something hit his shoulder, then everything was quite dark. He could still hear the roar of the whirlwind and, closer, Ishtar's sobbing. All the oil lamps had been blown out. He fumbled his way slowly up the ramps to the top level. Some daylight was filtering through the window spaces below the roof and he climbed a ladder to look out.

As far as he could tell the ark was holding together. There was no sign of the whirlwind. Somehow, unaccountably, the heart of the storm must have missed them. Retreating down the ladder he saw that Ham had found a pot of fire and lit a lamp. They walked carefully down to the door, Ham shielding the guttering flame with his hand. They examined the woodwork in the faint light.

'Dad! I don't believe it! The door's closed! Completely closed! Look down this seam. There's no daylight showing anywhere!'

They peered at it together. 'And see, there's even pitch forced out the whole way along! We've never got it this tight before!'

It was puzzling. The door seemed as rigid as the rest of the wall. The wind must have caught it and slammed it so hard against the frame that it had straightened out. The shock had even dislodged the heavy bars so they had fallen into their sockets. Noah tested first one bar then another, but they were all wedged fast.

Then they heard a pattering noise above them. It started gently, almost tentatively, but soon it became a steady drumming. And Noah knew. The Holy One had shut them in just before the rain began.

◆◈◆

Ehud was in party mood. Noah had worked them hard these past few days and he had earned a holiday. Of course it was only a village wedding but they were doing it in style. Why, they had even got in some dancing girls from the city! He had heard that they had a rather special routine. Still, he couldn't help feeling uneasy. Noah had been acting oddly recently. He had tried really hard to stop him leaving this morning, for one thing. And then there was that business of coming and grabbing Ishtar.

It was hot in the hall; he could do with a breather. As he got

161

outside he saw the cloud, stretching from the distant hills and reaching almost overhead. As he watched, it blotted out the sun.

'Great gods!' he exclaimed. 'I'd better warn the others!'

He had chosen a bad moment. The dancing girls were just starting their show.

'Leave off!' Kenan hissed, as Ehud pulled his arm.

'But the flood... Noah's flood... it's started!' he whispered loudly.

'Get lost!' Kenan's eyes were on the black-haired girl on the right who was just beginning to shrug off her robe, nice and slowly.

Frantically he searched the hall for Milcah. There was a loud cheer from the men as the dancing girl tossed her robe to them and began gyrating. Someone jostled his arm, spilling wine on his new robe.

Suddenly, he glimpsed Milcah in the far corner and grimly fought his way across to her.

'The flood's started!' he called. 'We've got to get back to the ark!'

She gave him a look of pure venom.

'You drunken beast! Go yourself! And take your dancing girl with you! I saw you eyeing her up and down!'

He tried to grab her, but she slapped his face. Then as several men began hustling him out he shouted, 'Stay here and drown if you want. I'm off to Noah!'

'Keep your bloody Noah and his stinking animals!' she screamed back. 'Get out! I never want to see you again!'

They shoved him outside. It was just then that there was a great roaring as the whirlwind passed, snatching up trees from the next field. Ehud cowered by the door clutching the post. It was several minutes before the noise died away. He stood up slowly, amazed he was still alive and unhurt. But there was no time to lose. He began running for his life as the first drops of rain fell. Within a dozen paces he was soaked to the skin, the rain was so heavy. He could see hardly any distance ahead and struggled to keep to the road. Once he slipped, falling heavily and winding himself. He scrambled up and limped on. His chest was bursting when he found the ark, more by luck than anything else.

He peered through the blinding rain. 'They got the door up,

then,' he gasped. 'Hope they can open it for me.'

He hurried up the ramp and started hammering with his fists. 'They must hear me!' He found himself sobbing.

His hands were numb and bleeding when he sensed someone calling. Looking up he could just make out Ham's face peering over the top of the wall through a sheet of water cascading off the roof.

'I can't hear you!' he yelled back.

'… shut … can't get it open… '

Ehud stared up at the ark wall glistening in the rain. There was no way up; the scaffolding had been taken down weeks before. He crouched in despair, trying to shield his head from the rain. Then he remembered that there was a ladder they had been using the week before when they were cleaning bird droppings off the wall. It had to be still around somewhere.

Desperately he fumbled his way round the ark, but could see no trace of it. As he reached the door again, he saw it floating in the water below the cradle. Throwing off his precious new robe he jumped down and began dragging it up the ramp. A ladder this size normally needed three men to carry it, but somehow he got it up single-handed. It consisted of a central pole with footholds on each side. The end had been snapped off, but it would have to do. Then came the difficult part. He lifted the broken end and began levering it up until at last the ladder was leaning against the wall of the ark

Just too short! The end was about four paces below the window space. If he could get up there he might be able to clamber in, but there was nothing to hold it in position. If only he could lash it somehow.

'Where's that rope they were using?' He wasted precious moments staring at the water swirling below.

'It's hopeless! I'll never find any in that! I'll have to try to balance somehow.'

The ladder stirred with his first step. He looked down at the water below; in just a short time it had risen further.

Rain was sluicing down on him from the roof; it was like climbing through a waterfall. The fifth step was missing and he nearly fell trying to get past. Somehow he steadied himself, saying a quick prayer before beginning again. It was the slowest climb of his life, setting his foot softly on each step before trusting his full weight, freezing with each slight tremor. But

163

at last he was at the top.

Here the eaves of the roof sheltered him from the worst of the water, but the wall seemed to be pushing him backwards. The last step was hard up against the woodwork; he could hardly get his fingers round it, but if he was to reach the window he would have to stand on it. Then he saw Ham just above him.

'Drop me a rope!' he gasped. 'Quick! I can't hang on much longer!'

Ham seemed to be gone for ever. Ehud's legs were trembling under the strain, but he willed them to stay still because the ladder shifted with the slightest movement. The wind had strengthened, gusting round him and buffeting him with spray.

'This is all I can find.'

Ham was tying something to an upright, then he dropped the rope down. The ragged end hung just out of Ehud's reach to the right.

Ham twitched it along, and Ehud stretched out a hand to touch it. The ladder lurched. He paused, then made a grab. If he had been a span higher he would have been all right. Instead, his fingers slipped on the wet strands. The ladder fell.

There was one awful moment of clarity. He saw the cradle far below him and the brown swirling water. Then he fell, smashing his thigh on one of the timbers. His fingers scrabbled on the wet wood, the pain engulfed him and he slipped the last three cubits to the ground. The cold water revived him. The overflowing stream was bringing with it a lot of debris and one large log was jammed between the brickwork piers. He grabbed hold of it and pulled himself halfway on top.

'Hang on!' he told himself. 'Ham knows I'm down here and he's sure to find some way of getting me out. Of course, I won't be much use till this leg's healed, but I'll soon be helping Noah with the animals again.'

The current shifted his log and swept it under the ark. Somewhere under the timbers he had helped lay he was in utter darkness. He breathed for a short time with his head jammed in a pocket of air. But then, slowly, it filled.

22

As if from a vast distance, Noah heard a voice shouting, 'Quick! Catch him!' He sensed arms round his chest, he closed his eyes against the spinning walls. Then nothing…

He woke on his pallet in his cabin. It must be night; there was only the faint glow from a lamp and nothing from the window spaces.

'He's opening his eyes!'

Zillah was smiling down at him, that special look she used to give her sons when they were little. Then he noticed she was shouting. There was a great roaring, and he realised it was rain lashing the roof. There was even water dripping on his legs.

'What happened?'

'You fainted. I thought we'd lost you! You're too old to go around manhandling your daughters-in-law. You've got to rest!'

'But I can't! There's so much to do!'

'You stay here! And don't move!'

He waited till she left, then painfully sat up. As his eyes adjusted to the gloom he saw spray coming through the window space, soaking the floor. He pulled himself up, hanging onto a post till the whirling sensation in his head ceased.

'Ham, Shem, Japheth,' he called weakly. 'We've got to get that shuttering up; the water's going everywhere! Get the men to… '

But, of course, there were no men to help. The full realisation swept over him. He stood, horrified, as he pictured them dying in that terrible rain. Only the Holy One understood how hard he had tried to warn them. He had saved Ishtar, but even she had done what she could to frustrate him.

'You stupid man! I told you to rest!' Zillah had returned.

'I will, I promise. But how's Ishtar?'

She snorted. 'Don't waste any time on her! She's got Shem attending to her every need. She's lying down – just like you should be!'

'We must keep an eye on her. I wouldn't put it past her trying to throw herself out of the window.'

'That wouldn't come amiss, I reckon!'

Then suddenly they felt the ark stir. Along with the battering of the rain there was a scraping and rumbling noise from beneath their feet.

'What's that?' Zillah gasped, clutching Noah's sleeve.

Gently he loosened her grip and put his arm round her shoulder. 'Nothing to worry about, my dear! We're just starting to float. We'll be scraping along a bit till the water's deep enough to lift us clear.'

The ark was coming alive. The deck started rocking under their feet and a chorus of new noises erupted as every joint creaked in protest at the movement.

'We're lost. We're falling apart!' she screamed, burying her face in his robe.

'No, no, my dear, that's nothing to worry about. Rafts always sound like this when they first get into the water before the wood swells. Of course, it's worse here because we've got walls round us and a roof too.'

But for all his words, he shut his eyes apprehensively. 'May every rope hold!' he prayed silently. 'How I wish I'd been able to check every single tie!'

Kenan left the wedding soon after Ehud. The rain beating on the roof was so loud that the dancing girls had given up. No one could hear the music. For a moment he hesitated by the door wondering what to do.

'Maybe I was a trifle hasty with Ehud. Not that this really *is* the flood that Noah's always on about, but I might as well grab my things and get over to the ark. Just in case.'

Outside the rain was so relentless he could hardly find the way to his own hut though he had lived there most of his life. Inside, the floor was deep in water and torrents were pouring through the roof. He grabbed some clothes which were floating past and out of habit wrung them out. Taking a deep breath, he forced himself outside again.

The rain was stupefying. It was hopeless trying to look for landmarks. The path was already knee deep, and twice the swirling water was above his waist. A strengthening current was making it hard to keep his footing.

Suddenly he saw a single tree through a gap in the driving rain. It looked just like the one by the boundary stone. He should be able to see the ark from here but the mist blocked out everything.

Now the water was chest deep. He floundered onwards, half walking, half swimming, buffeted by the overflowing stream. Then he was out of his depth and having to use the dog paddle he had learned as a child. His knee struck something hard. He reached down into the water and could feel a long piece of wood. It seemed to be fixed to something and he pulled himself along till he felt brickwork. A gust of wind tore the mist away long enough for him to glimpse a row of trees. He had often looked at them when he was working on the ark.

'I must be on the cradle!' he cried in horror. 'The ark's gone! I'm too late!'

Desperately he pulled himself up till he was standing on the beam. He looked all round but the mist had closed in again. He could see nothing.

'I must get back to the wedding. Someone will know what to do.'

He slipped into the water and tried swimming. But the current swept him away. Some huge logs were swirling round him. He seized one and clung on for a while. Slowly the cold seeped through him. It seemed the most natural thing just to let go...

Noah felt a gentle hand on his sleeve. It was Ishtar. He could hardly hear her above the roar of the rain.

'I'm sorry, Father-in-law, but I've been silly. Yesterday I washed my blue cloak and put it on the bushes to dry. I forgot all about it, what with going down to Mother's. If you could just open the door for me, it won't take me any time to fetch it!'

He looked at her, amazed. Her anger had vanished and she was smiling at him like a trusting child.

'Don't you realise? We're afloat! We can't open the door now!'

'But you must! That cloak's special, Shem gave it to me! And what about my family? We've got to let them in too!'

He almost choked. 'But, my dear... don't you realise? It's... too late! There is no way of letting them in.'

'But can't you... '

'I gave them every chance. I pleaded with them. I even tried again this morning and no one would listen. There's nothing I can do.'

'But... what'll happen to them?'

He paused a long time. 'I'm very sorry, my dear, but I'm afraid they're going to die. They're all going to die.'

She turned away and began to sob, her shoulders heaving as if she would tear herself apart.

Enosh had stayed at the wedding. He felt good; he had caught one of the dancing girls. She was sitting on his knee while he fed her grapes. When Marduk the bridegroom hauled himself to his feet and bawled out a toast, Enosh could only just hear him.

'To Noah, who's starting his voyage today!'

There was a chorus of cheers and ribald comments from the men.

'Got the right weather for it.'

'That old fool in his box must be splitting his gut laughing at us!'

'Why don't we go and burn his ark down?'

'What? In this weather?'

'Let's sort him out anyway!'

The men staggered to their feet. They had some difficulty locating the door and even more trouble opening it, but once outside they did not stay long.

'Hey! There's water out there, all right!'

'I fell in right over my head... '

' ... so we'll have to stay here till it eases.... '

'Pass the wine, Enosh... '

There was a sudden surge of water under the creaking door and the women screamed, scrambling on the benches to keep their robes dry. Enosh made a grab for his girl but she was gone, tiptoeing along a table. The party was over.

There was still some light from the torches flickering

overhead. He waded towards the door. It was just like a river out there with the current tearing away at the mud brick wall of the building. It was time to leave. Outside, he lost his footing almost immediately and was swept away helplessly by the current. It threw him against a tree but he managed to grab the trunk and haul himself up into a fork. Then there was a rumble and he turned to see the roof of the hall slowly collapsing. He was alone and trapped, gazing down on a circle of water hemmed in by mist and rain. Tree trunks, baulks of timber, even boats burst into view and raced across his view as the floodwaters swept them on. His tree was under tremendous strain; the trunk shuddered as floating debris struck it. Soon he was forced to climb higher as the water rose. He hung there, too frightened even to pray.

The light was fading when he sensed a dark shape approaching. With terrifying speed it became a wall of blackness stretching up and up. For a moment he saw it clearly, great walls and a roof streaming with water.

'It's the ark!' he screamed.

Then it was on him, crushing his body against the tree and hurling it into the torrent.

No one in the ark knew of Enosh's death. It was just one more thud among many as his tree was uprooted. But Ham was sitting, head in hands, shocked and grieving for Ehud. 'I killed him!' he kept reproaching himself. 'If only I'd been able to find a decent bit of rope!'

Shem and Japheth roused him to help lash down the shutters. Even Noah joined them, although he found it hard to keep his footing on the wet walkway. Zillah was waiting for him when he finished. Her face seemed to leap out at him as the wind caught the flame of her lamp.

'Noah!' she screamed over the noise. 'You've got to stop! You're not well!'

'There's all the animals to deal with,' he yelled back. 'It's going to get very rough tonight.'

Heth was in the city on business. He was engaged in a tricky deal with the priests and so preoccupied he hardly noticed the dark clouds gathering. The rain was only a minor irritation as they hurried from the city gate to the shelter of a granary built under the great tower. But some time later they noticed a pool of water on the floor. The chief priest dispatched one of his eunuchs to investigate. He came back soaked to the skin.

'I don't like the look of it out there, Your Holiness. It's fairly pouring down and the river's risen a lot.'

The high priest hastened to reassure Heth. 'We'll be safe enough here. But it might be a good idea to go upstairs till the slaves can sort this mess out.'

They went to an upper room and continued their business. There was no window and it was easy to forget the weather outside. But then the eunuch returned.

'Your Holiness, I beg your forgiveness for interrupting, but we can't get through that bottom door now. It's completely under water.'

The high priest went to investigate and came back looking worried. 'I've never seen a flood like it. I think you'll have to stay here tonight. I can offer you some food; there's always plenty left over from the offerings. And I'll arrange somewhere for you to sleep.'

By the light of their few oil lamps, they could see the water swirling ever higher up the stairway they had climbed. At last, they judged it wise to go outside onto the tower. The priest led the way through an old door to the external stairway. Heth pulled his cloak round his shoulders; the rain was falling so hard he felt as if he was being beaten with sticks.

'Maybe old Noah knew a thing or too, after all,' he mused. 'I wouldn't mind being with him in his ark right now!'

Then the first earthquake struck.

He threw himself against the wall, shielding his head with his arms. When the tremor died down, he looked up. In the gloom he caught a glimpse of the top stones of the tower as they collapsed on top of him...

The first tremor came without warning. Noah, having at last been persuaded by his wife to rest, had got up to relieve himself

170

when the deck suddenly rose under his feet and he fell sideways. He grabbed at a pillar to save himself, crying out with pain as he jarred his shoulder.

Then there was darkness; the lamps had fallen over. He was terrified. It felt as if he was dropping into a bottomless pit. Then, with a sickening shudder, the ark began twisting round crazily, its whole structure crying like a soul in torment.

Very slowly, the gyration eased. Noah let go and sank to the floor, but the deck was still heaving up and down. There was a hot feeling in his stomach which rose to his throat. In a moment he was vomiting helplessly in the blackness.

As the spasm passed he heard a rumble over the pounding of the rain which he knew instantly from his nightmares. He could almost see the great wave curling high above them. Suddenly he was thrown into the air, seeming to rise half way to the roof before crashing back on the deck. There he slid helplessly until he came up against something solid. Water splashed in his face. Was this the end?

Gradually he realised he was still alive. Cautiously he tried stretching his limbs, though the pain made him wince. Thankfully, he saw a flicker of a lamp.

Shamash had taken Noah seriously. He had stocked up his boat, and felt quite pleased when the rain started.

'Clever of the old man to guess this was coming. But I'd rather be in a proper boat than stuck in his box. He doesn't know the first thing about sailing!'

He waited till the bank was almost flooded before pushing off with his family.

'I've never seen the river like this,' he shouted to his wife. 'We'll have to keep an eye open for all that flotsam that's coming down. A tree trunk would finish us off and no mistake!'

When the earthquake came, the stream parted. For a moment the boat grounded on the riverbed, then the water roared back, capsizing it. Somehow they got it back upright, but the food and water had gone. They started bailing frantically with anything they could find.

Then in the distance Shamash heard a deep roar. He waited helplessly as it grew louder. A huge wave loomed through the rain, higher than the temple itself. He gazed in horror as it crashed down on them.

◆❖◆

'Good! We're all here.'

Somehow Ham had managed to keep one lamp alight, and now he had gathered everyone into his cabin.

Ishtar was terrified. 'We've got to sacrifice to Enlil or he'll kill us all!'

'No!' Noah shouted. 'Never use that name again. It's the Holy One who's brought us here. He'll protect us!'

Ham had been hunting through a heap of stuff that had fallen on the deck. 'There's some bread here if anyone's hungry. And one jar with some water, the others got smashed.'

They all drank a few mouthfuls, but no one felt like eating.

'Ham, any chance of getting a fire going?' Zillah asked. 'We're freezing!'

'Perhaps if … '

But Noah cut him short. 'It's far too dangerous! If the ark keeps jerking like this the embers will go everywhere. We'd better huddle together for warmth.'

'What on earth happened just now?' Shem asked. 'Did we hit something?'

'I think it was an earthquake. It set off a huge wave, like the one I used to dream about.'

'Are there going to be any more?'

'I don't know. But we can't afford to take any chances. We'd better stay here together tonight. Find something firm to hang onto or, better still, tie yourself down.'

'What if the ark runs into something?'

'There's nothing we can do about that!'

They settled down, but no one got much sleep. The night seemed endless. The rain hammered on and on and there were four more gigantic shocks. Noah retched repeatedly, though there was nothing left in his stomach.

Finally daylight showed through chinks in the shutters. Ham opened a shutter, but all he could see was driving rain, mist and an endless succession of angry waves smashing against the hull. A strong wind whipped spray into his face. But at least his water collection system was working well.

They checked the animals, all still rather subdued. They had enough stores to feed them for a day or two before needing to venture down into the bin area below.

The Great Valley was overwhelmed very quickly. Most of the river settlements were washed away before the first earthquake. Then the sea erupted over the land, engulfing men and animals as they struggled towards the hills. It even doused the sacred flames of the pitch lands.

Some men did reach the mountains, but were driven back by torrents of water and mud pouring down the hillsides. Huge rocks larger than houses bounced down the hills and were swept along the valley floor. All the forests were ripped out, leaving the hillsides bare.

The Cainites were the last to die. The priests continued their human sacrifices in the foundry till near the end. Then an earthquake blocked the river gorge and their valley filled with water. The slaves drowned in the blackness of the mines without ever knowing what had happened.

23

Noah's abiding memory of those days was of backbreaking toil. Every morning it was an effort to get his stiff limbs off his pallet.

'I used to complain things were difficult,' he reminded himself, 'but I didn't know how fortunate I was with all those servants to do the heavy work. I wish we had them now! Just eight of us to do everything! I ache all over.'

After the first few days, the animals livened up considerably. In fact, it was chaos. The ark echoed to the bellowing of cattle, roaring of lions and howling of wolves. Only the bears had settled down to their winter sleep.

'Before we feed the animals, we must make sure we soak the pulses and beans to soften them and also the fish to get the salt off.'

'Dad, we haven't got time for all that,' Ham complained. 'We're worked off our feet. Those wretched animals are always hungry or needing to be mucked out!'

'You should be grateful for the work – at least it keeps you warm! But, in case you're bored, I've got another job for you. Bilge water. We've had some pretty rough weather and I don't know how watertight the ark is. We need to check how much water has collected on the bottom level, then get rid of it.'

'Can't we leave it for now?'

'No. It would be very dangerous if too much got in – quite apart from spoiling our stores. Let's find Shem and Japheth and we'll all go down together.'

They edged carefully down into the blackness guided by a rope which had been fixed to posts down one side of the ramp. Noah's strained shoulder still hurt and as he reached the bottom a wave of nausea hit him. He paused, breathing deeply and swallowing, hoping his sons had not noticed.

Fortunately there was only a little water slopping around on the floor. Noah gave a sigh of relief.

'Well, that's a weight off my mind! I thought we must have

sprung leaks everywhere after that first night. I was even wondering whether this whole level might be flooded. But even so, I think we should bail it out as soon as possible. Tomorrow, you can yoke up some of the cows to help you carry the water back up. That is, if you can persuade them to go down the ramps in the dark.'

Next morning Noah was feeding the gazelles, marvelling that he was so close to these timid creatures. His sons had been working for some time and he looked up to see them driving the cows up the ramp with another load of bilge water. To his surprise Ham was stripped down to his loincloth.

'Why are you going around like that? It's freezing!'

'I got soaked as soon as we started. You should try scooping up filthy water and emptying it into a skin while you try to keep the cow still. And once you get to the top it's just as bad, trying to empty it out through a narrow slit without spilling it. Anyway, one more trip should do it, I reckon. I can't wait to wash this filth off and get warm again! I'm glad we've been able to get the fire lit at last.'

Noah delayed another two days before reminding them of a further unpleasant chore: filling the empty water jars.

'Do we really need to store that much?' Shem asked.

'I don't know how long we're going to be in here. We can't afford to run short. You can always blame Ham – after all, it was his idea to collect rain water!'

'That was before I knew how much work was involved!' Ham laughed.

Shem suggested hauling water up from the flood and lowered a small jar on a length of rope. After some manoeuvring he managed to fill it.

Tasting it, he made a wry face. 'It's salty! Like the sea. Remember that time we were down there with Shamash? Have we drifted that far already?'

'I don't know. It could be that the sea's poured in over the land and swamped everything.'

◆◈◆

It was hard to remember what it was to be dry. There were puddles all over the floor, the walkway was soaked with spray and everything was slippery. Patches of mould were forming on the walls and the ark smelt musty.

The task of cleaning out the animals was unending: raking up bedding and dung and stuffing it into baskets to be carried by the cows to the disposal point. The permanent gloom made it all the more difficult. There were rare moments of light relief like the time Japheth was butted by a goat and fell face down in the muck. But mostly they worked silently.

'The thing I really hate,' Ham remarked, 'is dealing with the lions and wolves. I can't drive the cows anywhere near them – they're unmanageable once they smell the dung. I think we'll have to carry these wretched baskets ourselves.'

'You should worry!' Japheth called down from the top platform. 'Just try shovelling everything out through this narrow gap; really we ought to fix up a chute to get it out. And as for the floor, it's so messy with all the spills that I keep sliding over.'

Apart from the sawdust and wood shavings, most of the bedding – reeds, hay and straw – was stored in racks fitted into the roof space. Here at least it was dry, but every time a bale was removed there were clouds of dust. The air was also full of soot from the fire. Soon, they had all developed coughs.

❖

'Have we got any chance of getting out?'

Zillah was in one of her black moods.

'Yes, of course. Let's be thankful to the Holy One we're all still alive... '

'*Alive* you call it! We aren't alive! I remember how the servants used to call your ark the coffin! Now I know why! It's the same shape, it's dark inside, it stinks and we're stuck in it forever! It's easy for you, working with the boys all day. You don't know what I have to put up with. The girls, for one thing.'

'What's wrong with them?'

'They keep complaining the whole time. They've had enough of your ark and they want to get out!'

'Just tell them to look outside! There's nowhere to go. They'll have to have patience!'

She glared at him. 'You men will never understand what it's like for us, having to live in this squalor all day, every day. I'm going mad! It's wet, it's cold and all the time there's that rain pounding, pounding, pounding, pounding on the roof. Then there are those filthy animals of yours bellowing at us, wanting food all the time and making a mess!'

'We'll really need the animals when we get out.'

'Need them! You care more about them than your own flesh and blood!'

'You should be grateful that you're safe!'

'*Safe* you call it! I'd be better off out there drowned! At least I'd be at peace. I feel so shut in that I could scream! The food's disgusting, we can't bake proper bread, and that straw you call bedding is damp! Can't we find land somewhere? Anywhere? I've got to get out and see the sky again and feel the sun.'

'You will, my dear. But you'll have to wait a little longer. Meanwhile, let's thank the Holy One for looking after us and giving us a future.'

'A future, that's rich! What kind of future is it going to be, living all by ourselves without any friends? Why did he have to kill everybody off?'

'Because of their wickedness. You know how evil the world had become.'

'The Cainites were pretty bad. They really had it coming to them. But what about all my friends? They never did anyone any harm. Don't you realise, whole families have been wiped out? Remember those children, Ea and Enkidu? And then there was Ehud. Why, he *built* half the ark – then he got drowned because he took a day off to go to a wedding!'

'I just don't know why that... '

'And another thing! With all those girls to chose from why, did you let Shem pick Ishtar? She's nothing but trouble! All she does is sulk. He was crazy to marry her, I said so at the time... ' She walked off angrily.

'And you've no idea how I feel either!' Noah said quietly after she had gone. 'I'd give anything to get out of here... a long walk alone with the Holy One in the fresh air. *I've* had enough of the ark, too – the darkness, rain, mess, stink. And vermin!' he added, scratching his leg.

He counted the notches he had cut on a pillar to mark the passing days. 'We've only been cooped up in here for two weeks! It seems much longer.'

He paced round the cabin. 'How dare Zillah blame me! If it wasn't for all my hard work, she'd be dead! If only I could go one last time to see the old ones. I'd give anything for a talk with them!'

In his mind he traced the journey up to the old homestead. He could picture every detail of it. Somehow he felt it must be still there just as he remembered it.

He shook his head. 'It's no good! They're dead and the whole place is probably washed away by now. There's no way back. But I would have loved to ask them why so many people died. I tried to warn everyone... It was all a waste of effort. Zillah's right about it being unfair. The Cainites really asked for it, but not Ehud. And certainly not all those innocent children and tiny babies. How could the Holy One do that?'

That night as he lay on his damp straw he tried to pray. But no answer came.

He was in the House of the Dead.

It was a huge, dimly lit hall stretching into infinite distance. He could see the spirits of those who had died. Each one was quite alone, trapped in their own alcove, unable to see the others.

He searched the faces for his mother, for Lamech and Methuselah, but there was no trace of them. Yet he recognised many men and women who had drowned in the flood. There was Ehud! He waved and ran towards him calling his name, but there was no response. He stood in front of him, shouting into his face, but Ehud just stared ahead, talking to himself: 'If only I hadn't listened to Milcah. If I hadn't gone to that wedding I could have stayed in the ark all day. I'd have been in time! It wouldn't have mattered about her; she didn't want to come anyway. Perhaps I should have made more effort to find some rope to tie the ladder. It was plain crazy going up it like that. I was always telling the men to prepare properly first... '

Noah stood listening to Ehud's regrets, excuses and thwarted plans, repeated word for word over and over again, the same things pouring out like the refrain of an old song.

Kenan was nearby. He was muttering too. 'It wasn't my fault! You couldn't really have expected it. Nothing like that ever happened before. How was I to know that there was really going to be a flood... ?'

Noah saw Reu standing silent, head lowered. And Heth, counting up something on his fingers. There was every kind of person there – some looking sullen, others with faces contorted with fury, cursing their fates and calling on the gods who had deserted them. He saw fire worshippers and shamans, practising their abominable rites as if the evil one was still interested in them.

And there were women. Some were naked, like those who had tried to burn the ark, flaunting themselves to the empty air. Beside them were respectable housewives, holding little ones and complaining about ruined homes. The children cried and begged to be allowed to go out and play.

Then he came to some Cainites. Although they were dead, he was still terrified of them. Perhaps they would guess that he had stolen their secrets and leap out to kill him? The soldiers were fingering their spears with the bloodlust still in their eyes. And their slaves were slumped, despairing and naked.

He saw many from the ill-fated wedding party. Marduk and his bride would always be separate, always waiting to consummate their marriage. Her parents were agitated, wondering if people would blame them for the rain. And there was Milcah, scowling with fury.

Then the Holy One came.

Noah had seen him in his brightness long ago in that vision of Eden. Now, strangely, his glory had gone. He moved awkwardly as if terribly injured. He hobbled slowly to each person and greeted them by name. Most ignored him, but others threw themselves at his feet. The Holy One came to Ehud. The man's muttering stopped and tears started trickling down his cheeks. Noah clenched his fists, willing him to kneel. A long moment passed and the Holy One had gone by. Then, too late, Ehud jumped forward and tried to follow him.

Now it was Kenan's turn. He was pouring out his story. 'I tell you, I was taken by surprise. I'd only gone for a few moments, just to get my things... ' He was too busy to see who was there in front of him.

Noah watched as, one after the other, his servants and friends made their excuses. And lost their last chance. The Holy One went along the line of the dead. Sometimes he leaned forward to pick up a baby. Often children or young people would run out to him. Noah was delighted to see Enkidu and Ea among them. To his amazement, he saw that several Cainites were following the Holy One, their faces beaming with joy. And many of the slaves came as well, stretching themselves up to their full height and striding out.

But most of the dead remained unmoved. Some even cursed or spat, threatening the Holy One with their spears or casting spells. Some of the women even tried to seduce him. But many watched their last opportunity disappear impassively.

Finally, the Holy One approached Noah. He remembered how he had boasted, taking credit for saving his family. He reddened with shame, staring at the ground. In that moment he relived the long years of building the ark, realising how he had been protected and helped at every stage. And he knew now that his men had not been rejecting him – but turning their backs on the Holy One himself.

Then, the vast hall was filled with light. And his confusion and sadness were gone.

24

'Is there a better use of this space?'

Noah and Ham were looking at the unused cabins, built for their neighbours and never used. They decided to turn them into a storage area, which would do away with some of the constant to-ing and fro-ing on the ramps. And it would mean less chance that some things would become damp.

Noah suddenly noticed a pile of clothing in one corner. 'Over here, Ham. Who do these belong to?'

Ham examined them, then turned away, choking. 'Those are the clothes that Ehud left behind to reserve his cabin. I suppose we might as well chuck them over the side.'

Noah picked them up. 'There's a lot of wear left in most of these. I'm sure we could use them. It may be a long time before we can make any more. He won't need them again, more's the pity.'

'Yes, Dad! And it's all my fault! I killed him! I can't forgive myself for that! If only I was quicker finding that rope, or got a better one. He actually got his hand round it before he slipped!'

Ham had hardly mentioned Ehud since his death, but now he broke down, sobbing. Noah put his arm round his shoulders.

'You mustn't blame yourself. You did everything you could.'

'Including finding a rotten bit of rope!'

'He brought his death on himself. If he had been here before the door closed he'd be alive now. He didn't have to be at that wedding.'

'It was that awful Milcah that made him go.'

'Don't blame her, either. If he hadn't married her there would have been some other excuse. He was an excellent worker, but was always putting things off thinking he'd get one more chance. I knew him quite well, you know. We'd worked together for so long, sharing in the planning of the ark and seeing the amazing things that happened. But deep down I don't think he ever believed in the Holy One or thought the flood would actually come.'

'And what about all the others – Kenan, Enosh, Shamash and Heth? And Reu of course, I almost forgot him.'

'Perhaps we could have said more to them. Looking back, it's always possible to see things you should have done better. But I don't think any of them believed the flood was coming and they weren't prepared to make fools of themselves by moving in with us. And, having made up their minds, they weren't prepared to change even when the animals started arriving miraculously. It's much more comfortable carrying on the same old way and hoping for the best.'

'But there must have been many others we never got a chance to warn. And youngsters like Ea and Enkidu who weren't free to choose for themselves. What about them?'

'The Holy One will look after them in the right way.'

'Easy for you to say.'

Noah shook his head. 'I had a dream last night. Perhaps I ought to tell you about it.'

But even after he had described it in detail, Ham looked puzzled. 'If the Holy One really appeared, I suppose some of the children might believe in him. But you'd never ever convince a Cainite!'

'I know it's shocking. That shook me completely. They looked as brutal as ever, before he arrived. But there's something about him. I couldn't hear what he said to people, but it was as if they had found out that someone cared for them and it broke their hearts! They were sobbing like babies, yet – and I know it sounds strange – they were bursting with joy at the same time.'

'What was it like when he spoke to you?'

'I can't really tell you. You'll have to find out for yourself. But it was the most marvellous moment of my life. Everything I'd ever owned... the estate, the ark, the lot... didn't matter once he was there.'

'And another thing. You said he looked as if he had been very badly hurt. What had happened to him?'

'I just don't know. And somehow I don't think I ever will...'

'Will this dreadful rain ever stop?'

Noah looked at Shem in surprise. In the last few weeks he

had said very little.

'The Holy One told me it would last for forty days in all. According to my tally it should be over in about three days from now.'

'You're not just saying that, are you? To cheer me up?'

'He's promised me a lot of things in the past and they've all happened. Remember the problems we had building the ark? I used to think we'd never finish it. People laughed themselves silly just looking at some of the fixes we got into! And here we are, safely inside. Just as surely as we built the ark, so the rain's going to stop soon.'

'This never-ending darkness… I can't stand it much longer. All we've got are these wretched lamps that keep blowing out. We can't even open the shutters or the rain comes straight in.'

'It won't be much longer – I promise.'

'Even the animals have had enough. And Ishtar's in an awful state.'

'I haven't seen her much the last few days.'

'That's because she's spends most of the day lying on her bed. I can't do anything with her. She won't eat, she won't even wash herself. She'll die if this goes on.'

'Why don't you ask your mother to have a word with her?'

'Mum's just as depressed as Ishtar.'

Shem had not exaggerated. Ishtar was lying down and ignored Noah completely as he put his head round the door of the cabin.

'We could do with your help, Ishtar,' Noah began. 'There's such a lot to do.'

There was no response. It wasn't until his third attempt that she roused herself and sat up.

'Go away! I never want to see you again! You murderer! You killed all my family! There's nothing left for me. I wish I was dead too!'

'But there's everything to live for! A whole new world for you to bring up your children in!'

To his surprise, she sprang to her feet.

'Children!' She spat. 'How dare you talk to me about children! Your Shem's useless! He can't give me a baby. None of your sons can make babies! I might as well be married to a temple eunuch!'

'But your children will come! The Holy One's promised!'

'You've never thought I was good enough for your precious boy,' she screamed. 'All you wanted me for was to drop a litter of grandsons! Well, sorry, I haven't obliged! And as for your Holy One, if he's any good, tell him to stop this stinking rain! Then I might believe!'

◆❖◆

Noah lay half awake wondering what was different this morning. He could hear the cattle stirring in their pens, the lions growling as they waited for their food, and even a cock crowing. There was the lapping of water round them, the creaking of timbers and the sighing of the wind.

'The rain's stopped!' he shouted.

The relentless hammering had gone. Noah paused just long enough to put his robe on, then he was up the ladder and opening a shutter.

It was true! A few drips still fell from the roof, but the surface of the water was smooth, no longer tormented by lashing rain. A thick bank of mist hid the horizon, but it was much lighter now that the heavy clouds had lifted.

He walked all around the ark opening shutters at intervals, but the distant view was always obscured by mist. Occasionally he saw some pieces of driftwood and once the bloated body of an animal. Banks of fog hung on the water and even as he watched the ark moved into one and everything was blotted out.

'Thank goodness the rain's stopped at last! Any idea where we are, Father?'

Japheth had climbed up beside him.

'It's still not possible to see the horizon.'

'Is it going to rain again?'

'I hope not – certainly not like the deluge we've just had. Help me finish off opening the shutters. We'll all be better for some light and fresh air.'

◆❖◆

There was a new spirit in the ark. Noah even caught Zillah singing.

'You sound cheerful, dear!'

She looked at him almost shyly, reminding him of the girl he had met many years before. 'I do feel much brighter today. I was thinking how fortunate I am... I'm sorry I've been very difficult to live with lately. That rain really got me down.'

Later Shem appeared. 'How's Ishtar today?' Noah asked.

'A lot better. She got up without being asked and even had a wash. She's going to give Siduri a hand with the birds.'

Ham was looking enthusiastic for the first time in weeks. 'I might try to catch some fish now the rain's stopped. I've still some of the bone hooks Shamash gave me.'

'I suppose it'll help feed the animals. This salt fish can't be that good for them, however much we soak it.'

'I won't need a very long line. It can't be more than about fifteen cubits down to the water.'

'Interesting,' Noah remarked. 'So the bottom of the ark must be a good fifteen cubits further down still. The water must be at least that deep or we'd have grounded by now.'

Ham found it awkward fishing through the narrow gap of the window, but he got several bites and soon had a good catch. But he gave up when the wind freshened and the ark began to rock.

'Do you think there's going to be another storm, Dad?'

'I hope not! In fact I was thinking that this wind might dry things up instead.'

Their new life settled into a routine. Meals were eaten, animals fed and cleaned out, water and food fetched from the stores and bilge water bailed out. But now there was more light and they could talk without shouting over the thunder of the rain.

From Noah's tally of the days he figured that they were passing from winter into spring. But it was unlike any season he had known. The sun was completely hidden behind clouds and a cold wind whistled round them. And the view was always the same: a circle of water surrounded by mist. They had no idea of the direction they were drifting in, or how long it would be before they reached land.

'We could finish up anywhere,' said Japheth, miserably.

'True. But I'm sure it'll be the right place. We'll have a huge job to do once we get out, and the Holy One's sure to find us

185

the best spot.'

'But what happens if we keep floating till we run out of food, or go mad? We should have planted our crops by now.'

'We've got to be patient.'

'Patient! Mother swears that that's the only word you know!'

Noah was in his cabin counting the notches again: one hundred and forty-eight long days since the flood began and they were still floating. Then suddenly Ham burst in.

'Quick! Come and take a look! I've seen land!'

They climbed the ladder to the walkway. But in front of them was the usual wall of mist.

'I'm sure I didn't imagine it. It was as clear as you are – a huge mountain.'

They peered in every direction but saw nothing. Noah was just going down again when part of the mist seemed to darken and thin.

'Look! There it is!'

As they watched, some rugged cliffs materialised for a moment in the greyness.

'I hope we don't strike one of those! It would smash the ark up completely.'

'We'll have to trust the Holy One to keep us safe. We haven't got oars or sails. I wasn't even told to make a rudder.'

The landing came as an anticlimax.

A fresh call from Ham that afternoon brought everyone up onto the walkway to stare into the mist for a glimpse of land. Then there was a scraping noise below them and they felt the ark catching on something.

'We've done it!'

'We've grounded!'

'Let's get that door open!'

But their enthusiasm was short-lived. The noises stopped and the rocking of the ark showed they were still afloat. This pattern of activity was repeated several times over the next two days and eventually they began to ignore it. They saw a few rocks sticking out of the water but the mist was thicker than ever. Then, on the one hundred and fiftieth morning, there was another jolt and a series of dragging noises.

'Here we go again!' Ham said in a resigned voice.' But this time the noises continued. Noah stood listening carefully.

'I think we might really have settled this time. Anyway, it wouldn't hurt to take a look around.'

At first they could see only the usual circle of water. Then the mist cleared for a moment and they glimpsed jagged cliffs about two hundred paces away.

'Look! I hope to goodness we're not sitting on something like that! We could tip over completely once the water runs away!'

Noah mopped his brow. 'Don't say things like that!'

For a time the ark continued to rock, then at last with a series of groans it came to rest.

Zillah was delighted. 'I've been living for the moment I could walk on something firm. I can't wait to get my feet back onto solid earth!'

Noah was more cautious. 'Before you get too excited, we need to know just where we've landed. If we're stuck near a precipice we may need to watch our step!'

Just after midday, Ham came down the ladder.

'I'm sure the water's going down. I've just had a look over the side and there are several rocks I didn't notice before.'

Noah stared at the floor. We're on a bit of a slope, but it's not too bad. We shouldn't have any difficulty getting the door open.'

All that day they waited anxiously, startled by every creak and groan. But by nightfall all movement had stopped. Next morning the cliff was in clear view and most of the water on that side of the ark had gone, leaving an expanse of mud and small rocks. By afternoon, the other side was clear too, with just a stream running down the hill about thirty paces away.

Noah called Zillah to look. She was puffing by the time she pulled herself up the ladder. 'I don't think much of that! Doesn't it look bare! Trust you to land in a desert. There isn't a single tree!'

Japheth had followed them up. 'But, Mother, I doubt if there are any trees left. Rain for forty days will have washed out everything. Let's hope there are a few seeds left to sprout.'

'Well, it should be spring,' said Noah. 'And it does feel warmer. We'll just wait a... '

'No!' Zillah was quite definite. 'The girls and I want to get out *now*. Can't we open the door today?'

'I'm sorry but you'll have to be... '

'Patient! Patient! Why can't we just open that door?'

'You remember the job we had getting it closed. If it hadn't been for that whirlwind slamming it shut... I'm afraid it's jammed solid. We're going to have to break it down and I don't want to do that until we're certain it's time to go. I'm not happy about the animals getting out until things are ready for them outside.'

'So you propose sitting here and doing nothing until we go mad!'

There was nothing he could say.

◆❖◆

'So, Ham, what have we got in the way of stores?'

'I don't see why it matters. We'll be out of here soon!'

'Perhaps not. Everything's going to take a lot longer than you imagine. For one thing, we'll have to wait till there's some decent grazing.'

'Everyone's desperate to go, animals included!'

'So am I! I'd love to drink fresh water from that stream over there. But we've got to wait till the Holy One shows us it's time to go. I doubt if anything's growing yet. I can't see any green from up here. We have to stay put and we need to check our stores.'

'How much food do you think we need?'

'Enough to take us well into next year.'

'We could sow some crops now.'

'It's too late. It'll be summer soon, even if it doesn't look like it. There wouldn't be time for anything to ripen, even if the sun came out now.'

Japheth was getting agitated. 'Are we ever going to have proper seasons again?'

'I certainly hope so, otherwise I don't know how we'll survive. But for now, we've got work to do. First, we have to make a check on the bilge water. I know we bailed it last week as usual, but we may have had some more leakage while we were scraping along the bottom.'

The lowest level smelt very wet and musty. As the ark had settled, a pool of water formed at one end, covering the bottom of several grain bins.

'We must get this dried as soon as we can,' Noah ordered. 'Today if possible.'

Once the water had been bailed, they examined the wet bins.

'A lot of this will be spoilt,' said Japheth, prodding the grain.

'Save as much as possible,' Noah replied. 'Throw the rest outside.'

Ham was of the opinion that someone would need to get right inside the bins to make sure all the spoilt grain was got rid of.

'I wonder if we could ask one of the women to do it? Perhaps Naamah – she's the smallest.'

Naamah clambered into the bin and started filling baskets with grain and passing them out to Japheth to empty into sacks. But after some time she poked her head over the side.

'I'm sorry, but I'll have to come out. I feel quite sick.'

'Well, it can't be due to the ark moving around any more!'

'No. To be honest, I've felt a bit sick for days.'

25

The news of Naamah's pregnancy delighted Zillah. 'Marvellous! Just what I've been waiting for. At last I'm going to be a grandmother! If only this had happened years ago. I was hoping I'd have half a dozen grandchildren by now.'

'Perhaps it's all for the good that we had to wait. It would be difficult looking after babies in here.'

'We'll manage fine!'

Ham and Shem did their best to congratulate Japheth, but it was a stark reminder of their own failure to father children. Siduri and Ishtar were also rather subdued but there was no time to brood with all the animals still to look after. Naamah was given lighter jobs, but nobody could be spared completely.

One day Naamah and Ishtar were cleaning out the birds together.

'Disgusting things, these vultures!' Ishtar remarked. 'They make the whole place stink!'

Naamah nodded grimly. She was holding a rag to her face.

'Bit sensitive, are we, this morning?' Ishtar continued. 'Does our little mother-to-be find it a bit trying for her delicate nose?'

'Just let me alone, please. I suppose you couldn't get me some water?'

'Water, is it? And what else would you fancy? Perhaps some nice fruit? Or flowers?'

'Ishtar, please! You know how it is... '

'No! I don't know how it is! It's all right for you, with a husband that's a real man!'

Zillah had to intervene in their shouting match. Naamah lost the baby that evening.

Next morning Noah found Zillah sobbing.

'It was the only grandchild we're likely to have. And everything was going so well. I'd love to get my hands round that Ishtar's neck!'

'Don't be hard on her. It's not her fault. She's bitterly disappointed she's not had a child.'

'Maybe. But I never… '

'Stop!' Noah ordered. 'Listen to me. I've had about enough of this. Whatever you feel about Ishtar, she's still Shem's wife. And, whether you like it or not, he's not going to find another one! When we get outside, there'll still be just the eight of us. Any descendants will have to come from these three girls. We've got no option. We've got to work together. Even if Ishtar was to blame for what happened last night – and I'm not saying she was – we still have to forgive her!'

Ham finished clearing the spoiled bins, throwing the wet grain over the side. Soon there was a green mound where it had sprouted. But meanwhile another very unattractive pile was accumulating, made up of dung, soiled bedding and general rubbish. The smell pervaded the ark.

'I never thought I'd miss the flood,' Noah remarked to Ham as they emptied another load on top, 'but at least it washed everything away.'

'It didn't get rid of these flies though, did it? Or the ants. Or those weevils we have to dig out of our food before we can eat it. You know, Dad, I wish it would start raining again!'

Noah raised one eyebrow in surprise.

'Then we could get fresh water off the roof,' Ham continued. 'I'm tired of scraping muck off the surface every time we open a new water jar from the store. The taste makes me sick.'

'Where exactly are we?' The arguments went on interminably as they looked though the narrow slit of window at the mud outside.

'Well, we seem to be on a mountainside.'

'It could be anywhere.'

'We could be miles from home – swept out to sea.'

'Perhaps we've fallen off the edge of the world!'

But, almost imperceptibly, the mist began to lift day by day. Cliffs appeared in three directions, with hardly a level place to be seen. And in the distance was a deep valley.

'I reckon we've been pretty lucky,' Ham remarked. 'Can

you see anywhere else flat enough for us to land? If the ark had been caught on one of those rocks it could have broken in two – then we'd have drowned just when the flood was over!'

'We should be very grateful to the Holy One for bringing us here safely.'

Then one morning Noah heard Japheth shouting excitedly from the walkway. He hurried up the ladder.

'Sorry, Father, it's gone! The sun! I saw it a moment ago! The very first time since the flood! I'd almost forgotten what it looked like!'

Just then a pale disc showed momentarily through the clouds. Noah stood staring at the place, willing it to come back.

Slowly the mist continued to rise during the rest of the day, revealing huge crags, sheer precipices and tumbling streams. They even saw patches of green – but not a tree in sight.

Then, seventy-four days after they landed, they saw the top of the mountain rising above them. Something stirred in Noah's memory as he stood with Japheth looking at it.

'I think I know where we are! I came here with my own father when I was a boy. We'd made a long journey northwards to a large lake near here. We must have come along that valley down there.'

'But, where are we?'

'This is Ararat. The great mountain! Yes, I'm sure it is. I'd know that peak anywhere. When I saw it before, it was very different because all the lower slopes were covered in trees. That's what confused me.'

'But what's the country like round here?'

'Very good. The valley below catches the sun so it rarely gets cold down there. And the soil's magnificent – you could grow anything you liked. I think it's an excellent place to live. The only reason we didn't stay was because father hated the idolatry. The local people worshipped the mountain. When it was covered in clouds they said the gods had come down. They believed these gods would only be satisfied with human sacrifices.'

'It sounds dangerous.'

'Yes, even the Cainites used to think twice about coming this way.'

'Then we're asking for trouble! The ark's not going to be much protection if anyone attacks us.'

'Haven't you forgotten something? They all drowned in the flood! This is a great place to live – and perfectly safe.'

The sun was stronger. It was warm inside the ark and everything began to dry out. The animals dozed in the afternoon heat while the family stood on the walkway, catching the breeze. One day Zillah found Naamah singing quietly to herself.

'Well, Mother, seeing the sunlight makes all the difference, even if we can't walk outside yet. There's a lot of green down there.'

But, despite everything, Naamah's eyes were sad.

'How are you – really?' Zillah asked.

'Losing the baby seemed like the end of everything – but maybe there'll be another. The argument with Ishtar was so foolish. She was unkind to me, but she was miserable herself.'

'I've seen you talking to her the last day or so.'

'Yes. You can't avoid each other in here, so you might as well be civil. We're both longing to get out of here and away from those flies and that dreadful smell. Why doesn't Father-in-law just open the door and go?'

'He says he's waiting to hear from the Holy One.'

'But can't you persuade him?'

'When you've lived with him as long as I have, you'll know he's stubborn. And, of course, he's frustrated at the moment.'

'But why?'

'He's never been happy unless he's got something to do, like building up the estate. Just when I thought he'd ease off, he got started on the ark. Now he's bored.'

'He'll be better when we get out.'

'Yes, but I think he's frightened about what he may find.'

It was over a month since the mist disappeared and Noah was wondering how to check around outside without opening the door – since once this was done it might be impossible to make it secure again. Ham suggested lowering an animal or even one of the family out of the window by rope. But memories of Ehud were still vivid.

'How stupid I've been!' he said one morning. 'I can send a *bird* out and see what happens.'

He wandered round the cages. A raven caught his eye. It was pecking at a putrid piece of fish which had not been salted properly. Few other birds would have touched it.

'It's big and tough so it ought to survive,' he decided.

The bird came to him quite easily and perched on his hand. Slowly he edged over to the lattice which ran along the top of the wall in front of the aviary. The whole section could be pushed sideways to leave a gap, but it was very stiff; the wood had swelled with dampness.

'I miss Enosh,' he thought, as he tugged at it with one hand. 'He'd have had this open in no time.'

At last he managed to shift the lattice and pushed the raven out. It had not flown in months and seemed to stagger in the air for a moment before perching on top of the ark wall, looking down at him reproachfully.

'Shoo!' he shouted, waving his arms. 'Shoo! Go and see what you can find!'

It spread its black wings and flew, circling the ark a few times before striking out towards the deep valley.

He saw it several times in the next few days, winging its way overhead. Once it even came swooping close to the ark. But it never returned.

'Isn't that good news?' said Japheth. 'It must mean that there's food out there. Why don't we go and see?'

'It's not as simple as that. Perhaps it wasn't the best idea, sending a raven.'

'But why?'

'A raven will eat anything, including the stuff we'd never touch. It may have even found a rotten body left over from the flood. I think we need to let its mate go and hope they find each other. Otherwise there won't be any more ravens – that's the only pair we've got. Then I think we might try a different bird, one that eats food we like. How about a dove? We've got seven pairs of them. It ought to be safe enough; we've got all the hawks shut up in here!'

Noah launched it carefully next day through the lattice. It

was as reluctant as the raven, but at last flew away. He climbed the ladder several times during the day to look for it, but it was evening before it reappeared, flying round the ark and searching for a way in.

Noah pulled back the lattice and pushed his arm out. Immediately the dove settled on his outstretched hand. It seemed grateful for the rest.

'Poor little thing,' he said, 'you look tired. I don't think you found anywhere to settle.'

A week later, he let it fly the second time. Again it returned in the evening. As Noah pushed his arm out to collect it, he could see something in its beak.

He gently prised it out. It was an olive leaf. He had never realised how beautiful it was, silver green with the sheen of new life. He savoured the faint smell of foliage and for a moment imagined the barren hillside covered in olive groves.

'You've done well, little bird. I wonder where you found this?'

He hurried down the ladder, calling the family.

'The dove's back! With an olive leaf. A fresh one! They must be growing out there somewhere!'

After a week, he launched the dove again. There was no sign of it that evening. He never saw it again.

26

A month dragged by. There was something different in the air, a hint of coolness in the mornings. Despite the extraordinary year with the seasons turned upside down, they all sensed the coming of autumn.

'Aren't we ever going to open the door?' Ham pleaded. 'I mean… how much more proof do you want that the flood's over? You saw that olive leaf the dove found. I tell you things are growing out there! We should be getting the animals out and the ground ready for sowing, not moping around in here!'

'But we've… '

'Don't say it! We've got to be patient! Till you get your sign from your Holy One! And in the meantime we rot in here!'

Noah sighed, rubbing his forehead in exasperation.

'I know how you feel. I'm just as desperate to get out of here as you are. But it's no good rushing things. If we got all the animals out and there wasn't food for them, we'd be in an awful mess.'

Ham's head dropped in frustration.

Wearily Noah went on, 'I've been trying to see what it's like over there since the mist cleared, but you can't really tell. Those rocks block the view. You'd need to be up on the roof to see over them and… '

Ham looked interested. 'So why don't we get up there?'

'I don't want anyone clambering around on top. It's far too dangerous. You'd never keep your footing.'

Ham tilted his head back, staring at the beams and the darkness above. Then he caught his father's arm.

'That's it! Why don't we make a hole in the roof? If we cut through the thatch up by the ridge we'd be able to see everything without having to mess around outside. There's lots of spare wood around. I'll soon fix up a ladder or something.'

◆❖◆

Now he had an objective, Ham worked quickly. He harnessed two cows and dragged timber and spare rope from the lower decks so that he could rig up ladders and a walkway over the roof trusses. Once on top he edged his way along, crouching low under the ridge before cutting away the thatch with a bronze knife. Soon he was coughing helplessly.

'It's filthy up here,' he gasped. 'Soot everywhere.'

It was hard work cutting between the bundles of reeds with the pitch constantly catching his blade but soon glimmers of light began to show. Suddenly a large piece came away, almost knocking him off the walkway. He hardly noticed the soft thump as it landed on the deck far below because he was so overwhelmed by the sky.

The brightness hurt like a blow and he hid his face behind filthy hands. Slowly and carefully he levered himself up, forcing his head and shoulders through the hole. As he gazed around, a deep joy flooded him. He twisted round so excitedly that he almost lost his footing.

High above the sky was unbelievably blue – as blue as the veins in the rock from which they had made strong metal. White clouds drifted past, inviting him to travel with them. The sun was warm on his shoulders and a gentle breeze was carrying autumnal smells which took him back to childhood and visits to Methuselah and Lamech.

He pulled his head back inside and shouted. 'It's marvellous! You can see right into the valley. The water's gone and there's a lot of green around.'

For Noah it was a terrifying climb up the makeshift ladders into the claustrophobic darkness with only one small patch of light to aim for. His palms were wringing wet long before he reached the top, edging up a rung at a time, gritting his teeth against the void below. The final plank shifted ominously as he fidgeted, waiting for his eyes to get used to the light. He longed for the security of the deck but, having got this far, he was determined to have a look. At last he pushed his head cautiously through the hole. He had a moment's panic when he saw the ground so far below. He forced his gaze towards the valley, scanning the view quickly – frightened to stay long and yet unwilling to face the horror of the descent.

'You're right about the valley, there's a lot of grass there,' he said after he had climbed down.

Ham was jubilant. 'Why don't we go there this afternoon?'

Noah shook his head slowly and sadly. 'It's no good. It still doesn't feel right. I just wish I could hear from the Holy One.'

He watched Ham's excitement drain away. 'But, Dad, what more can I do to persuade you?'

◆❖◆

The next two weeks seemed never-ending. The family talked of nothing else but their plans for the future. Noah could hardly look them in the eye and took to spending whole days by himself on the lower decks. Even the animals seemed to accuse him with a new restlessness; it was as if they sensed freedom.

Noah's mood did not improve as he cut the three hundred and sixty-fifth notch on the beam by his bed. A whole year in the ark and they were no nearer release.

Six days later a gale howled round the ark, bringing the first flakes of snow. Smoke from the fire swirled in their faces, but there was little heat. Noah pulled his cloak tightly around him as he hurried through the day's chores. That night he lay awake shivering, listening to the wind moaning outside, and it was far into the night before he fell into a fitful doze.

But that was when the Holy One came.

Brightness like the midday sun flooded round him and a voice rumbled like thunder, shaking the very fabric of the ark. Rousing himself, Noah rolled over to lie face down on the floor in worship, sensing rather than seeing the figure in front of him. He heard the command to leave the ark and to release every bird, animal and crawling creature.

A deep peace soaked through him like that of a baby rocked in its mother's arms. He lay there long after the brightness faded, unwilling to lose his joy. He smiled as he recalled the worries and frustrations of the last few months. It had never really been necessary to send out the raven or the dove or to make a hole in the roof. All he had needed was to wait for the Holy One.

Suddenly he remembered his family and the animals. They must have been terrified by the visitation! Groping for his robe in the dark he pulled himself to his feet and hurried to make his inspection. To his surprise and relief they were all asleep. The vision had been his alone.

The next morning was bright and clear and the wind had dropped. But the family were lost in their own thoughts. The first taste of cold weather had reduced their enthusiasm for getting out and they seemed resigned to another winter in the ark. When Noah made his announcement there was none of the excitement he had expected.

Shem was puzzled. 'Is the Holy One going to break down the door?'

Noah shook his head. 'I reckon it's up to us. Let's get those locking bars loose for a start.'

His mood soon changed to frustration. The bars were so tightly lodged that they seemed part of the structure. Each man took it in turns to try to shift them, but there was not the slightest movement.

'I suppose there's nothing for it but to smash the bars,' concluded Ham. 'Stand clear and I'll have a go.'

Taking a bronze hammer, he attacked one with all his force. Soon it began to splinter and he was able to pull the wood clear in pieces.

'That's shifted the first bar! Five more to go and we'll open the door. Then we'll just slacken off the ropes round the bollards and let the door go slowly, encouraging it with a hammer as needed. We'll need four people on each rope.'

Despite their combined efforts, the door remained obstinately firm. Tempers began to fray. Ishtar began to shout about them being stuck inside until they died.

Finally, the men decided to use a large log to batter down the door. There was a sharp intake of breath as they felt the shock of the impact through their hands. At the third stroke there was a noise of splitting timber and a line of daylight showed down one side. Grimly they concentrated their pounding on the other side. On the second blow, daylight showed all along the top and side. Then the door began to fall outwards.

'Grab those ropes!' Ham shouted.

But it was too late. By the time they had dropped the log the ropes had pulled loose from the bollards and the door was falling freely. With a thunderous crash it hit the ground and the sound reverberated round the ark.

Ham alone had managed to grab a rope. Now he found himself balanced on the very edge of the deck looking at the ground twenty cubits below. Somehow he managed to edge his way back to safety.

But his near mishap passed unnoticed in the shock of the sudden brightness. The whole family cowered, overwhelmed by the daylight, shading their eyes and blinking like bats at midday. A cool breeze swirled around them, stirring the stagnant air and tugging at their clothing.

Noah was the first to pull himself together. He had dreamt of this moment so often, but now it seemed unreal. He hurried down the ramps from the top level, still keeping his head down because of the glare. It was almost as if someone else's feet were doing the walking, carefully side-stepping patches of mould and filth which had been unnoticed in the lamplight. As he crossed the open door he saw that several timbers had been broken. 'We won't get this shut again in a hurry!' he muttered.

Now at last he was walking through the long, clean, autumn grass. A sense of wonder came over him; no man or animal had passed this way before. He strolled on, relishing the feel of the firm ground beneath his feet, the smell of vegetation warmed by the sun and the grass stems tugging at his legs.

At last he paused and turned, lifting his head for the first time. It was a shock to see the old familiar ark in such a different setting. It looked quite insignificant against the mountains while his family were toy figures, still standing where he had left them.

'Typical!' he laughed to himself. 'They complain for months about being cooped up. And when they do get the chance to get out, they're afraid to move!'

He went a little further, marvelling at his freedom. Then a childhood memory surged back. He must have been about seven at the time and living at the old homestead. He had climbed the hill up to the stone of sacrifice when suddenly he had realised he was on the edge of the world; there was not another living soul beyond him. The mountains with the valley on the other side and the ice fields were all uninhabited. But suddenly the emptiness had become a nameless horror. He had run crying down the hill to his mother.

Now, all these years later, the realisation that there were no people anywhere except those of his own family cringing in the doorway came like a sharp blow. Every direction was the edge of the world now. Panic gripped him as the great emptiness began crushing him.

'Holy One, save me!' he gasped – and, just as quickly as it had come, the fear left. Instead a warm feeling began in his belly and spread upwards, engulfing him – a mixture of relief, joy and wonder. All the years of toil and misunderstanding had been worthwhile. The Holy One had saved him and his family and given them a new world. Stiffly he got down on his knees, then lay down on his face in the rough grass in worship and thanksgiving.

At length he got up and started walking slowly back, his ankles protesting at the unaccustomed exercise of walking over rough ground.

'Come on out, all of you!' he shouted as he neared the door. 'It's wonderful!'

The others slowly picked their way down to the ground. Then, spontaneously, they begun shouting and playing like children. In a moment, Ishtar was rolling over and over in the grass while Siduri was turning somersaults.

Laughter. Helpless laughter. That was what had been missing for so long. Now it rose in a great crescendo of delight, releasing the horrors of the last year and making the hills re-echo. He smiled to see Ham lying helpless on the ground clutching his belly, while even Zillah was shaking uncontrollably, dabbing at her eyes and nose with the end of her sleeve. Soon he too was chuckling and then roaring out loud with joy. Very unwillingly he dragged himself away. There was work to do.

The squalor of the ark was unbearable. In the stark light of day he saw great heaps of rubbish, pieces of dried fish alive with maggots, piles of dirty straw, fungi sprouting from the wet wood. Worst of all was the stench, and he gagged after the fresh air outside.

The family were still romping in the sunlight. Regretfully, he called out, 'Time to come in. We've got to release the animals.'

'We'll start with the birds,' he told them as they joined him on the top deck. 'Let the clean ones out first. We'll keep the eagles and vultures till last.'

They must have known what was coming. That morning they had been apathetic, moping in their cages. But now, as Noah and his sons began forcing the lattice open, there was a great beating of wings. As soon as they were released they poured out in clouds, blundering into the men's faces in their eagerness to be gone. A few rested for a moment on the ledge, testing their wings before they flew away. The cages were soon empty apart from a few disconsolate pigeons and doves kept back for sacrifices. Noah gazed out of the window as the last flock disappeared, irrationally irritated that they had shown no gratitude for the months of care. Then he smiled at himself. 'I'm glad we won't have to clear this mess out again. But this last layer of dung will be good manure for next year's crops.'

The animals, too, had suddenly come alive. Some paced impatiently round their enclosures, others crowded round the doors or shook the bars. They let them out – first the deer, all following the dominant stag. Then the sheep, the rams pushing ahead and sniffing the air before hurrying through the long grass up the hill.

As other pens and cages were untied, the rest of the animals behaved as if they knew exactly what to do. Tears pricked Noah's eyes as he saw the wolves, lions and bears leaving. Often he had patted them or stroked their heads – but he would never be this close to them again. Now they were free again – and dangerous.

The hippopotami left almost last of all. During their time in the ark they had grown enormously and there had been little room left in their pen. Instinctively they headed downhill towards water.

The domestic animals were still waiting patiently in their pens and there were also a number of boxes holding the insects and smaller animals. Again Noah's eyes filled with tears as he remembered Enkidu and Ea and their enthusiasm. Ham walked by with a large box. 'What have you got in that?' he asked.

'A pair of snakes.'

'I wouldn't take them outside now. They're very sluggish in the cold. They're best left till next spring when it warms up again. The same for the crocodiles and lizards. Just check their pens to make sure they are all right. And, talking of animals sleeping all winter, I hope those bears find somewhere for a den.'

'They've got enough fat on them to see them through the winter. The last few weeks they've done nothing but eat! But how do you think those lions and wolves will manage?'

Noah frowned. 'I've been worrying about them. I think the only thing we can do is to keep on putting food out for them till they get established. There's still several bins of that salted fish. If we don't, I reckon they'll finish off the deer and sheep before they get a chance to breed. It's going to be a long time before everything's back to normal.'

Reluctantly, Ham helped Noah and Japheth fetch a load of salt fish and spread it near the open door. Turning to go in, they saw one of the wolves looking through a gap in the rocks. It ran off as it saw them. Suddenly it was wild again.

The sun was setting. A chill wind ruffled Noah's cloak, an omen of the winter to come. Silently he prayed to the Holy One for protection through the cold months.

'Pretty soon all our animals will be mating so that they can replace all those that were drowned,' commented Noah to Ishtar.

She shrugged. 'They didn't show much urge to breed when they were in here. They were about as successful as us!'

Noah smiled. 'Think of all the extra work we'd have had if we'd got a lot of young ones to care for! To say nothing of the food they'd have eaten. I think that was all part of the Holy One's plan.'

27

'First, we need some fair-sized rocks,' Noah told his sons. It was their first morning of freedom after leaving the ark.

'I'm going to build an altar for our sacrifice. I want to thank the Holy One for saving our lives.'

Ham paused, lowering a bundle of dirty straw he was carrying. 'Dad, wouldn't it be better to leave that till we've got ourselves sorted out? We've still got an awful lot of clearing up to do.'

'That can wait. Let's get the altar set up first and pick the animals for the sacrifice.'

Japheth's face clouded. 'But we've got so little stock. If we wait till they've bred we'll have a lot more to chose from.'

'No. It's important to do it *now*. While everything's fresh in our minds.'

'And what are you going to do for fuel, Father? We've burnt most of the wood we brought with us and there aren't any trees or branches round here. We haven't even found that olive tree the dove discovered.'

'We'll get what we need from the ark. We're going to have to burn a lot of it to keep ourselves warm this winter, anyway.'

It was noon before preparations were complete. The altar had been built on a flat rock overlooking the ark and they had piled a large heap of wood on top. Noah had chosen the pick of the flock for the sacrifice, much to the annoyance of Ham who wanted it for breeding. It came willingly to him as he opened the pen, hardly noticing the loop of rope he dropped round its neck as it trotted by his side down the ramp. Noah felt a sense of betrayal as he took it up the hill. His sons were waiting expectantly. For a moment Noah paused, pushing his hand nervously into his pouch, reaching for the flint knife and fingering the blade. Of course, it had always been necessary to slaughter animals when they were sick or too old to work, but that was a task he had been happy to leave to the men. On occasion he had also watched Methuselah offering a lamb at the stone of sacrifice. Now it was his turn. He had never killed an animal before, though there was the dreadful memory of the woman he had stabbed. The horror of that moment came back; the sickening feel of his knife as it plunged through living flesh. He hesitated, tickling the ram behind its ears and running his fingers over its neck.

'Come on, Ham, and you too, Japheth. Give me a hand. Hold the head firm while I cut its throat.'

Japheth and Ham together took hold of the horns and forced the head back to expose the throat, but the ram began to struggle.

'Easy, there,' Noah said, stroking its head softly before putting the point of his knife against its neck. Suddenly the ram reared up, knocking it out of his hand.

There was a suppressed giggle. Looking up, he saw Ishtar hiding her face in her cloak. He bent down awkwardly and picked up the knife. His sons had regained control of the ram. Waiting till it was still, he drove the point deep into the neck and dragged it sideways. Blood spurted through his hands and he desperately fumbled for the bowl to catch it in.

Soon the ram's struggles became weaker and the animal sank to the ground. Noah looked in disgust at the sticky redness of his hand and the blood in the bowl. He started retching and swallowed desperately.

It was some time before he could perform the old custom of sprinkling the altar. His sons lifted the carcass onto the wood while he tried to clean his hands on a patch of grass; then he rummaged about in a bag to find twigs for kindling. He blew on his bowl of fire till it glowed, then lit the twigs before piling dry wood on top. Soon a wisp of flame appeared and the whole heap caught fire. Noah raised his hands in worship, conscious of Ishtar fidgeting. Perhaps she was remembering more spectacular rituals with robed priests and dancing girls. The smoke billowed out, carrying that strange smell of burning flesh. Suddenly the flames leapt high and, with a roar, the heart of the fire blazed like the midday sun.

Noah rose first, pulling himself up stiffly from the ground. The rest of the family lay round the altar as if dead. Gently he went to Shem and patted him on the shoulder. He seemed in a trance, but eventually Noah roused him and he stood up, eyes glazed. Slowly the others began moving and Noah led them back to the ark. Not a word had been said.

That afternoon Shem came to find him. 'The Holy One came, didn't he, Father?'

'Yes, Shem, he did.'

'It was terrifying. I've never been so scared in my life. I thought I must have been struck by lightning!'

'Yes, he's like that. But did you hear what he was saying?'

'I heard nothing except that awful thunder. Then I think I must have passed out.'

Noah paused for a moment. 'Strange! It was so clear to me. What about the others?'

'Just the same as me, Father.'

'Well, it was the Holy One sure enough. To start with, he told me he'd accepted my sacrifice. I was quite nervous about that. I was afraid he might reject it just as he did Cain's. And then he said he wouldn't curse the land again because of man.'

'Because of man?'

'You know that the first curse came on the ground because of what Adam did. That's why it's difficult to grow crops.'

'I understand all that. But things are different now. We're much better people than Adam was.'

Noah shook his head. 'I'm afraid we're not. In fact, the Holy One said we're just as bad as the folk that were drowned. We're evil through and through and we've been like it since we were children.'

Shem looked annoyed. 'Surely, Father, that's all wrong? I mean... it might be true of the Cainites... we all know what they got up to. But we... well, we're different and we've got a new start.'

Noah looked bleak. 'I wish it was true.'

Shem shook his head in disbelief. 'And did he say anything else?'

'He promised that he'd never destroy all the living creatures again.'

'You mean, there won't be another flood?'

'That's right. And he said that there would be seasons again, summer and winter, and also day and night, for as long as the world lasted.'

'The same as it used to be?'

'Exactly. He spoke it out as a poem, so we could remember it better. Let me see... it went like this:

As long as the earth endures,
seedtime and harvest,
cold and heat,
summer and winter,
day and night
will never cease.

Shem looked at him carefully. 'I only hope it's true. This has been the most extraordinary year ever; half the time we haven't known whether it was summer or winter.'

'We're going to get back to farming, Shem, and come the end of next year we'll have a harvest.'

Shem was silent for a long time before he spoke again.

'That's all very well and I'm glad to hear it. But... well, what's the good of it all? Who's going to inherit this new world? Deer? Birds? Those wolves?'

'The Holy One's planned this world for us and our children!'

'Children! There aren't any children – and there won't be any!'

'At the proper time... '

'There's no chance of me being a father. You don't know what it's like. Ishtar treats me as a joke! And Siduri's the same with Ham. If there had been any other men around they'd have been off long ago! As it is, they're always making eyes at Japheth, because at least he managed to start Naamah off, even though she lost it! And that's not the worst of it... the women have been saying they get more satisfaction from each other than they ever do from their men!'

'I think we should go back to the altar today,' Noah suggested the next morning.

There was an embarrassed shuffling of feet. Shem in particular seemed very uneasy, perhaps regretting what he had said the previous evening.

Ham spoke at last. 'It's a good idea... and it's not that we don't want to worship the Holy One. But we've got quite a lot to do round here.'

The others murmured agreement and Ham started to walk away.

'Come back here!' Noah called. 'I know you were all scared yesterday. But I'm sure the Holy One's got more to tell us.'

'That was quite enough for me!' The whisper was just audible but Noah chose to ignore it.

'And that includes the women.'

'No chance of that, father,' Japheth said. 'They were frightened out of their wits yesterday. I've hardly had a word from Naamah since.'

After some discussion they agreed to leave the women behind. Noah led his sons up the hill. It was a cloudy day but suddenly as they reached the altar a shaft of sunlight lit up the hillside. They formed a self-conscious half circle, gazing at the pile of ashes and the few pieces of charred wood and bone left from the sacrifice. A gust of wind whipped some dust into the air.

Ham kicked nervously at a piece of rock. 'So what precisely are we doing here?'

'We're waiting for the Holy One.'

'But there's so much to do... '

The younger men lapsed into sullen silence while Noah closed his eyes trying to meditate on the Holy One. It was hopeless! He could not concentrate. His head ached and his shoulders were tense with anxiety. That conversation with Shem haunted him.

'I should have guessed,' he reflected glumly. 'It's every bit as humiliating for my sons not having children as it is for their wives. Only they find it harder to talk about.'

Suddenly the earth shook and light blazed. For a moment he glimpsed the others falling terrified to their knees. Next he himself was prostrate in worship, paralysed with dread until he became conscious of the Holy One's blessing. His head cleared and the tension in his shoulders eased. Instead of lying on hard ground he seemed to be floating in a warm river. A voice filled his head. The Holy One was telling the family of Noah to have children and repopulate the world.

Noah gasped, overwhelmed by depression at his sons' failure to be fathers. He knew now how they felt, confronted every day by their frustrated wives, cold contempt grinding down any self-respect. Anger welled up and his fists tensed, but just as quickly it died away. He sensed something of the sadness of his daughters-in-law, each aching to hold a child in their arms and put it to the breast.

Then realisation dawned. 'Those words of the Holy One... they're not a promise or a pious hope... they're an order! The Holy One's *demanding* that they have children – but how... ?'

There was no time to think. The Holy One was speaking again, describing how he would put the terror of man into every living creature, and that they would be given to man to do whatever he wanted. Noah was reminded of the trust and respect that had built up between man and the animals in the ark. Soon that would just be a memory.

Then the Holy One said something shocking and obscene. He was giving them authority to eat those same animals – as food!

'But that's blasphemy!' Noah gasped in disbelief. 'I've never eaten meat in my life. I've kept to fruit and seeds according to the ancient law.'

Sickening images overwhelmed him: wolves tearing chunks of flesh from the living bodies of their prey, Cainite perverts laughing as they roasted great joints of meat. He sweated as he remembered how he had killed that ram yesterday. That was bad enough but now, as well as cutting an animal's throat, he must rip the body to pieces. He gagged at the thought of gobbets of flesh, quivering and dripping with blood, being forced down his throat.

But almost as if the Holy One was answering him, he was given a solemn command. Meat must *never* be eaten with the blood in it since this was the life of the animal. More important still, anyone or any animal that spilled *human* blood would be answerable to the Holy One personally.

Somewhere inside him he heard a new song forming:

Whoever sheds human blood,
by human beings shall their blood be shed;
for in the image of God
has God made humanity

'Of course!' he shouted aloud. 'That's what happened to Abel!

Cain killed him, spilling his blood over the ground. And the Holy One held Cain responsible!' And then he remembered the sacrifice, that ritual of Methuselah's he had followed blindly, sprinkling the blood round the altar after he had killed the ram. Why, that must be a sign, too! Somehow the sacrifice that was so unpleasant to him was in token for human blood that had been spilt.

He raised his head for a moment to glance at his sons and see whether they had noticed his outburst. But they were silent, still bowed. A dreadful thought came to him. 'I wonder if they'll be killers, too?'

As if to reassure him, the Holy One was repeating his command to multiply and fill the earth.

'The Holy One loves them – and he's chosen them just as he chose me,' Noah murmured to himself.

◆❖◆

'I had no idea he was like that,' Shem confided.

He was walking down the hill with Noah. The others had gone on ahead.

'Well, Father, I saw the fire. And this time I heard him too.'

'Isn't he amazing? He's so much bigger than you can imagine and so full of surprises. I never ever know what he'll do next.'

'I feel... stunned!'

Noah smiled. 'I know how you feel. Perhaps you realise what it's been like for me all these years, being warned about the flood and ordered to build the ark.'

Shem paused, struggling with his words. 'But... about us having children... surely that can't be true?'

'I know it seems impossible, but everything the Holy One says comes to pass.'

'At the moment I feel so worthless... as if I'm not really a man.'

Noah put an arm round him. 'You can't rush the Holy One. You've got to wait his time. Meanwhile, there's work to do!'

Where to live was the immediate issue. They dismissed using the ark. It would be cold and damp with the door open all the time, and the hole in the roof wouldn't help. Besides, they were enjoying the fresh air.

They found their next home in a cave in the cliff within

sight of the ark, next to a smaller one they used for storage. The floor of the cave was covered in silt but at least it was dry. Ham and Japheth brought wood from the ark to fix up a windbreak and to light a fire in the entrance.

To their surprise, Zillah approved of their new quarters. 'I'm so glad to be away from those flies! Give me a day or so and I'll make this place look like home!'

But no one felt quite at ease as they settled down for the night. It would be their first outside the ark for over a year.

'Shouldn't we set a watch?' Ishtar asked nervously.

'There's no one out there to harm us,' Noah reassured her.

'But what... but what about the ghosts? The ghosts of all those people who died... I feel them all round me and I'm scared to go to sleep tonight.'

Noah smiled. 'Don't worry. The Holy One's looking after us.'

But several times that evening Noah noticed her keeping as far away from the cave entrance as possible and, when she thought no one was looking, she was making the sign against the evil eye.

His own slumber was disturbed with dreams of Cainites marching and of great walls of water crashing down. He awoke in the darkness in a cold panic and managed to get up from the straw without waking Zillah. He pulled his cloak around him against the autumnal chill and forced himself to walk towards the cave entrance. The moon was full, visible now and again behind racing clouds. Memories stirred of those terrible nights when the women from the city had tried to burn the ark. He stared at the dark shadows, half expecting to see dancing silhouettes emerge, writhing naked in their demonic dance.

The wind was sighing round the rocks but he heard nothing else.

'Of course! There aren't any animal noises. I wonder if I'll ever stand in a forest again and hear birdsong.'

He slept late, waking when the sun was breaking through the early mist. The women were tidying the cave, apart from Ishtar who was grinding corn. Ham was building an oven with bricks taken from the ark.

'I can't wait to bake proper bread again,' Zillah was saying. 'You could never do *anything* with the fire in the ark!'

Shem and Japheth had gone down the hill, and Noah could see them laying out more fish and hay for the animals, patting them affectionately as they nuzzled round the piles of food. Then Noah noticed two large black birds tearing at a fish.

'It's the ravens!' he said in relief. 'They've found each other!'

28

Ham burst into the cave and grabbed Noah's arm, hustling him to the entrance.

'Look there! It's starting again!'

A long line of black cloud lay over the distant mountains – just like that terrible day the flood began. Noah gazed, stupefied. In a moment he was back in his old nightmare, waiting for the dreadful rain.

'Holy One, you've betrayed us!' he breathed. 'How could you save us only to drown us now in a new flood?'

He felt faint, grabbing at the wall to save himself falling. He forced himself to remember the promise the Holy One had made to him. Breathing deeply he bunched his fists and glared at the sky, shouting, 'There'll never be another flood!'

He remembered that Ham was standing next to him. He half turned, embarrassed that he had voiced his fears aloud. But his son was oblivious, white-faced and shaking, staring at the cloud. At last he groaned, 'We're lost!'

Noah seized him by the shoulders and shook him, speaking through clenched teeth. 'Ham – *there's not going to be another flood*!'

'But those clouds... '

'An ordinary storm. Just because we've had a flood doesn't mean it's going to stay dry for ever!'

Ham pulled away. 'Dad! We've got to get back to the ark!'

He ran two steps then halted, his shoulders slumped. 'The door! I'd forgotten! We'll never get it closed!'

He began sobbing hysterically till Noah slapped him hard across the mouth. He paused, staring at his father with blood trickling from a cut lip.

'Ham – stop! It's just a bad storm. Find the others and get them into the main cave.'

Ham dropped his eyes, turned and slipped away like a naughty child.

Soon all four men were standing in the mouth of the cave

watching the clouds blank out the sky. Zillah was behind them with her arms round Naamah and Siduri. Ishtar stood defiantly apart.

Noah lit a lamp from his bowl of fire and walked off towards the back of the cave.

'Where are you going?' Ham called anxiously.

'Somewhere quiet so I can pray.'

'Can't you pray here with us?'

'No! You'll be all right.'

The first heavy drops were falling. Soon the rain was a solid curtain, blotting out the mountains and even the ark. The ground was awash and the brothers edged back into the cave as a pool formed around the ashes of their fire.

But after some time the rain began to ease, the ark reappearing like a grey ghost as the mist lifted. There was silence apart from the dripping of water from the rocks. Slowly, the sun came out, the light at first hazy then crystal clear as if the sky had been washed. Every rock glinted like a jewel and the mountains glowed against the dark sky. Then the rainbow formed – clear and vibrant, the most perfect one they had ever seen.

'Look at that!' Japheth gasped. 'Have you ever seen anything like it?'

They stood laughing at the beauty, willing it to last for ever. The bands of light were unbelievably beautiful after a year of darkness and a world starved of colour.

The Holy One was there too.

Instinctively, Noah fell to his knees, then lay on his face in worship as a great voice rumbled round him. Afterwards, he pulled himself to his feet, ignoring the mud on his face and robe. His sons were still kneeling, staring open-mouthed into the distance. The women crouched behind, heads buried in their robes.

The voice of the Holy One echoed around the valley as the rainbow began to fade. *This rainbow is the sign of my covenant.*

They waited till it disappeared, then Ham walked outside.

'It really was just a rainstorm. I thought we'd had it!'

'I was worried too,' Noah confessed.

◆◆◆

'So, let's get this straight. Every time we see a rainbow we'll remember it's something to do with the Holy One?'

It was that evening and they were sitting round the fire at the cave mouth. Noah picked up a piece of wood that had fallen out of the flames and threw it back.

'Yes, Ham. The rainbow's his special sign.'

Shem looked puzzled. 'But, I don't understand. I mean... we've all seen rainbows before.'

'My mum told me it was the goddess Ishtar's jewels,' Ishtar said quietly.

Noah twisted round. 'Enough of that! I don't want talk of goddesses here!'

He turned back to Shem. 'I know it's not new. But now it's got a special, new meaning. It's the sign of his *covenant*.'

'So what's this *covenant* then?' Shem enquired.

Noah thought a little. 'Well, I suppose you could say it's like one of those agreements I made when I ran the estate. Say I was buying some land. We'd make the sale, then write down the details on a tablet. So every time I looked at the agreement, I knew the fields out there belonged to me.'

'So we've got a rainbow instead of a tablet? But what's this agreement with the Holy One about?' Japheth asked.

'A promise... a promise that there'll *never* be another flood big enough to destroy all life. He told us that when we made that sacrifice. But I think we all forgot it today, didn't we? So now we have the rainbow as a reminder to us – and to him too!'

'And how long will this agreement run?'

'For ever! It's a promise to every generation from now till the end of time. And not just for us but for all other living creatures too. We obviously do need a reminder, otherwise there'd be a risk we'd panic every time we saw rain and we'd be running back to the ark. We'd never get anything done.'

Noah suddenly had an idea.

'Do you remember Tiras? He was so proud of that bow he'd made. He was always testing it out. But when he'd finished for the day, he'd stack it away, with the curved side up... '

'What's that got to do with it?' Ham interrupted.

'Don't you see? It looked just like that rainbow, curved side up. The Holy One's been shooting arrows at us. Only now he's finished – so he's put his bow down!'

'Do you think he'll keep his word? What happens if we do bad things again?'

'Yes, I'm sure he will. In fact it's the second covenant he's made with me. When I started building the ark, he promised we'd all be safe, including the animals. And he's been as good as his word.'

◆

Winter arrived. A bitter wind howled down from the mountain bringing banks of grey cloud and the promise of snow.

Noah called his sons together. 'We'd better get as much stuff as possible from the ark while we've got the chance.'

Shem was unconvinced. 'We've shifted an awful lot already. Haven't we got enough for now?'

Noah shook his head. 'If we get deep snowdrifts it might not be possible to get to the ark, let alone carry anything back. Anyway, we need a lot more wood right away so we need to start breaking up some of those empty food bins. And – another thing – we need extra hay. We'll need to take most of the domestic animals into the caves with us. And as much feed as we can manage. I'm afraid that includes the smoked fish. There'll still be wolves and lions to feed.'

Ham looked disgusted. 'It'll stink the place out!'

'Put it in the smaller cave and cover it up to stop the animals getting at it. They've already raided a couple of the bins in the ark.'

The three brothers set to work, carrying full loads on their backs. The labour warmed them, though the rising wind was cruel, with no trees to break its force. There were odd snow flurries during the morning but it was only as the light faded that it began to settle. At dusk Noah went outside one last time.

'Ham. Could you come down with me to the ark? I need to collect the writings.'

'Can't they wait till tomorrow?'

'No. They're the most precious things we've got and I want them safe.'

Inside the ark it took them several attempts with frozen hands to light a lamp. They climbed the ramp, carefully shielding the flame. Dark shapes moved round them; some of

216

the animals and birds had come back for shelter. One of the dogs rubbed against Ham's leg, making him jump. It took some time to find the tablets, but eventually Noah spotted them under a pile of old clothes. They were in two sacks. Ham slung one over his back but Noah held the other carefully to his chest.

◆

The next few months were grim. They were all crammed together in the main cave with the cattle and sheep penned up at the back. The animals were restive after their few days of freedom.

'Poor things!' Siduri remarked to Naamah. 'They must wonder if they'll ever get onto grass again!'

The snow had its uses. They built a huge pile as a windbreak which blocked out the worst of the north wind. But the days passed miserably. They spent hours crouched over the fire in the cave mouth catching fleeting warmth from the flames, or huddled further inside the cave, choking every time a stronger gust swept smoke inside. Day blurred into day; a bitter struggle to stay alive. Unless it was blowing a blizzard, the men stumbled most mornings through the drifts to the ark for more fodder. The freezing conditions left their calloused hands cracked and bleeding.

The women took their turn mucking out the domestic animals and leaving food for those outside. The stream had frozen, so they piled snow into a water jar and dropped in hot stones to melt it. Their food was still the stale provisions from the ark.

Zillah took it harder than the rest. Often during the day she lay sullenly on her bed, inert or rocking monotonously.

One afternoon when the rest were outside, Ishtar found Noah slumped near the cave mouth. 'Are you all right, Father?' she asked, smiling.

He looked at her in surprise. It was unusual to hear anything from her except complaints.

'It's Mother, isn't it?' she asked.

'I just don't know what to do. If she'd only talk to me... But everything I do seems to be wrong. I might as well not be here for all the good I'm doing.'

217

Ishtar smiled again. 'It's not your fault, Father. I think she's very sad. I think it was harder for her than for any of us, living in the ark. She had lost her home, which was so important to her. She'd really prided herself on it, making it as nice as she could. Then suddenly – it was gone. And she's missing her old friends.'

'But they've been dead a year or more.'

'She still grieves for them. She told me she dreams about them almost every night. In her dreams she's still living in the settlement and the wives of the other landowners drop in for a chat. She told me how she used to have a large platter of sweetmeats made with honey. When her friends turned up they'd nibble them and have a good gossip.'

'I'm going to build a proper house for her as soon as I can, and maybe we'll even find some honey... but I'm afraid there's nothing I can do about her friends.'

'Still, she'll enjoy being a grandmother.'

She said it in such a casual way. Noah lifted his head and stared at her.

It was the first time he had ever seen her blush.

'That's right. Next autumn some time I'm going to have a baby. And perhaps I shouldn't be telling you, but Naamah's expecting again too – and Siduri.'

29

'I can't stand this place a moment longer!'

Zillah was definitely feeling better.

'Look at the state of it! It's worse than the ark!'

She bent to examine something on the floor then recoiled in disgust.

'Just look at this! Animal droppings everywhere! What will the neighbours think?'

It was not the best time to remind her that there were no neighbours. But it was a relief to hear her complain; anything was better than that awful silence.

'Just as soon as we've finished planting, I'll make a start on the new house,' said Noah.

She snorted. 'Oh yes! I've heard that before!'

With the first hint of spring in the air came a new terror – snow slides. Noah was the only person outside when the first one came and he was buried up to his waist. An agitated Ishtar was the first out of the cave to see what had happened.

'I reckon most of the snow on the mountain came down. It only missed us by a few paces,' said Noah, struggling to free himself.

'It's Tiamat, isn't it? He's trying to kill us!'

Noah ground his teeth in frustration. 'Can't you forget that superstitious rubbish?'

He took Ishtar's hand. 'There's no chaos monster trying to destroy us. The Holy One protects us.'

Now the snow drifts were shrinking, dark earth showed through the footprints on the path to the ark and patches of brown appeared on the hillside. Then they heard the first faint gurglings from the brook. Soon they were ankle deep in mud and new streams were springing up everywhere as the last stubborn mounds of snow melted.

It was a magic time; the finest spring since the creation of the world. Puffs of white cloud floated in the deep blue sky and the air was warm and tasted sweet. The frustrations of winter were vanishing; everything was possible. Birds were singing again, foraging for materials to make nests among the rocks or even in the ark itself. The ewes were heavy with young. Soon there was enough young grass to introduce the animals to a wonderful new diet.

Despite their disillusionment with cave living, the men knew that crops must be sown before a house could be built. Shem urged moving down into the valley floor to take advantage of the better soil and warmer climate. But Noah was adamant about staying where they were.

'The priority this year is getting a harvest or we'll starve. But once we've sown the crops and built the house there may be time to go down and take a look.'

They chose land near the stream where the melt water had washed the soil and the grass grew strongest. The plot included land round the ark and a long, gentle slope below. Ploughing was a challenge. With all the cows in calf and none of the bulls gelded they had to hitch two donkeys to the plough. It was backbreaking work. They planted wheat close by the stream, with millet on the edges where the land was poorer. Near the ark they put in beans and peas and sprinkled patches of herb seeds.

The women meantime were struggling with the family's clothing. There had been little opportunity to wash since the flood began and their robes were thick with grease and vermin and in urgent need of repair. The three younger women spent days by the stream, spreading the clothes over rocks and pummelling them, pausing only to let the feeling come back into their cold hands. Some afternoons they sat in a sheltered crevice among the rocks where they could enjoy the sun and watch the lambs playing. But even then their fingers were busy, twirling their spindles and spinning woollen thread. Ham had promised them a loom as soon as the house was up. There would be babies to clothe come the autumn.

The men spent several days arguing about the best place to

build. Eventually they agreed on a spot below their field. An outcrop of rocks protected it from any avalanches, while the plot itself had a slight dip in it.

'We'll dig this out further,' Noah explained. 'It'll be a stable for the animals in winter. They'll keep us warm. We'll put our house on top. We'll use stone and whatever wood we can get by breaking up the ark.'

Despite Noah's optimism they had never been more aware of how few they were. The ground seemed to be solid rock; every piece had to be prised free and manhandled. It took weeks to excavate the cellar. Then they began building the walls, placing stones carefully on each other to get the best fit. The women helped, carrying baskets of pebbles, cow dung and mud to fill in the gaps. They used the best of the ark timbers to shape a roof, shifting them to the site on smaller logs acting as rollers. They trimmed them with a bronze saw.

Finally, they had made a framework with smaller pieces of wood lashed to the main joists. Noah had intended to use some of the reed thatch from the ark to roof the house, but when Ham climbed up into the rafters he soon returned, discouraged and covered in pitch.

'It's no good, Dad. The reeds are really stuck fast with all that tar we poured on.' So they used turf instead.

By late summer they had finished. Zillah examined the work critically.

'It looks just like one of those huts the servants lived in.'

Noah sighed. 'It's the best we can manage. At least we've got separate rooms. It's a lot better than the cave.'

Ploughing, sowing, house building, harvesting... it was a time of learning for them all, making do with the few tools they had. But at long last the wheat was gathered, threshed and stored. They gathered to celebrate. Their new home was filled with the smell of baking bread from the fresh flour. Suddenly Noah rose from his corner seat and hurried outside, rubbing his eyes with the corner of his robe.

Japheth slipped out after him. To his alarm he saw his father lying stretched out on the ground. He bent over him anxiously.

'Are you all right, Father?'

Noah slowly lifted his head. His eyes were filled with tears.

'Yes, I'm fine. I was just thanking the Holy One for his kindness. Come on, give me a hand up.'

They stood watching the sun dipping towards the horizon.

'These last few weeks have been hard, and I suppose we've all been too busy to remember the Holy One. But just then, smelling that bread, I realised just how he has kept his promise.'

'Giving us a harvest?'

'Of course, and so much more. He saved our lives and he's given us land. He helped us build this house. Even the ark provided building wood.'

They walked back inside where the family was impatiently eyeing the new bread on the table. Noah picked up one of the loaves and broke it in his hands.

'The Holy One promised us there would be harvests while the earth remained. Here is the proof. This is a special day for us, a very special day indeed. Let us all thank him.'

At last they were eating, delighted by the first fresh bread in two years and the sharp flavour of goat's cheese.

'I've never tasted anything like it... '

'... best bread I've ever had ... '

'Pass that other loaf ... '

'Look! Not a weevil in it!'

Ham was particularly excited. 'We can throw all the old stores away.'

Noah held up his hand. 'Not so fast! I doubt whether there's enough new grain to see us through till next harvest. We may be very grateful for that old stuff before we've finished!'

They sat until the oil lamps glowed bright in the darkness. Then one by one they went to do the final chores of the day. Ishtar and Shem were left alone. She giggled as he patted her belly.

'Our first son!' he laughed. 'What do you think of your husband now?'

'I've met worse. I'm certainly not looking for anyone else! But maybe we'll have a beautiful daughter.'

◆

The babies all arrived within a week of each other.

Ishtar was the first to go into labour. It was a wild day with an autumn gale lashing the mountain. The fire gave little heat, and smoke swirled everywhere.

'I wish Erishkigal was here!' Zillah said to Noah.

'Erishkigal? That old woman from the village? The one that smelt like a goat?'

'She was a brilliant midwife.'

Noah was suddenly alarmed. 'But... don't you know what to do?'

'I think so... only I've never done it before.'

Ishtar's labour seemed to go on for ever, but then the baby came quickly. It was a girl – a healthy looking scrap with a wisp of black hair and a loud bellow. Zillah wiped her carefully, wrapped her in a shawl and gave her to Shem to hold while she hurried out of the room for more rags.

Ishtar looked up at him, her eyes brimming with tears. 'I've failed you, love! I didn't give you a son.'

But he was gazing at his daughter, his mouth open at the miracle of her tiny fingernails. 'She's ours!' he murmured. 'She's ours! Our very own!'

When Noah was allowed into the room he stared at the baby, overwhelmed by a sudden fierce joy. He reached down and cradled her in his arms.

'Holy One, you have been good to us,' he said, his voice as low as a lullaby. 'You have blessed us. You have kept your promise.'

Siduri's first son Cush arrived two days later and two days after that Naamah gave birth to her boy, Gomer.

The babies seemed to take over the entire home. A week earlier there had been so much space, but now everywhere was cluttered. Noah marvelled how three such tiny people could monopolise the women. Ancient memories stirred; he wrinkled his nose at long-forgotten smells and learned to ignore bouts of inconsolable crying. He had seen so little of his sons in their early years. There had always been women to help Zillah and he had been out most of the time dealing with the estate. Now there was no escape. Meals were late and the rooms were strewn with cradles and piles of dirty rags. But there was joy too. He had missed his sons' first smiles but now he sat entranced, happily gurgling at these precious babies, even suffering the indignity of having his beard pulled.

A deep contentment came over him. Zillah had come to

life, delighted to spend hour after hour rocking and talking to the babies. Her criticisms of Noah became muted and she was showing a little of her old tenderness.

There were other births that autumn too. The first calf arrived.

'At last!' Siduri exclaimed, watching it greedily nuzzling its mother. 'There'll be proper cow's milk. How I've missed it!'

It was a race to complete the winter sowing before the first blizzard. There was more land to plough this year; during the summer they had cleared stones to add another field. But, for all that, the winter seemed easier than the one before. The new house was much warmer and more comfortable than the cave, and even the old chore of leaving out dried fish and hay for the animals were bearable. But supplies were running low. Next year they would have to fend for themselves.

In the spring Noah, Shem and Japheth travelled to the valley and were gone for three days.

Shem was enthusiastic. 'We've found the ideal place! It's down by that lake you can just see. The land's beautiful! Flat – and there's thick grass there already! It's sheltered too, and it'll be even better when the trees grow back. Lovely soil – deep, and hardly any stones to dig out.'

Japheth broke in. 'To begin with we'd just put up a shack for the summer. After harvest we'd come back here. We could start tomorrow. If we hurry we can plant crops for this year.'

30

The next few years were the happiest of Noah's life. In no time it seemed there were children everywhere. The family had spread out over the valley and Noah was enjoying the comfort of a splendid new cottage near the lake close to Ham and Siduri's house.

These days he left the heavy farm work to others. But life was busy. He was always there when the children needed him, helping them onto their favourite rock ledge, or standing by the lake as they splashed in the shallows. He became expert at fixing broken toys, inventing new games or wiping away tears. He was constantly surrounded by children clamouring to hold his hand and tell him their news. Each afternoon he would find his favourite seat and the little ones would crawl over him or sit by his feet while the older children watched and giggled in the background, waiting to pounce if he should nod off. They knew his stories word for word and corrected him if he missed anything out.

And what stories he told! There was the story of how the Holy One made the world and the beautiful lost garden. Then there were the adventures of Adam, Cain, Seth and Enoch. But best of all was the Great Flood. They never tired of hearing about it. Noah would explain how he had built the ark, tracing everything out with his stick on the ground. He would tell about where they had got the materials and how the animals had come to him. Then he'd describe the terrible day the waters rose and the amazing ways the Holy One had looked after them and brought them floating to the new valley.

Sometimes they would visit the remains of the ark itself. They would start in the early morning before the mist had cleared, clutching bundles of food for a picnic. Around mid-morning they would pause by the stream for a rest and it was noon before they reached the final slope. They passed the old house, empty now apart from a few wild animals, while the fields they had toiled in so hard were becoming overrun with scrub.

In the early years it had been possible to see the ark from the lake but now it was hidden by pine trees. It was always a surprise when they suddenly glimpsed the skeleton of the walls towering high above them through the trees. The door had rotted away and they clambered up rough steps to the entrance. Noah found it almost impossible to recall the moment when he had stood there watching the whirlwind bearing down on him.

Inside everything was open to the sky. The roof and upper floors had been taken out long ago to build houses. Trees and bushes grew inside and the shell reverberated with bird song.

Then the ritual began. Noah would point with his stick, explaining what each part of the ark used to look like. He finished by indicating a piece of the walkway still attached precariously to a section of the wall high above their heads.

'That's where we used to stand so we could see out.'

'Can we climb up there, Grandpa?'

Noah would shake his head. 'It's much too dangerous.'

Then they would eat their midday meal. Afterwards he told them the old familiar story of the flood. Then, while he had a doze, the children would play at looking after the animals or hide-and-seek.

But life was not all idyllic. Noah frowned when he found out that somehow the children knew stories about the Cainites and played games of beating slaves. Often young warriors would come bursting through the bushes brandishing sticks.

'We're the Cainites! We're going to burn the city down!'

Then there were secret games. Once Noah chanced upon several little girls stark naked, daubing themselves with mud in a credible imitation of the women who had tried to burn the ark down. After a major row, they were sent to bed without supper. That evening he summoned the family.

'So which of you has been telling the children about those women? They're far too young to know about things like that!'

He searched each face in turn, but no one spoke.

Noah went to bed glumly. 'I never thought it would happen in my family,' he said to Zillah. 'I pray they're not meddling in witchcraft. I'd better get the whole family together so that we can offer a sacrifice to the Holy One asking his forgiveness.'

◆❖◆

Nothing was quite the same after Zillah died. She slipped away so quickly that he scarcely realised what had happened. Called to her bedside, she still seemed to be asleep and he half expected her to stir. He stared at her. She looked young again. The deep lines in her face had softened almost as if she was the beautiful girl he had married so very long ago.

It was the first funeral in the new world. They laid her to rest near the lake in a natural bower sheltered by some large rocks. It had been her favourite spot in these last years. Noah watched as his sons gently lowered her body into the grave and piled the earth back, leaving a rock on top to prevent the animals disturbing her. He walked forward to commend her to the Holy One. Despite the coldness inside, his voice rang out clear and strong as he gave thanks for her life.

But the pain followed. Over the next few months Noah took to sitting in Zillah's old place, looking at the grave, the mound of earth slowly settling.

'I wonder if she ever really forgave me for building the ark?' he mused.

Again and again he thought back over their time together, questioning himself as to whether he could have been more understanding. So often he had left her alone, but what else could he have done? Always there had been pressure, first to make a success of the estate, then to build the ark. She was the last link with the old life. There could be no one else now, no one at all. He wept, longing for the chance to put his arm round her once more.

If Noah was unprepared for the first funeral, he was also unprepared for the first wedding. Japheth's son Gomer sidled in one evening after supper to ask permission to marry Ham's daughter Milcah.

'But they're so young,' Noah said to Siduri.

'Old enough to make up their own minds. I reckon you weren't much older than that when you married Zillah.'

Noah was on his way to harvest his latest crop – grapes! Some time back he had found a large vine growing up a tree and as he poked among its leaves he found some dark fruit. Soon his hands and beard were stained purple and old memories stirred.

'Of course! Heth had a vineyard. I remember those stakes he put in so they had something to climb up. Then, when the fruit was ripe, he'd crush it and make an excellent drink.'

By autumn his young vines were ready for planting. Ham's youngest boy Canaan had helped him. They marked out a plot on a hillside facing south and after clearing the ground the young man drove in stakes and built a lattice to hold the vines. By the end of the summer it was smothered in leaves.

'It'll be a year or two before they are bearing fruit properly,' explained Noah. 'First, we've got to do some ruthless pruning.'

The vineyard flourished and became Noah's favourite haunt. On winter days he would slip off to see his rows of leafless plants and trim the odd branch. Then in spring he would sit for hours in the shade of the new leaves, looking at the small flowers.

'I could make myself a tent here,' he thought. 'Just something simple with matting. I'll get the boys to give me a hand.'

Summer saw him thinning out the young fruit clusters, but autumn was his particular delight. He would take enough food along to camp out for several days, checking his grapes till they were ready to pick – black, juicy and sweet with a slight bloom on the skin. By the fourth year he had grown so many that even the children were getting tired of them.

'Do you remember that wine they used to make in the city?' he asked Ham.

'I certainly do! It tasted marvellous on a hot day. But it could make you do some funny things! Are you going to try to make some?'

Noah looked slightly embarrassed. 'I thought I might make a bit. Just enough to taste. It's a shame to waste the fruit.'

'Well, take it easy. It can be powerful stuff. They used to drink a lot of it down in the city after the autumn sacrifice and there were always fights afterwards. Once they even knifed one of the priests.'

They discussed how to go about making the wine and the next day Ham arrived with a donkey carrying a large bronze bowl and an earthenware jar.

Noah set to work picking his grapes, piling the bowl full before hitching up his robe and stepping in gingerly. By the time he had filled the jar with juice his clothes were splattered.

Next morning when he woke in his tent there was a strong

yeasty smell. The juice was foaming out of the jar and had split on the floor. He tasted it cautiously, finding it sweet and fruity. It took a lot of self-control to leave the jar alone, but after four long weeks the bubbling stopped. He dipped in a small cup and sipped it carefully.

'Ah! This is really good! I'll take some along tonight when we have our special supper to celebrate the end of harvest.'

The sun was very warm. He filled his cup and, sitting in the shade, took a deep swig. He had not felt so relaxed in years. He refilled the cup twice and by midday felt like a nap. Somehow he managed to pull himself up, stagger inside the shelter and collapse on his pallet.

He lay flat on his back with his mouth open, snoring. His robe had ridden right up to his armpits.

'Grandpa! Are you there?'

It was late afternoon and Canaan was walking up the path. Normally by now he would have spotted his grandfather but today there was no trace of him. Suddenly he felt worried. The old man was getting on in years and no one had seen him for days. He hurried across to the shelter and pushed his head inside.

For a dreadful moment he thought Noah was dead. Then he heard the snoring.

'So that's what happens when you drink that wine stuff!' he sniggered. 'I'd best get Dad.'

Ham was working in a field near the lake. Canaan could not hide the smirk as he spoke.

'Come and look. I've found Grandpa fast asleep – and he's got hardly any clothes on!'

Ham was shocked for a moment when he reached the tent, but then started to chuckle. 'Would you believe it? I told him to be careful. He's just like those drunks in the city. Legs wide apart – showing everything he's got.'

Japheth was outraged to hear Ham's amused account.

'Haven't you any respect for him? He is your father! Isn't he entitled to some dignity?'

'Dignity? He got himself drunk, didn't he? Made a complete fool of himself.'

'But if he makes silly mistakes we must... cover up for him.'

'Well, he's not very good at covering himself too well, that's for sure. I shouldn't wonder if all the children aren't queuing to take a peep!'

Japheth hurried to find Shem.

'Quickly! We must get there right away! Grab one of those large cloaks!'

They raced up the path to the vineyard. Outside the tent, they arranged the robe with the two sides over their shoulders. Then they shuffled into the tent backwards carefully, kicking with their heels to stop themselves tripping over anything. When they saw his feet they began lowering the robe. Noah, now properly covered, stirred in his sleep.

'Let's hope Ham's had the sense to keep his big mouth shut,' said Japheth grimly. 'If the others hear about this, Father will be a laughing stock. And we must never forget that this family would be nowhere without him.'

31

Noah awoke in the late afternoon, feeling sick. His head was pounding. But when Japheth told him what had happened his face blazed red with anger.

'You don't mean that Canaan actually saw me like that? And Ham too? And they left me exposed – without doing a thing about it?'

Unsought, the ancient shame of his visit to the Cainites came flooding back. He could still feel the soldiers' rough hands as they groped for the gold round his waist while the official looked on with contempt. Shock, shame and, finally, rage gripped him. He paced up and down.

'That Canaan! I'll throttle him with my bare hands. In my day they *killed* sons for less than that. How dare he?'

Japheth raised his hand. 'Please, Father... why don't you sleep on it before you do anything rash?'

'No. I'm going to have it out with him and his father at tonight's harvest supper.'

As they sat at table, Noah asked Ham about what had happened, but his son only gave a lame excuse for his conduct. As a hush fell over the rest of the family, Noah went on, 'By now you all know what happened today. And I call on you all to hear that I am solemnly *cursing* Canaan. From now on he will be the lowest slave for his brothers.'

Ham glared at him.

Next Noah turned to Shem. 'I bless the Holy One, the God of Shem! May Canaan be Shem's slave.'

Finally, he faced Japheth. 'And may the Holy One expand Japheth's lands. Japheth will live in Shem's tents and may Canaan be his slave!'

There was a long stunned silence. Then Ham's voice broke through. Noah had never heard such anger in his voice.

'So that's all the thanks I get for looking after you all these years. You curse my son and you curse me! And it was your wretched fault in the first place! If you think my family's going

231

to spend their time crawling round after you, you can think again! We'll never put up with that!'

He thumped on the table.

'Forget our nice cosy family feast! I want you all out of my home! *Now*! And take that drunken old fool with you! I never want to set eyes on him again, with or without his robe!'

In a moment, they all found themselves outside in the courtyard. There was a chorus of crying as the younger children were woken up and thrust out of the building after their parents, but Noah hardly noticed them. He stared in amazement at his son, who was swearing at him from the open door.

'Come home with us, Father,' Ishtar said, taking his elbow. 'We'll look after you.'

The next few months were a torment. Again and again Noah relived the awful shame of Canaan and Ham looking at him naked. He spent long hours reproaching himself for having made the wine, pacing the floor in impotent rage. Ishtar watched helplessly, waiting for any chance to distract him by asking for help with the animals or her grandchildren.

'Don't worry about it. You said only what was needed. It's up to Ham and Canaan now – they're the ones who need to apologise.'

The rift with Ham hurt badly. He had been the one with all the drive, all the ideas. Noah knew he couldn't have coped without him. But now he had isolated himself, even from his brothers. Japheth had called on him but had been threatened with a large dog.

'He said he would turn it loose on me if I didn't get off his land right away,' he told his father. '*His land*. I ask you! After all the help I've given him!'

'I just don't understand. I can't think why he shamed me like that. We taught him to respect his elders, particularly his parents.'

'He's proud, that's the trouble. Give him half a chance and he'd have us all bowing down to him. And the thing is, now you've... you've humiliated him in front of everyone.'

'As he humiliated me, don't forget!' shouted Noah. 'He's lucky to be alive. Back in the old days, fathers killed their sons for less than that. But... I still love him. I'd give anything to get him back.'

'Why did you curse Canaan? I know he's a spoilt brat – but

shouldn't it have been Ham?'

'As my old grandfather Methuselah used to say, *If you judge a man, you judge his father.* If I'd condemned Ham directly, it would have come back on me. Between them those two destroyed my authority and if that had gone there'd be chaos round here. Anyway, the words weren't mine. I heard the Holy One telling me what to say. It was the Holy One that showed me that Ham's family is always going to take second place. And that you and Shem would be blessed. For you, it's only a fulfilment of what has been promised all along. When you were born we called you Japheth because it means *enlarge*. The Holy One's going to enlarge your family and your influence.'

'And Shem?'

'That means *name*, of course. Every time we mention him we're reminded of the name of the Holy One. Once I'm gone it'll be his responsibility to keep worship going. Ham is *hot*, just as his name implies. The pity is that his hot temper has cut him off from the Holy One's blessings.'

It was the hardest winter yet. Shem had chosen the site for his house carefully, facing south and sheltered on the other three sides, but even here the snow piled up in great drifts. For months they only went outside to feed the animals. Noah continued to feel distressed about Ham, worrying about the harshness of the punishment.

'And it was all my fault in the first place!'

'No, Father,' said Ishtar. 'You may not have realised, but he was always laughing at you behind your back. He often called you a stupid old man – or worse. He reckoned you'd gone soft in the head. Then there were the jokes he made about you... playing with the girls, suggesting that you were... you were... well, abusing them.'

Noah's face had turned scarlet and his hands shook.

'What? You can't mean it? He never said that... that I defiled my own granddaughters? But why does he have to say that?'

'I think he was trying to shift his guilt onto you.' Now it was Ishtar's turn to flush. 'You just have to hear the way he talks to the young girls. He tells them what they used to do in the city – you know, with prostitutes. Who do you think taught the girls that horrible game where they took their clothes off and painted themselves?'

❖

As winter turned to spring, news came that Ham and his family had packed up and moved, and that he had staked out a new estate in the Great Valley. Noah was inconsolable. He felt he knew how Adam felt as he watched his firstborn son striding away into eternal exile. He took out the old tablets of writing.

'Why don't you write some more?' suggested Shem. 'Tell how you made the ark and all about the flood so that people in the future will know what happened.'

'Of course! You're right! I promised Methuselah and Lamech I'd do that! And I need to teach you to read them for yourself.'

'I'm too old to start reading. You'd be better off teaching one of my boys.'

Shem's third son, Arphaxad, proved the most apt pupil. Soon he could read as well as Noah and had learned to make the signs on wet clay.

'I think we can start on the new writings now,' Noah remarked one day, with some satisfaction. 'I'll tell you what I want to say and you can write it down for me. We'll begin by completing the history of my family, with the details of Methuselah and Lamech. And we'll go on to my own birth and those of my sons. Then, I must tell of the evil of the old world, of the Nephilim and the sons of the Holy One who sinned, of how men's minds were corrupted and of how the whole world was filled with violence.'

'And how the Holy One judged everyone?'

'Yes, Arphaxad, we'll come to that. But first we need to write of the Holy One's sorrow and the dreadful pain the evil hearts of men and women caused him. And how, for some reason I can't understand, he chose me to do his work.'

It took days to write that much on the tablets.

'Next we come to the building of the ark. We must be careful to get everything correct – the type of wood, the pitch and each dimension. And the animals.'

'And, Grandfather, we could mention the problems you had finding the wood, the pitch and the tools and...'

'No! Nobody wants to hear all those details. All you need

say is I did everything I was commanded to do by the Holy One. That will be sufficient.'

Then Arphaxad wrote of the flood, of how the ark came to rest, of the birds Noah sent out and of the Holy One's command to open the door.

'And now we come to the important part,' Noah insisted. 'The covenant the Holy One made with us and all the animals. We must record all his promises and tell of the sign he put in the sky.'

At last the history of the flood was complete.

'I do believe we've finished, Grandfather.'

'We haven't written yet about that time when I was drunk.'

'Grandfather! You can't possibly put that in! You'd look a fool!'

'We're going to be completely honest. If this record's to be complete I have to explain what Ham did and how I cursed Canaan.'

The news from Ham and his family in the Great Valley was disturbing. Reports talked of hunting parties with spears roaming the countryside and killing animals for sport. Two of Shem's grandsons were attacked and robbed by these same gangs. Canaan, it was said, had moved on from the Great Valley, taking a number of young men with him and moving over the mountains. They returned from time to time to make use of any women who were willing. But the news that hit Noah hardest was that they had gone back to worshipping the old gods.

'They're doing all the same awful things as in the old days,' reported Shem. 'Witchcraft, throwing live babies into fires to appease their gods, building temples and moving prostitutes in there. There are shrines everywhere for sacrifices.'

Noah wept, feeling intensely the pain of the Holy One. He had never imagined that the family the Holy One had rescued would spawn such blasphemy, such idolatry.

'It's all been a waste of time,' he called out into the darkness of his sleepless night, his clenched fist striking the wall above his pallet.

'The world is as bad as it ever was! I thought the flood would give us a new start in a new world, but we carried the evil with us. Like seeds. The evil has taken root within us all!'

His remorse over his drunkenness never diminished.

'I'm no better than any of them. One drink too many and I cause a huge rift in the family.'

But Ishtar and Shem tried to cheer him up.

'The Holy One knew what he was doing when he chose you to build the ark,' said Ishtar. 'No one else could have done that. And if it wasn't for you, none of us would be here today. When I think of you bursting into that wedding celebration and carrying me off over your shoulder with hardly a stitch on... !'

Noah grinned, despite himself.

'You know, all my life I'd carried lucky charms and worshipped different gods. I was frightened of them but also relied on them. But now... now I realise that there's only one true God, and that's the Holy One you've served so faithfully all these years. And I'm not the only one who thinks that, because of what you've done.'

'So, Ishtar, do you mean... do you mean you believe in him now?'

Yes, Father. I know he's the one who saved us from the flood and gave me my children. I'm going to worship him for ever.'

For the first time in months a broad smile spread across Noah's face.

That night he dreamed he was a boy again, listening to Methuselah tell the familiar story of Enoch: 'Enoch stood up for the Holy One against an angry mob one day. He told them that the Holy One would come to judge them with hundreds of thousands of believers... '

Then he understood. 'Hundreds of thousands – why, that's more people than have lived in the world yet! That must mean there's another, greater judgement to come and that there will be many more believers in the Holy One, like Ishtar.'

Then he dreamed again, and he was in a great city, totally unlike the city he'd known before the flood. It gleamed so brightly that it hurt his eyes. There was a river lined with great trees bearing flowers and fruit. The shining streets were thronging with happy, singing people who were somehow more alive than any people he had ever seen.

The he saw the Holy One wearing a robe brighter than snow,

with a girdle of gold and eyes burning like a furnace. And for the first time he looked into his face.

When Ishtar came in next morning to see him he was ecstatic.

'You look happy, Father.'

'It's wonderful! I've seen the Holy One face to face and I feel marvellous. Recently I've been so helpless and I've wondered if my children will remember me when I'm gone. But now I don't mind any more. One look at the Holy One and I forgot all about myself and my worries. Once you've seen him, nothing else matters – nothing at all!'

FOR READING GROUPS AND DISCUSSION GROUPS

If you have enjoyed this novel, why not invite some friends to read it too and then get together for a discussion? To help you, we have posted a suggested outline for a group discussion on THE DAY THE SKY OPENED on

www.scriptureunion.org.uk/noah